CHILDREN
OF THE
FIFTH SUN
ECHELON

T0159854

OTHER BOOKS BY GARETH WORTHINGTON

Children of the Fifth Sun: Echelon (Book II)

Forthcoming From Gareth Worthington

Children of the Fifth Sun: Rubicon (Book III)

Books by Stu Jones and Gareth Worthington

It Takes Death To Reach A Star

Forthcoming From Stu Jones and Gareth Worthington

In The Shadow Of A Valiant Moon
(It Takes Death To Reach A Star, Book II)

CHILDREN
OF THE
FIFTH SUN
ECHELON

GARETH WORTHINGTON

Echelon

This is a work of fiction. Names, characters, places, and incidents either are the product of the author's imagination or are used fictitiously.
Any resemblance to actual persons, living or dead, events or locales is entirely coincidental.

Cover Design by John Byrne

ISBN: 978-1-944109-63-9

VESUVIAN BOOKS

Published by Vesuvian Books
www.vesuvianbooks.com

Printed in the United States of America

10 9 8 7 6 5 4 3 2 1

PRAISE FOR CHILDREN OF THE FIFTH SUN

2019 Eric Hoffer, Honorable Mention, Best Sci Fi Novel
2019 Eric Hoffer First Horizon Finalist
2019 Eric Hoffer Grand Prize Finalist
2018 Silver Falchion Finalist
2018 Hollywood Book Festival, Winner Best Sci Fi Novel
2018 Cygnus Award Finalist
2017 London Book Festival, Winner Best Sci Fi Novel

"An action-packed, globe-hopping science fiction thriller... pedal-to-the-metal pacing and relentless action make it easy to turn pages..." -*Kirkus Reviews*

"Insane! A wild ride researched on par with a Michael Crichton novel." - Jonas Saul, Bestselling author of the Sarah Roberts Series

"A bit Tom Clancy, a hint of Dan Brown." - Charity Scripture, Reviewer

In development for Film/TV

CHILDREN OF THE FIFTH SUN: ECHELON

While this is a work of fiction, many of the places described are real and the theories and mythologies based in solid research.

PROLOGUE

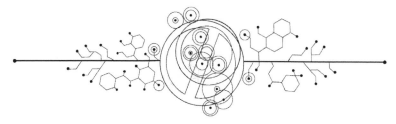

Location: Somewhere on the Southern Indian Ocean

No one saw the attack coming.

The first blast tore a hole in the hull at 1:37 in the morning. By 2:15 the aft portion of the supply vessel, Marion Dufresne II, was pointing to the starless sky, while its nose was dipped below the frigid black ocean. A cutting wind battered the exposed keel and the remaining crew who managed to hold on to the outer railings.

Freya Nilsson clung to the thick frame of the eighteen-ton oceanographic crane, though it too was already slipping beneath the waves. She cried out, but her voice was drowned by the howling Antarctic maelstrom and the ship's three, huge, Wärtsilä diesel engines, now churning nothing but air. Freya shivered uncontrollably, her hair and clothes frozen to her skin. "KJ!" she cried out, again.

Her son didn't answer.

Freya sobbed, tears freezing halfway down her cheeks. "KJ, where are you?"

A flash of lightning illuminated the angry ocean and a thick layer of clouds covering the heavens, but the attacking vessel was nowhere in sight. A deafening clap of thunder filled the air

1

followed by a wave of needle-like raindrops that shattered across her face. The vessel reared up and the engines roared. A muffled explosion beneath the water cleaved the ship in two and the nose began to sink.

Have to jump, Freya thought. *Can't let them take KJ!* She pushed off the crane and dropped into the icy ocean below.

Despite already being frozen, the shock of the glacial water stole the breath from her lungs. Before she could swim to the surface, Freya was sucked under. Tumbling down, down, down, she struggled to find her bearing. Her lungs burned, poisoned with carbon-dioxide. Instinctively, she kicked and fought and pulled until somehow, as if pushed upward, she eventually broke the surface.

Freya took a massive gulp of life-giving salty air, only to be pulled beneath again as a piece of the ship crashed into the ocean beside her. The falling debris dragged her farther and farther into the deep. She jerked and thrashed, but it only served to steal the energy from her stiffened limbs.

Blackness enveloped Freya's mind, the cold claiming her will to fight. Yet, even as death stalked her, she couldn't let go. KJ needed her. She couldn't die. Refused to die. Freya summoned her last drop of power and kicked. Once. Twice. Three times. And then, she could breathe again. The wind whipped her jet-black hair about her face, and the rain stung her eyes. But she was alive.

The silhouette of the supply vessel bobbed in the distance, ass up, before gurgling down into its watery grave. Gone. Still the attackers were invisible. With only the lasting image of where the Marion Dufresne II had just sunk as a destination, Freya paddled forward. Fighting against the chop of the ocean, she inched along. The spray blinded her and the salt burned, but she had to find him.

"KJ where are you?" she called. "Answer me, baby. Please."
Only the squall howled back.

Her legs tightened and Freya plunged below the surface again, choking on yet another mouthful of seawater before once again scrambling upward—to a light. A bright circle of light rippling on the surface.

A strong hand clasped her under the armpit and pulled. Freya was lifted from the water, her hip smacking into the hull of the lifeboat. She fell backward into the bow, panting and coughing. "KJ ... have to find KJ."

"Cover her. Someone cover her," a familiar voice said from above.

"I got it. Are there any more?" a woman asked. "We've got to get the hell out of here."

"I don't think so. I only saw her," the first voice answered.

Freya lay in the boat, covered in a thermal blanket, her eyes screwed shut. "I'm sorry, Kelly," she whispered. "Our son. I'm sorry ..."

CHAPTER ONE

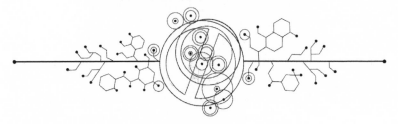

Location: Connecticut, USA, six weeks earlier

"Mommy, Mommy!"

Freya leaped from her bed and sprinted to her son, stomping on a Lego piece along the way. She careened into the room, but came to an abrupt halt and breathed a sigh of relief at the sight of Kelly Junior in the dark, holding his portable nightlight.

"What happened, Mr. Man? Are you all right?" Freya asked, rubbing her sore foot. "Bad dream, again?"

KJ nodded. "Mhmm."

"Same one?" she asked, although she didn't need to hear the answer. Of course it was the same one. It was always the same. A hole. A deep, black hole, with bright blue eyes staring out and voices from within calling to him. That was the dream. It had been since he was three. And she knew in her heart there was a link with Siberia—with a sinkhole that had opened up two years earlier. KJ was obsessed with it.

"Yeah, I hate this dream, Mommy." KJ sniffed and ran his forearm across his face. "I wish I could make it go away."

She took a seat on the bed next to him. "Me too, sweetie. Me, too."

"Can I have some chocolate milk? To help me sleep." KJ looked up at Freya, his big blue eyes shining like sapphires in the dark.

"Help you sleep, huh?" Freya raised an eyebrow.

KJ just gave the same grin that his father used to give.

"C'mon then. But, then straight back to bed." She picked up KJ who clamped himself around her body and rested his head on her shoulder.

Freya skipped down the stairs and into the kitchen. Once KJ was placed on the counter, Freya busied herself about making his warm chocolate milk, keeping one eye on her son in case he fell.

Clasping his now full Iron Man cup, KJ climbed down off the side and meandered into the living room. Freya followed him in, wearing only a T-shirt, panties, and thick wool socks. She may be a mom, but for Freya, pajamas were a step too far.

"Do you think Minya and Nikolaj are awake?" KJ asked, snuggling into Freya on the couch.

She looked at the clock. Three in the morning. "Yeah, it's about 11:00 a.m. for them." She pulled her ponytail tight and squinted at him. "Why?"

"Maybe they'd like to Skype?" he asked, hopefully.

"I guess we could … wait, are you doing that thing you do?"

KJ smiled. "What thing?"

"You're too clever for your own good, you know that?"

"I know," he said.

"Well, maybe it would be good to say hi."

Freya's friendship with Minya had been a surprise to them both. Over the year that followed the battle with the Shan Chu in Teotihuacan, they'd had to interact numerous times to assist the Secretary of State, Lucy Taylor, in cleaning up things. An initial dislike for each other had grown into respect. And as Freya's belly grew with KJ, Minya had thawed considerably. But it was when KJ was born the friendship solidified. Minya was another mother who understood everything that had happened. With KJ's special abilities increasing every day, she had been the only one with whom Freya could talk. In the end, Minya was the only one who knew *everything*.

The video call hummed its dialing tone.

Almost two minutes passed.

"I don't think they're in, Mr. Man," Freya said, leaning for the remote to hang up.

"Wait, just one more minute," he pleaded.

Freya sat back and waited.

Sure enough, the call connected. Minya's high cheekbones and almond-shaped eyes filled the TV screen.

"Freya. A nice surprise. It's what, three in morning there? Kelly Junior, you wake up your mother again?" Minya had always refused to call him KJ. "She needs her rest, young man."

"Bad dreams again," replied Freya for her son.

KJ nodded, slurping on his chocolate milk.

"You know my thought on this, my friend," Minya said.

Freya sighed. "I know."

"What do you have to lose? You fly here. We check out the site, Kelly Junior feels better. You go home."

"And if that's not what happens?"

"You will never know what your son needs unless you try. Kelly Junior has too much of his father in him. If you don't take him now, one day he will go alone."

KJ sat listening, wide eyed, hiding behind his cup.

Freya's chest tightened. "You're right about that."

Minya shook her head. "Freya. Your son is tiny version of that man. You know this. I know this. Everyone knows this."

Freya glanced at KJ. The wavy brown locks that fell about his face. His piercing blue eyes. That half-baked smirk. He was a miniature version of Kelly Graham. Each day that passed, more of his father came to the surface. He was far too confident for his own good.

"He's only five," Freya began.

"Freya, my friend. You and I both know that is not true. He may have the body of a five-year old, but his brain ... that is something different entirely."

Freya squeezed her son. "It's too dangerous. I can't risk it. Can't risk KJ."

"Where are we going?" A tall boy with blond hair and chocolate-colored eyes squished himself into the camera shot.

KJ sat upright. "*Privyet!*"

"*Privyet*, KJ," replied Nikolaj. He was quite a bit older than KJ, but he was always kind to her son.

"Where are we going?" repeated Nikolaj.

"We're coming to you, Nikolaj," KJ said, his voice full of excitement.

"No we're not," Freya said, firmly.

The boy smiled. "Oh, good. I look forward to see us."

"You," corrected Minya. "I look forward to see you."

"*Da*, sorry, you," Nikolaj said.

Freya scowled. "Hey, has everyone gone deaf? I just said it's not happening."

"Freya—" Minya began.

"Look, I gotta go, Minya. KJ should be in bed. I'll call you soon okay?"

Freya cut off the call, and the TV screen was once again black.

7

"But mom—"

"But nothing, Mr. Man. I said we're not going and that's final. Go brush your teeth and get into bed, I'll come tuck you in in a minute."

KJ slid off the couch his head hung low, then dropped the empty cup in the kitchen sink. As he trudged up the stairs, he called to Socks—their cat—who came bounding from the hallway and duly followed him to his room. Besides her white paws, Socks was an all-black, sleek and decidedly bad-tempered, cat who scratched anyone who came too close. Anyone, that was, except KJ. For KJ, the razor-clawed little monster was a playful kitten. Most of the neighbors found it cute. Freya knew different. All the more reason not to go.

Location: Yamal Peninsula, Siberia

Svetlana was nowhere to be found. The ice-laden wind whipped about the leathery face of her mother, Anuska, rendering her blind. Defying the storm, she pulled the thick reindeer-skin hood over her raven-haired head and trudged onward through the snow, away from the tents, in the only direction her daughter could have gone. With unsteady steps, she called into the blizzard but her voice carried no more than a few feet.

"Svetlana!"

Nothing.

Pushing farther on, Anuska searched with outstretched hands, feeling her way forward. The snow concealed jagged rocks that cut into the leather of her reindeer-skin boots, letting frigid water seep in and freeze her toes. Still, she pressed on. She was Nenets; used to the perils of living in the open—and children often became lost. Though, this was different. Svetlana had not been herself. Not been awake. She'd wandered off several times since they set up camp near the sinkhole. Normally a girl who always completed her chores, tending to the reindeer, Svetlana had become obsessed with visiting the deep crater and peering over the edge for hours at a time.

Anuska could only hope her daughter had not tried to visit *it* on a night like this.

Before long, she stood at the edge of the sinkhole. More than one-hundred feet wide, it was an almost perfect puncture in the Earth's crust. Here the wind seemed to swirl around the black hole, but never over it. Anuska could make out the twenty-foot thick rim of gray rock that encircled the hole, and the pitch black center that absorbed all light, even during the day. She edged her foot forward, sending crumbling rock into the void.

"Svetlana!" she called again.

Anuska held her breath, squeezed her eyes shut and listened—hoping against hope.

"Mama …"

The Nenets mother faltered at the edge. "Svetlana?"

The wind howled. But on its very edge, the voice came again. "Mama …"

"Svetlana!"

Anuska scrambled to the ground and crawled backward into the hole, searching for a foothold. Through snow-soaked boots, her toes found an outcropping. She tested it for stability. It didn't move. Anuska allowed her weight to rest on it, then lowered herself a little more and with her other foot began the search for another base.

Slowly, she climbed down into the pit, one awkward step at a time. Her reindeer-skin mittens prevented the dexterity needed to properly grip the rock face, yet she clung to it with all her might. Her forearm muscles burned and her legs ached.

As she lowered farther and farther down, the storm's power lessened. The wind didn't bite as hard, and visibility got better. She chanced a glance below, but it made her stomach roil with vertigo. The gray lip of rock was almost at its end, and there seemed to be nothing more beyond but a bottomless quarry. As she stared into the pitch, her vision blurred and her world spun.

"Mama ..." came the voice from the void.

Startled, Anuska lost her footing. She scrambled to regain purchase, but it was no use. Her legs slipped out from under her and she slid down the remainder of the rocky gray rim. Her knees smashed into a ledge, and then she fell screaming into the darkness below.

Location: Chongjin, North Korea

Jonathan Teller tore off a piece of his shirt sleeve and tied it just below the knee as tightly as possible. The blood flow from the gunshot wound in his calf subsided. The bullet seemed to have passed straight through. Hunched behind the blast furnace, careful not to press his back against the hot surface, Jonathan wiped a grimy arm across his forehead, then inspected his M9A3 Beretta. Ten rounds left. No additional clip. This was not going how he'd imagined.

The sweltering heat in the furnace room made the clothes stick to his skin and sweat run into his eyes. Jonathan wiped his face again, blinking away the sting. His crew wasn't answering over the radio and there was only one way in or out of where he was. He had to hold his ground and hope his entire team wasn't dead.

A loud *clang* from the back of room echoed off the metalwork. Jonathan eased back the hammer on his Beretta and exhaled. *Time to go to work.* He quickly glanced around the huge furnace. Two men edged their way forward, flanking his position either side of the oven. In one movement, Teller stood, pivoted to the left of the furnace, and fired two clean shots into the chest of the first attacker. The man spluttered blood down his chin, stumbled to the side, then fell into the bright orange river of molten steel. His wet body hissed and the river spat droplets of metal onto the walkway. Jonathan ducked back down behind the giant kiln and gripped his injured leg.

More clanging rang throughout the room as the second soldier rushed down the right side toward Jonathan. The man paused at the edge, and crouched down.

Teller laid on his side and, between the metal framework, took aim at the man's ankle. He gently squeezed the trigger. The enemy's Achilles tendon exploded and his shrill scream filled the room. Jonathan scrambled to his feet and hobbled around the furnace. Without hesitation, he fired a kill shot to his attacker's head. The screaming ceased.

Jonathan slumped to the floor beside his assailant and clutched at his own calf. *Focus, Jon*, he thought. He breathed away the pain and then pawed at the dead man's fatigues searching for clues. The gear was definitely North Korean Military, but something didn't add up. His morphology seemed more Japanese than Korean. And his weapon—Jonathan picked it up and studied it. The markings had been filed off, but it was a Markov for sure. A Soviet sidearm. And the strangest thing of all: the tattoo. Hidden behind the man's left ear was a small black Arabic nine. What the hell was going on? What was the connection?

Teller rubbed his temples. North Korea was created by a former Soviet commando, Kim Il Sung, and the Korean People's Army with help from Moscow. The KPA brought together those Koreans who were either veterans of the Soviet Red Army or anti-Japanese guerrillas based in China. Was that it? Were the Russians supporting North Korea now? If so, why did this guy look Japanese? And why have an Arabic number tattoo?

He shook his head. This wasn't helping. He had to get out of there.

Men's voices drifted through the doorway. *Shit.* Jonathan shuffled back behind the furnace and checked his Beretta again—not that he needed to: six rounds left. He concentrated on the ringing footsteps. That was more than six people. It was an outfit.

One last time, Jonathan clicked on his radio and whispered as harshly as possible. "Delta team. Come in Delta team. I'm in the furnace room. Over."

Static.

"Come in Delta team."

Still nothing.

Jonathan tapped the radio on his forehead and then switched it off before hooking it to his belt. "Okay, looks like I'm gonna have to shoot my way outta this one." He stood on his good leg and readied his weapon. "Here we go."

Rapid gunfire echoed out from the hallway followed by shouting and muffled screams.

Then, silence.

"Sir?" a man yelled.

"Teller?" called another.

Jonathan sighed in relief at the sound of American voices. His teammates' voices. "In here, boys."

Six soldiers dressed in arctic combat gear shuffled into the room, swinging their camouflaged assault rifles left and right, scanning for further threats.

"It's okay, boys. It's clear."

"Jesus, Teller what happened back there?" one soldier asked.

Teller slid out from behind the furnace and smirked. "We were gonna lose the opportunity. I had to move."

Tony Franco knelt down by his commanding officer and inspected the gunshot wound. "We didn't get to do anything other than save your ass."

"You shouldn't have. The needs of the many ..."

"Don't. Not another Star Trek reference. It's no wonder you can't get laid, boss." Tony laughed, his wide smile revealing perfectly polished teeth. "So, same guys?"

Teller winced as his wound was poked. "Yeah. A mixed bag of gear, and totally the wrong ethnicity."

"And the tattoo?" said another soldier, stepping up.

"Yep. Same one, Gibbs. Take some pics, let's see if we can ID these guys. And radio the angel, I want outta here ASAP. We followed them back here, but I don't wanna stay longer than we have to."

"Any idea why they came here at all? Why a steel works?" Tony scanned the room again.

"I don't know. But, this mill has history," Teller replied. "This was the Seishin Iron and Steel Works, built in the 1930s by the Japanese who stayed after the Russo-Japanese war. They used to manufacture steel for the military here, but it was shut down following the depression years ago."

"What's your point boss?" Tony asked, bandaging up Teller's leg.

"Does this look shut down to you?" Teller raised his eyebrows expectantly.

Gibbs and Tony glanced about the room, noting the molten river of steel pouring from the furnace.

"Okay, so it's fired up. Then where are the workers?" Gibbs asked.

"I think they got a heads up we were coming," Teller replied. "These clowns probably thought they could lose us in here. It's how they got the jump on me. I'm still piecing it together. But I'm telling you there's more to this than we can see right now. We'll do a quick sweep, then get the hell outta here."

"I can actually hear that big brain of yours whirring, boss. Now's not the time. Get your heavy ass up."

Tony grabbed one of Teller's arms, swung it around his neck and hoisted up his friend.

"Umm, sir? You have a message on the sat phone," one of the soldiers said.

"Fort Meade?" Jonathan asked.

"Someone called Freya Nilsson?" the soldier replied. "How the hell did a civilian get this number?"

Teller smirked again. Freya Nilsson was no civilian.

CHAPTER TWO

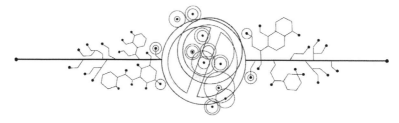

Location: passenger plane *en route* to Siberia

The hum of the engines rumbled through the business class cabin. It had been expensive, and the other passengers had thrown unhappy glances at her as KJ sat in the adjacent seat, but Freya felt it worthwhile. The journey would be a long one, and next would come camping out in tents at thirty below zero. They both deserved a little comfort. Not that it was helping her sleep. Going back to Siberia, all she could think of was Kelly. Of course, if Kelly could see her now, he'd be laughing at her for being a princess in army boots—always ready to shoot someone if necessary, but flying business class and turning up her nose at foreign food. Freya smiled a sad smile. She'd never hear his voice again. Five years later, and it still hurt. This is what it had been like for him all day, every day. A hole that never went away.

It was hard on KJ, too. Never knowing his father. Watching other kids and their dads. It didn't help that Freya often talked about him; sometimes as if he was still around. KJ asked questions, but seemed to know it was a difficult subject. Usually his queries were simple ones, about how much he resembled his dad, or just how much Freya loved him. "Very much," was all Freya could say. How does someone explain to a five-year old everything they had been through? How would she explain what it was she loved about

15

Kelly Graham so damn much, despite his arrogance, and how he was a broken man who shut out the world? Love isn't black and white. You don't love someone for their eye color, or their sense of humor. You love them because you do. And if she loved Kelly, then what she felt for KJ was more than words were able to describe.

Freya pulled her gaze from the window and studied her son, now curled up in a ball on the seat-cum-bed. Kelly had lost his wife and daughter. What would she do if she lost KJ? She had known of Kelly's loss before. She'd sympathized. But no one can truly understand that pain until they're a parent themselves. It didn't bear thinking about. Yet here she was, on a plane to Siberia with her son, with no idea what to expect.

She'd been adamant that it wasn't going to happen. Stalwart. There was no way she was going to Siberia with her son. But sat alone in the dark after her Skype call with Minya, the conversation had rattled around in her head over and over. Time wasn't on Freya's side. KJ's nightmares were only getting worse and one day, he'd only go alone.

Freya had called Minya back, keeping the TV volume low.

"If we came, I need a guarantee KJ will be safe. And, if anything happens to me ..." Freya had said.

"Da, my friend. I know the arrangement. Of course," Minya had replied.

Freya had simply nodded.

"I will need copy of your passports, for Salekhard Border Division. We will need to mention every settlement and region we plan to visit in Yamal. You know where you wish to go?"

Freya could only guess it was the last sinkhole that had opened up on the peninsula. So that was where they had decided upon. Minya would sort out the necessary visas and meet them in

Salekhard.

But, for the rest of the night, Freya got no sleep. She must have changed her mind a thousand times. Debated and worried about how she was going to keep her son safe. Terrified of what she may find.

That's why she'd called Jonathan.

It had been a long time since she and Jonathan had spoken. A year of madness and press had followed the incident in Teotihuacan. And they'd had to be in contact to tie up loose ends. But their relationship was over. Just like Kelly, she'd been unable to move on. Jonathan had hung around, and for a while she'd let him. KJ needed a strong male role model, and Jonathan was a good man. But he wasn't Kelly. She just wasn't able to give him what she knew he wanted—not now and definitely not later.

Despite that, Teller had religiously given her the sat phone code each time it changed. If she ever needed him, she could call. She hadn't done so in four years. Hadn't even had the urge. But now, selfishly, she'd called in the favor. And ever the white knight, Teller had responded to her cry for help. He was already on his way. Perhaps she was using him—playing on his feelings for her. Right now, only one thing mattered: KJ. And if this was a way to protect him, so be it.

A flight attendant wheeled her trolley up to Freya and KJ. "Something to eat? Drink perhaps?" Her sickly-sweet smile matched her overuse of makeup and inordinately complicated hairdo.

KJ stirred at the sound of her voice, and then immediately sat upright and alert. Freya eyed him as he had one of the stronger traits from his father—a healthy interest in pretty women. Any time one walked by, KJ's mood brightened.

17

Freya turned to the attendant. "Just some water, please."

The woman handed over a glass of ice water. Freya rummaged around in her bag and pulled a small bottle from an inner pocket. In a practiced motion, she popped the lid, shot two pills into her mouth, closed the bottle, and placed it back into her purse—all without KJ seeing. A mouthful of water and the pills were gone.

"What a handsome boy with such pretty eyes," the attendant cooed. "Would you like a snack?"

KJ's trademark half smile spread across his lips. "I'm KJ," he said. "What's your name?"

"I'm Susan," the woman replied.

"Well, Susan, my mom thinks I'm not old enough to drink alcohol, but I am."

The air stewardess smiled again. "Is that so?"

"Yep. I mean, we are in business class, after all. Surely, I'm allowed? And if you think about it, we are over international water. So, what legal rules apply?"

Freya's eyes narrowed.

The woman swayed a little on the spot, staring into KJ's cobalt eyes. "You have a point there, KJ." The woman fished out a flute from the cart. "Perhaps some champagne, if your mom says it's okay?"

"Are you crazy?" Freya shooed the woman away before turning to her son. "International water? Legal rules? KJ, where did you even learn that? Did you ... was that? Did you do that thing again?"

KJ hunched his shoulders and stared at the floor. "I just wanted to see if I could have some."

Freya slipped an arm around him. "I know, Mr. Man. But you can't use that on people. It's not nice."

"I can't do it with everyone, Mom, only people who aren't

strong. It doesn't really work on you."

Freya pulled away and squinted at her son. "So, you've tried?"

"I'm a kid." He giggled mischievously. "I'm supposed to try."

Location: Chongjin, North Korea

Hiroki Ishii sat on his haunches and pushed his long pinky fingernail into the perfectly round hole in the middle of Masamune Ikeda's forehead. It was wet and cold. He pulled his finger from the bullet hole and wiped the blood onto a hand towel that he immediately passed to one of his followers.

He stood and beckoned his second in command aside.

"The Beast has been here and killed our men, Master Ishii-san," the stocky man said.

Ishii ran his fingers down the strange fern-shaped scar that cut its way across his right eye socket disappearing into his black beard, and stared in contemplation with his one good eye into the molten river of steel at his feet. "They can chase us all over the world, but they will never catch us. Just as a man can no more catch the very air. The Beast thinks only in the physical. We are an idea. Everywhere. Always. They cannot stop the bringing about of Shōhō. It is inevitable."

"*Hai*, Master Ishii-san. Still, we must be more careful. They are closer to us than is comfortable."

"Did they find it?" Ishii asked.

"No. We handed it off before we came across the border."

"Then there will be no retribution. At least for now."

"Understood, Master Ishii-san. So, we proceed?"

"*Hai*. But not you. You need to go on an errand. Take a *kuru*. Twenty men. Tell me what you find." Ishii handed his commander a tablet glowing with the image of a map. "Be careful, Takashi. Do not engage. Reconnaissance only. Do you understand?"

Takashi bobbed his head. "*Hai*, Master Ishii-san."

Hiroki stared into the black eyes of his subordinate, then grabbed the man's wrist and lifted it up to his own face. "Last time you lost a finger. Next time you lose an arm."

Takashi Suzuki stared at the stump where his little finger used to be, then lowered his gaze to the floor. "Hai," he said finally.

Location: New York Times Building, New York City, USA

"Keeping you up, O'Reilly?"

Catherine woke with a start, then stared at her desk in a daze. A large brown envelope that had been slapped unceremoniously on her keyboard stared back. Slowly, she turned to see Frank Thompson sitting on the corner of her desk, his supersized butt cheek enveloping the wood.

"I was awake," she said.

"Sure you were." He studied her with beady eyes. "This just came for you." He nodded at the envelope.

"Just?" She checked her watch. "It's like, gone 10:00 p.m. Who delivers a parcel at this time of night?"

Frank shrugged his heavy shoulders. "Someone who knows you'd still be here instead of at home wrapped around some Porsche-driving, no chest-hair-having, pretty boy?"

She rolled her eyes. "Keep your fantasies to yourself, Frank."

"No need to roll those freaky eyes at me, O'Reilly. Your—"

"Yes, leprechaun-like, magical eyes. Blah, blah, blah. Every time we speak, Frank. Yes, I'm Irish. Yes, I have one blue and one green eye. No, I'm not a leprechaun. No, I'm not magical. And no,

I won't go on a date with you."

Frank shrugged again, but didn't move.

Catherine sighed. "Are you waiting for something?"

"For you to open it. Maybe it's from an admirer. Or from a PI whose been taking your pic—"

"Piss off, Frank!" In the UK, being a redhead had been seen as a form of leprosy. Friday nights were lonely. In the States, she was some kind of ginger-goddess. She'd only been there six months, but it was already tiresome.

"Woah, okay. Someone's PMSing." He shuffled his sizeable weight off the desk and meandered away.

"This is why you're stuck doing the back pages, Frank," Catherine called after him.

He didn't reply.

She tucked a bright orange curl of hair behind her ear and studied the envelope. No stamp. No sender info. Just her name, hand scrawled across the front: *Catherine O'Reilly, New York Times.*

Just open it, Cat, she thought.

Catherine turned it over and peeled back the sticky tab. Inside was a wad of aerial photographs, several printouts of maps and two newspaper clippings. She spread them out face up on the table, then grabbed one of the maps. A red marker had been used to encircle the land mass protruding into a large body of water. A sea or ocean maybe? Google would tell her. She shook the mouse to wake up her computer and then Googled a map of the world. Catherine matched the coastline in the photo to that on the screen.

"Why there?" she whispered to herself.

She snatched up the newspaper clippings. One was foreign, written in Cyrillic. It appeared to be a weather article. She didn't understand the words but the temperature and symbols suggested

… warmth? A sunny day? Why was that significant? The clipping was from two days ago. The sender wanted her to know these images were recent. She studied the other newspaper excerpt. It was … one of her own articles. Written five years ago for *The Guardian*. She studied it closely. *Why this article?* She'd been shut out of this, the whole thing mothballed. Every source had dried up, every contact gone silent. Her boss had almost fired her for pushing the story so hard.

Reviewing the photos more closely, she now saw they were in fact enlarged shots of the first aerial map. Close ups of the land mass. Catherine pawed at them, turning them around and around until, eventually, she saw it.

"No fuckin' way." She leaped from her seat and pounded over to Frank's desk. He'd apparently gone home. *Good.* She rummaged around his desk until she found them: his glasses. She raced back to her bureau and hovered Frank's thick lenses over the photos, magnifying the images.

There it was. Faint. Perhaps blurry. But there.

"Holy shit." She rubbed her slender face. *What now?* No time for approvals, this window wouldn't last long. Someone had given her the jump, and she couldn't let anyone else scoop this story. Catherine grabbed up the papers, stuffed them back into the envelope, then snatched up her keys and leather jacket, and raced out the door.

CHAPTER THREE

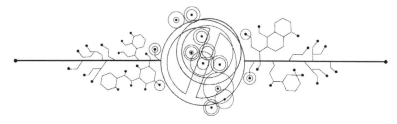

Location: Salekhard, Siberia

Salekhard by any standard was a modern town, with all the amenities one could want. Shops, restaurants, pharmacies. It even had a small airport and a railway at Labytnangi on the opposite side of the river Ob. Yet the Siberian winter showed Salekhard for what it was: a man-made town and no match for mother nature. The long-awaited bridge across the Ob was still not finished. In the summer, a ferry operated. In the winter, vehicles crossed the river by driving over the frozen river ice. But, during the floating ice seasons—currently—Salekhard operated in standalone mode, completely cut off from the world. Freya and Minya, with their children in tow, had taken snowmobiles to get as far as they had.

KJ shivered, so Freya pulled him close and ensured the fur lining to his hood still protected his delicate face.

"It's c-c-cold, Mommy," KJ stammered.

"I know, Mr. Man. The chopper's here now."

"W-why, won't they let us get in?"

"We're waiting for Minya to get the okay. These things take time."

"But I can't feel my fingers," KJ complained.

Freya crouched down to meet her son's gaze peering out from

the fox fur frame of his cowl. "Mr. Man, I know you're cold. I am too, but we have to wait. If we don't do this properly, we won't be allowed in and you won't get to visit the hole. Do you understand?"

KJ nodded, albeit sheepishly.

Minya stormed back from the chopper, bracing against the stabbing wind that pulled at her fur coat. "*Khorosho*, we can go."

"Finally," Freya said.

Minya placed a hand on Freya's shoulder. "No weapons on board, *da*?"

"*Da*," Freya bobbed her head.

Minya eyed her. "Freya, you are sure? No weapons? It's not safe and you know it."

"I'm sure, *davai!*" Freya flashed a smile, pulled her ponytail tight, then turned to KJ. "Okay KJ, *bistro, bistro!*"

KJ ran off ahead and was helped into the chopper by Nikolaj.

Minya grabbed Freya by the arm, stopping in her tracks. "The stupid *kozel* also wants more money."

"What?" Freya squinted as the icy wind knifed at her face.

"*Da*. He say it is bad weather and risky. He wants more."

"Of course he does. Does he also want to keep his teeth?" Freya asked, her jaw clenched tight.

Minya smiled. "My friend, this is not good example for Kelly Junior, no?"

Minya had been a voice of reason. For the last year, any time Freya felt she might lash out, a call to Minya helped. The woman was infinitely calm, with seemingly never-ending patience. Freya had put it down to her time in the Gulag—mastery of her emotions. Whether she was raging on the inside was another question. Of course, other than setting a good example to KJ, Minya's wise counsel had also touched upon the young man's uncanny likeness to his father. If KJ were to have the same lack of impulse control as Kelly Graham, and this was combined with his unnatural abilities, there was no telling what havoc would be wreaked.

"I suppose."

"*Davai*," Minya said, her hand on Freya's shoulder.

The two women padded off through the worsening snowstorm toward the chopper.

The KA-27PS was about as comfortable on the inside as it looked from the outside. While referred to as a HELIX-D by NATO, and used the world over in various forms, often for search and rescue, one look at the monstrosity was enough to remind Freya this was an aircraft originally designed for anti-submarine warfare. A forty-foot gray monster with two Isotov TV3-117V turboshaft engines, and coaxial rotors removing the need for a tail rotor. Of course, the torpedoes, cannons and machine guns had been removed and replaced with searchlights and winches.

It hurtled along the snow-laden inner peninsula at one-hundred-twenty miles per hour—far too fast for Freya's liking given the gales outside were gaining strength the farther north they ventured. KJ was curled up in a ball on the floor, covered in a blanket. His head poked from the top and every so often he'd grunt or murmur as his recurring dream took hold. All Freya could see was Kelly—the exact same picture some six years ago having dragged him half-drowned from the South China Sea. History repeating itself. KJ needed him now more than ever. Hell, Freya needed him now.

A gentle nudge and KJ stirred from his sleep. "Mommy?"

"Hey, Mr. Man. Dreaming again?"

"Uh huh, about the hole and the people."

"People?" He hadn't mentioned people before.

KJ giggled. "Yeah, they look funny. Wrinkly skin and fur hats."

"They sound like Nenets, sweetie."

"Ne-nats?"

"Ne-*nets*, Mr. Man. They're the people who live where we're going."

The chopper abruptly dropped a few feet. A garbled instruction from the pilot sounded over the loud speaker: they were in for rougher weather. Freya beckoned KJ to her and strapped him into the adjacent seat. His little face was white, his eyes wide.

"So," Freya began. "Did you know the Nenets herd reindeer?"

"Really?" KJ asked, his demeanor brightening.

"Yep. They use the reindeer for everything; fur for clothes, meat for food. They eat it raw, or boil it up and mix it with the blood. Ewwww." Freya wrinkled up her nose in feigned disgust. "And they sell the reindeer for money—or vodka."

"Vodka?"

"Alcohol. Never mind. Anyway, they move across the land with the reindeer following the food for them. They haven't had much to do with outsiders, and they don't speak Russian, really. Even the government left them alone. The Nenets pay the government in reindeer each year."

"All of the reindeer?"

"Actually, no." Freya smiled. "Each Nenets has a special reindeer, one that is just for him or her. And they are not allowed to eat it, or harm it. They have to look after it until it's unable to walk. It's kind of a spirit animal."

"Like daddy and K'in," KJ offered, a broad smile spreading

across his face.

Freya's heart skipped in her chest and her stomach knotted. "Yeah, just like daddy."

The decision of how much about his father to reveal to KJ was a difficult one. Freya had decided to answer as honestly as possible, in a way that a five-year old could understand, any question he asked. As it turned out, five-year olds have a lot of questions. And so, he knew his daddy had a special animal friend, one that helped him when he was sad. KJ had wanted his own special animal friend. Freya had settled on a cat—Socks.

Another jolt and the HELIX-D banked hard to the right. The contents of Freya's stomach rose into her mouth as they sharply plummeted another twenty feet. Nikolaj gave a whoop of excitement.

"Is this fun to you?" Freya asked.

"*Da*, it's like a fair ride," he replied.

Minya shot Freya a glance only other mothers would understand.

"It's too windy and too cold. Visibility sucks—" Freya said.

"*Da*, welcome to Siberia!" Minya yelled back, holding onto her harness.

Freya climbed into her own harness and strapped in. "Mr. Man. I want you to put your head as close to your knees as you can, and cover your head with your arms, okay?"

KJ complied. "Okay, Mommy."

"Not bad advice for us all, *da?*" Minya said as the chopper shook yet again.

Freya nodded and took the brace position.

A severe crosswind pushed them west. The chopper's engines whined as they defied the Siberian winter, forcing the chopper east, and most importantly toward the landing site. Veering too far off course would mean several hours before the Huskies could pick them up. Hours they couldn't afford in the Siberian cold.

Location: St Petersburg, Russia

The smell of the *dyestskii dom* was far too familiar. The old wood, the stench of cheap cigarettes used to barter between children and of cheaper vodka that lingered on the breath of the staff. Long before Polkovnik Aleksandr Vladimirovich Vetrov was a sleeper agent in the USA, or a Colonel in the FSB, he was an orphan. A true orphan, his family dead. Not a social orphan, like the half a million abandoned children who now clogged up the system as a result of the collapse of the Soviet Union. Their families often poor, jobless, ill, and in trouble with the law, unable to care for their offspring. No, he was alone from the age of five. And had found himself in an institute just like this one. Stripped of his family title, he'd simply been called Sasha Vetrov.

Sasha pawed at empty bedsheets and side tables in the room crammed with more than twenty cots. It was disgusting. These days the children were herded through a maze of state structures operated by three government ministries. Depending on how they're classified—disabled or not—the orphans were sent to different kinds of orphanages after the baby houses. Never given a chance. In that respect, Sasha was lucky. He'd been picked up by a military program to become a sleeper agent. Taught how to fight and survive. It had served his life well.

This orphanage was supposed to be closed some five years ago. But there was no dust on the tables. And the bedsheets were fresh. Sasha wedged his cap under his arm and slowly paced from room to room, examining every corner and every wall. In the last bedroom, he found a crayon drawing pinned to the inside of a closet door. It was crude, the red wax used to sketch out the rough shape of a man and perhaps several small children at his feet. In the hand of the man was what looked like a gun. And on the man's face, next to his jug-like ears, in black crayon, was the number nine.

Sasha pulled the drawing from the door and studied it closely. Who was this man? And what was the significance of the number nine? He folded the picture and slid it into the inner pocket of his tunic, then continued his search of the dilapidated building. He had tracked the terrorists here, following intel from his contact in China. When he'd discovered it was an orphanage, only the worst implications came to mind.

A soldier calling from downstairs broke the Polkovnik's train of thought. Sasha stomped down the old wooden stairs, which creaked and protested under the weight of his muscular frame. Around the corner, three of his men waited, one holding open a door-shaped piece of wall—a secret doorway. Sasha's eyes narrowed. He indicated for his men to ready their weapons, and cautiously followed them into the dark room.

Nothing. No one. The room was abandoned.

The soldiers inspected the closet-sized room, searching for clues. The room appeared to have been scrubbed. There were clean spots on the desks where computers and monitors may have once sat. But other than that, nothing.

The Polkovnik's boot clanged on a metal wastepaper basket sitting under one of the desks. He crouched down and fished out a few pieces of burned paper. Whomever had been here had attempted to scorch all of the evidence, but these had not been completely destroyed as hoped. He studied the fragments. One appeared to be in either Japanese or Chinese, simply typed out on white paper. The other was an aerial photograph. Sasha pulled his smart phone from his tunic and launched the translate app. He hovered the camera over the text, allowing it to auto-detect the language and then translate. The unburned text was immediately recognized as Japanese and translated. It was a prayer. A very specific prayer, only used by one group. That didn't make any sense. They were a defunct terrorist cell. What the hell was going on? And why had they left so quickly? Had he been so clumsy as to be detected?

Sasha rubbed his chin in contemplation, then turned his attention to the photograph. For this he didn't need any technology to understand. He knew exactly where this was. The question was, why did this obscure group have any interest in that place at all? Sasha barked orders to his men: they must prepare.

CHAPTER FOUR

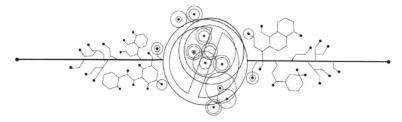

Location: Yamal Peninsula, Siberia

The Husky team had not arrived. Or maybe the chopper had been blown too far off course to be found. Either way, the foursome was alone, huddled up and freezing, in the hold of the KA-27PS. Freya placed KJ in the arms of Minya who pulled him into her embrace with a shivering Nikolaj. She then slid the cargo door open, hopped down to the ground, and closed it behind her with a *clunk*.

Taking stock of her surroundings, Freya scanned for danger. As far as the eye could see, the landscape appeared bleak; a wind-blasted tundra hidden under a layer of permafrost, fractured by serpentine rivers and dotted with dwarf shrubs. The permanent dusk was covered with a film of wispy gray clouds.

Freya swiveled on the spot, swinging her gaze a full three-hundred-sixty degrees. It wasn't until the third pass that they came into view; two men, driving a sled pulled by six Huskies. The dogs pounded the permafrost, moving at an incredible speed, yet it took a full thirty minutes for them to actually reach her.

"*Privjet*," one man said, stepping down from the sled when they arrived. While he spoke Russian, his accent was poor.

"*Privjet*," Freya replied, eying the man. He had typical mongoloid epicanthic folds and dark hair streaked white.

"American?" the man asked.

"*Da.*" Freya nodded.

"No need for speak Russian. I speak good American."

Freya cocked her head in amusement. "Okay, American it is. You want me to throw in some slang here and there? The occasional, *y'all?*"

The Nenets man didn't reply, or even smile.

"Got it, no jokes."

"It is as if the ghost of Kelly Graham is here with us," Minya said, hopping down from the chopper. "Sarcasm is not understood here."

"He speaks American," Freya said.

Minya nodded. "More and more Nenets have learned. Many tourists come here, especially after the sinkholes."

Freya turned back to the men, studying their red noses and dried out skin. "I'm sure it helps to be able to ask for vodka in multiple languages, too."

The two mothers and their sons perched on the back of the reindeer-skin-covered sled, their belongings wedged between them. KJ squirmed and wriggled for two hours straight, constantly complaining things were poking his back, or the terrain was too bumpy and it hurt every time they flew over a snow drift. Freya couldn't blame him; the awkward posture was exacerbating the pain in her hands and feet, making her muscles twitch. However, eventually, KJ fell asleep, mouth agape, snuggled up to his mom.

The landscape didn't improve much on their journey; still a frozen wasteland, but at least it didn't get any darker. This far north, the sun never really disappeared behind the horizon. Why anyone would want to live here was simply not fathomable to Freya. And she actually liked Russia; its cities, old and cold—both in terms of climate and its people. But, this—this was something else entirely.

Bleak was the only word Freya could think of. Of course, to the Russians it wasn't bleak. It was a veritable gold mine—or at least, gas mine. Eleven gas fields and fifteen oil, gas and condensate fields were discovered on the Yamal Peninsula and its offshore areas. Nearly sixteen trillion cubic meters of explored and provisionally evaluated gas reserves, with another twenty-two forecast. The pipelines to rape the land of these reserves were set up a few years earlier. Perhaps this was what had set off the appearance of sinkholes. Perhaps it was the change in climate—global warming. Whatever it was, she didn't like it.

Sleet began to swirl the sled, obscuring their view. Freya pulled the scarf from her nose, her warm breath misting the air. "How far?" she called to the driver. "The weather is closing in and I want to be under some kind of cover before it gets worse."

"Not far," he called back. "Camp is much close. Not long wait."

He hadn't lied. Twenty minutes later, behind a wall of sleet, shapes began to form in the distance. Another thirty minutes and they had arrived at a small camp. Maybe twenty conical tents, *mya*, draped in red cloth, arranged closely together.

Freya nudged KJ who stirred, then immediately jerked awake and hopped down from the sled, stretching his arms and rubbing his butt. Freya stepped down beside him and placed a hand on his shoulder to keep him close. The camp seemed relatively empty. Fewer than fifteen tents in all. On a hill, a small triangle of sticks was erected, decorated with strips of red cloth and fish hanging from its top. Women and old people shuffled from *mya* to *mya*. There were few men and no children at all.

33

Minya marched with Nikolaj and their drivers to a makeshift sled parking lot to meet with two middle-aged men. She greeted them in Nenets, but quickly switched to Russian. A few glances back at a shivering Freya and KJ later, and they were ushered inside the nearest *mya*.

Dogs lounged by the entrance but didn't move as Freya and the others pushed through the flap. Freya almost walked straight into an old graying reindeer as it sauntered past. It used its antlers to poke the flap open, then trotted outside. Freya shot their Nenets driver an amused glance.

"Pee time," the man said.

"Indeed," replied Freya.

"Please sit," said the driver.

"I'm sorry, I didn't ask your name," Freya said.

"Andrei," he replied. "Sit."

Freya and Minya sat, urging their children to do the same. Their hosts, three older women, two younger women, and an old man, all dressed in reindeer skin and embroidered coats, busied themselves with making fires using dried low-brush willow. In the small pots, they boiled water for tea and to cook fish. The oldest woman broke a loaf of stale bread into chunks, then handed KJ and Nikolaj a piece each. Both accepted it, but neither took a bite.

As the evening passed, Freya and Minya played good tent guests. Now adorned in Nenets's felt boot liners, tanned knee-high boots and reindeer hide coats, they leaned back into bundles of furs that padded the tent walls and listened to an epic tale told by the old man together with a younger woman. The story seemed to be broken into minute-long portions. The young woman's sole task was to repeat the last few words of each segment—much like in a gospel church, echoing the pastor's sermon. Nikolaj and KJ slept at their mothers' side, warmed by the smoky fire.

The old man finished, so Freya sat up and cleared her throat. "I hope they don't mind me asking, but where are the children? Nenets's camps usually have children in them."

Andrei turned to the elders and repeated the question in Nenets. They responded, their faces solemn.

"They were taken by Ngha, the evil son of the creator Num," Andrei conveyed.

"Interesting," Minya said. "I thought communist regime had crushed shamanism. It appears not."

"Where did Ngha take them?" pressed Freya, before popping two pills from her bottle into her mouth and taking a mouthful of tea.

"Into the earth," Andrei said, verbally confirming the physical gestures of the oldest woman. "One of the mothers went looking, but never came back. She must have been taken, too."

"The sinkhole," Minya said, glancing at Freya.

Freya pulled KJ closer. "How far is the sinkhole fr—"

The two older men from earlier rushed into the tent, firing a string of panicked words in Nenets. Despite the calamity, both Nikolaj and KJ remained asleep, exhausted from the day.

The hosts' eyes widened, and they quickly clambered to their feet before shuffling out of the *mya* and into the cold.

Freya glanced at Minya and then at their kids. "Do we follow them?"

"Of course. We leave children here, safe in tent."

Minya and Freya carefully freed themselves from their children, resting them comfortably in the reindeer skins, and then made a hasty exit. The air was clean, crisp and free of snow. The sky was a permanent dusk-like orange, despite it being the early hours of the morning. The women followed the footprints in the permafrost to the edge of the camp.

There, fewer than fifty feet away, stood a small girl no more than five years old. Still dressed head to toe in skins and furs, she seemed unscathed. In fact, her stance was tall and confident. And even at this distance, her cobalt blue eyes—just like KJ's—shone out from beneath the fur-lined hood.

"Svetlana!" called an elderly woman who then began to trudge toward the child.

Freya glanced at Minya who just shook her head and gave a small shrug.

"What's going on, Mommy?" KJ had sidled up to his mother.

"*Da*, what is emergency?" Nikolaj said, rubbing his eyes and yawning.

Freya pulled KJ to her legs. "No idea, guys. You're supposed to be asleep in the tent. We should keep our dis—"

The sky burst into life—a bright green ribbon of light snaking its way across the heavens. Fluttering and dancing, other ribbons appeared, emerald green and fire red, alive with oxygen and nitrogen ions, twirling together yet in different rhythms. The Nenets child on the hill took a step forward as if to make room for someone else. Against the supernatural backdrop of the *aurora borealis* came another silhouette—padding along on all fours. A silhouette Freya knew all too well and thought she'd never see again. Freya drew a sharp breath and fired a worried glance at Minya.

"It's not possible," Minya said.

The creature sidled up to the Nenets girl, who rested a hand on top of its head.

Freya stared at it until details could be seen within the silhouette. The same snubbed mouth and small nostrils. The same trapezoid head and set of six blood red, feather-like gills, bobbing with its movements. It looked just like K'in, yet different. Smaller and fatter, and its skin was a translucent blue, not pink.

"It's ... it's ..." Freya stuttered.

And then, they came. One after another, the camps' children appeared as featureless figures on the horizon, and with them each another creature. Another of K'in's kind. Every one slightly different to the last, some rounder, some thinner. Some with long gills, some with short. But they came and sat, attentive, at the side of the children.

Freya's stomach churned and she clamped onto her son. It was a nest. A nest of Huahuqui. And they'd bonded to the children.

The view through binoculars was limited. Takashi Suzuki was a long way from the American's camp. But from here, even with reduced visibility, he knew what he was looking at. It was not supposed to be possible. The Chinese Green and Red Societies, the Shan Chu, had fumbled that chance years ago. The creature they had fought to capture had been killed, and every orb demolished. The Americans and the Chinese government had destroyed all data on that race, so it could never be cloned again. Yet, here in the Siberian Tundra ...

This was his chance to prove his worth again to Master Ishii. Takashi beckoned one of his soldiers closer and handed the man the binoculars. The soldier laid in the snow, his arctic camouflage fatigues blending into the environment, and peered through the device, adjusting the focus to align with his own eyes. For a few seconds he lay still, then slowly pulled back and stared in disbelief at his commander.

Takashi nodded once. "*Watashi wa watashi no meiyo o kaifuku shimasu [I will restore my honor].*"

Location: on a plane from New York to Moscow

Catherine sipped on her economy-class coffee. The bitter liquid attacked her tastebuds and scalded her tongue. She placed it as near to the edge of the fold-down tray as possible to leave enough room to spread out the photos and examine them for the hundredth time.

There it was. As plain as day, staring out of the sinkhole in the ground. A pair of sapphire-blue, wise and knowing, eyes in the blunted face of a creature—the very same creature whose existence had been leaked by a Google technician and then covered up some six years ago.

Catherine had chased down the story while at the Guardian newspaper in London. Quieting US newspapers was one thing, but the CIA or the NSA, or whomever, had far less control of British journalism. She had wanted—needed—the truth. Proving their existence, proving that everything humans had achieved was owed to another species, was vindicating. Every rally she'd organized. Every Greenpeace protest she'd attended, vilifying what humans had become—selfish and disconnected from nature. A species with whom we need to be whole, was her version of the Holy Grail. She was an environmental journalist. Well known and disliked by corporations the world over. Before chasing this story on the creature, she had been key in running stories on the Deepwater Horizon tragedy. She liked to think her dogged approach to keeping that story in the public eye over a full four years had directly influenced the outcome. Transocean, BP and Halliburton were forced to pay out billions for negligence, violating clean water acts and killing eleven crew members.

On the success of the Deepwater Horizon stories, Jim, her editor, had been supportive of her running the story on the mysterious creature cloned by the US government. For a full year he had let her chase it down. Much to the annoyance of Freya Nilsson. The woman had been a stone wall. Unmoving. Unwilling to speak. Her stubbornness on the subject beyond all reason. *Why wouldn't she tell the truth? Tell the world? Why keep it a secret, even after the leak? Why be a part of a poor cover-up, that the rest of the world seemed to happily swallow?*

Catherine had pushed too far. Cornering Freya outside the pre-school of her young son, Kelly Junior. The military woman had almost knocked Catherine's teeth out in front of all the other mothers. After that, things changed. Jim suddenly lost interest and any contacts Catherine had, had gone silent. The trail wasn't cold—it was dead. Just like that.

Only Jonathan Teller had been somewhat co-operative. He never really told her anything. He was with the NSA after all. But he didn't stonewall her either. Most of the time, it felt like he was gleaning information from her, not the other way around. On their very last call, he'd said something cryptic:

"We don't see the world as it is. We see it as we are. Perhaps one day, we will be mature enough to see it with wiser eyes."

And that was the last she heard.

So why now? The creatures are back? Had the government been hiding them in Siberia? Too much conjecture. Too few facts. Soon, she'd be in Moscow, then she could charter something down to Salekhard and scam her way across the border into Yamal.

The only question was: who was her benefactor here? This was satellite imagery, so either a government or a corporation. Or maybe a private hacker. No demands had been made. There had been no exchange for this information. That wasn't good. Catherine sighed and sipped on her coffee again. Everything had a price.

CHAPTER FIVE

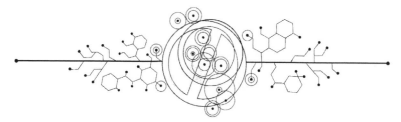

Location: Nenets camp, Yamal Peninsula, Siberia

The Nenets had been surprisingly accommodating. Perhaps they were glad to get their children back. Perhaps they understood what the bond meant. Much like the peoples of Peru Freya had encountered some six years ago, there was an inherent acceptance of the Huahuqui —an understanding. Without the prejudices of modern society, these tribes' people's hearts were open to something more advanced societies weren't. And that included Freya. She didn't like this one bit. To start with, no one seemed interested in where they came from, and were unwilling to take her to the sinkhole to investigate. Then, there was the fact the creatures seemed to preferentially bond to the children, the adults unaffected. Was this a choice? Did they see something pure in the children? Or were these little people easier to control?

As far as she saw it, things would go one of two ways: a bond like the one Kelly and K'in had—benevolent and healing; or a bond like Victoria and Wak—painful and torturous. There were no guarantees. No way to ensure anything one way or the other. And that wasn't even considering the wider implications. *Could the government cover up a whole nest? Would the Russian government be co-operative? Would the Russian government even tell anyone else?* Freya knew all too well how these things went. There could be no black boxes. No secret experiments. The only way to protect these children, and maybe even the creatures, would be to expose everything to the world. Truly leak it.

That was the scariest part of all. She'd spent the best part of five years protecting KJ. Hiding his gifts from everyone, especially the government—even Jonathan. And yet now, exposing KJ to the world might be the only way to save him. Maybe her son being part of this in its entirety was a blessing. *They* could steal KJ and no one would miss one child. But, a whole nest and family of special children? That was harder.

KJ sat on the ground beside his mother, staring wide-eyed through the open *mya* flap at the creatures as they padded around on the permafrost, their blue skin shimmering in the morning light. There were twenty-two tribe's children and all had bonded with a Huahuqui. At least ten Huahuqui remained unbonded.

One in particular had repeatedly come to sniff around the *mya* in which Freya and KJ sat. Freya shooed it away several times but, unfazed, it had come back again, nuzzling at the tent material. It reminded her so much of K'in. A smaller, slightly fatter version perhaps, but it had the same soft face and strangely calm demeanor. The same child-like curiosity. KJ was giddy with excitement, inching closer and closer on his butt to the entrance to get a better look.

"She's back again, Mom," KJ said.

"She?" Freya asked.

KJ smiled a big toothy grin. "Sure, she's a she."

Freya edged closer to the opening and studied the creature as it sniffed around the tent, shaking its long red gills. "How do you know that?"

"She told me," KJ replied, flatly.

"Told you? Told you how?" Freya grabbed her son by the shoulders.

"In my head. Not in English. Or in Russian. Just … told me." He broke his gaze from the creature to concentrate on his mother. "What's wrong, Mommy? You look worried."

Freya couldn't speak.

"She can be my special friend, like daddy's," KJ beamed.

Freya's heart sank, her insides cramping. The creature had him already. She cast a painful gaze at the animal and then back to her son, whose smile was still fixed from ear to ear. What was she supposed to do? There was nowhere to go, nowhere to hide. Where the hell was Jonathan? Why hadn't he arrived yet? He could have choppered them out of there, before her son had bonded. *Damn you, Jonathan,* she thought.

"Have you chosen name?" Minya stood in the opening to the *mya.*

"Uh-huh!" KJ replied.

Freya's nostrils flared. "Are you actually encouraging this?"

Minya stared a knowing look at Freya. "Have you considered he may need this? Not now, but—"

"That's not the point," Freya snapped. "Do you not remember what happened to Victoria?"

"Of course. But that was different situation. Different creature. A monster made by government. These are not monsters. They are like K'in. And remember what that creature did for Kelly. You know this more than anyone."

It was true that K'in had helped Kelly heal. Such a bond might do the same for KJ in the future. But, that didn't change their present situation. "So, KJ becomes bonded. You think it will stop there? He'll be put in a box and experimented on. He needs protection. They all do."

"And that is our job, no? We are mothers," Minya said with a determined smile.

Minya was right. But saying it and doing it were two different things.

"K'awin," KJ piped up.

The women stared at him.

"I'm sorry?" Freya said.

"That's what she's called. K'awin. It's Mayan. It means spirit." He reached into his rucksack and pulled out a large tome that was altogether too advanced for a child his age. KJ opened it to the correct page and thrust it into his mother's arms. "K'awin," he repeated again, tapping on the hieroglyph and associated English word.

"I like it," Minya said.

Freya gave her friend a worried glance.

On the floor, KJ stroked the nose of K'awin. The creature responded in kind, fluffing out her red gills and making a low warble akin to a cat's purr. He giggled and shuffled forward a little more. Then when close enough he threw his arms around K'awin's neck and hugged her.

Jealousy is the only word that accurately described the feeling washing through Freya. Not fear, or worry for her son's safety, as perhaps it should have been. No, it was definitely jealousy. It hurt like hell to see him so happy with something, someone, else. For so long it had been him and her. Now it was him and her—and K'awin. And Freya knew all too well the strength of the bond.

"Okay, Mr. Man. We need to get some rest; you've been up all night. You can see your pet later." Freya tugged on her son, gently easing him away from the creature.

CHILDREN OF THE FIFTH SUN: ECHELON

"She's not a pet," KJ said. "She's too clever to be a pet."

Freya sighed. "I know, sweetheart. Trust me, I know." She pulled him inside and laid him on the soft reindeer skin, before turning back to Minya. "Can you watch him? I need to make a call."

"Call? There are no cell towers here."

Freya pulled a clunky, square, cordless phone with a long aerial from her bag. "No, but there are satellites above our heads." She exited the *mya* and trudged off to an empty spot in the open, away from prying eyes and ears. Satisfied she was alone, Freya pulled her ponytail tight then stretched out a finger to dial. It trembled, failing to press the buttons on command. She clenched her fist until her knuckles were white then released. She dialed the number and let the phone ring. Five full minutes passed until the call connected.

"Hello? Who's this? Do you know what time it is?" a female voice asked.

"Hi, Lucy, I mean, Madam Secretary. It's Freya—Nilsson. I'm sorry to bother you, but we need to talk."

Location: Washington DC, USA

That was not the phone call Lucy had been expecting. Four hours later, she was at her desk in the White House preparing for an emergency meeting with the President later that morning. *This can't be black-boxed. No experiments this time,* Freya had pleaded. And, of course, she was right. Lucy had spent a year after the incident in Teotihuacan cleaning up the government's mess. Wiping the slates clean, battling the press, and ensuring that all projects were shut down. There would be no more cloning. Wak was supposed to be the last.

45

Now, this. Now, there wasn't one creature—but a nest. The Huahuqui, Freya called them. And they'd bonded to the children in that remote part of Siberia, and to her son. Lucy had only met KJ once. He was the absolute image of his father, right down to his half smile. The world owed Kelly Graham a lot. With Kelly gone, doing all she could for his son was important. Yet, the incident—secrets within secrets—had left her jaded. So many lives lost, both in the USA and in China. And she'd had to be part of it. The cover-up supposedly protecting the world at large. Could she really make a difference or would political bullshit overwhelm everything?

Her career didn't matter now. It was time to make amends. Lucy hadn't felt this way since her college days. Leading rallies fighting pipelines that ran through Native American homeland, or petitions pleading for changes to the environmental laws around carbon emissions. Fighting the good fight, for the good fight's sake. The only agenda: justice.

Lucy stepped into the Oval Office and patiently waited as President Michael Trainor finished up some paperwork. He'd not been in his position long, and was young compared to every President before him. His wavy black hair and strong blue eyes, under even stronger eyebrows, gave him presence. He was a man of the twenty-first century and steeped in his democratic beliefs. Half his cabinet had family names that stemmed from the first boats that entered New York's Liberty Island port many decades earlier. Most of all he liked Lucy—respected her need to fight for what was right—and so had kept her on as Secretary of State, even after his predecessor had departed. But his young age, new status and early provocative cabinet appointments meant he was now erring on the side of caution. Relationships with Russia and

China were at an all-time low and he was unlikely to ruffle feathers.

"Good morning, Lucy," the president said. He put down his pen, rested his hands on the desk, fingers interlinked, and raised his gaze to meet Lucy's.

"Good morning, Mr. President."

"Michael, please. We've been through this. Please, sit."

Lucy pulled up a plush chair and sat down.

"So, what's up, Lucy?"

She swallowed hard. "Do you know why our relationship with Russia and China is so fragile?"

The President frowned. "Decades of mistrust on all sides. Opposing world views. Econom—"

"Yes, of course. But now? Why it's so fragile right now?"

"From your tone, I assume you're going to tell me."

"Do you remember a few years ago, there was an incident with China. We came close to war."

He nodded. "Military ops in Chinese-owned waters. We overstepped some boundaries. They overreacted. I wouldn't say we were almost at war."

"Trust me, we were." Lucy sucked in a breath, then let it out slowly. "You may not believe what I am about to tell you. But, I suggest you let the evidence speak for itself." She slid a heavy folder from her handbag and dumped it with a *thunk* on the large wooden desk. "When I'm done, I need you to help me avoid war again."

Michael stared at the folder, then pulled it toward him. "With the Chinese?" he asked, his brow creased with worry.

"With everyone, Michael. And I mean everyone."

Location: Salekhard, Yamal Peninsula, Siberia

Salekhard was freezing. Not New York, a big, duck-down jacket will make it go away, cold. This was bone-chilling, muscles don't work, death seems preferable, Siberian cold. Catherine O'Reilly patted and rubbed her arms over and over, breathing into gloved hands and stamping her feet while she waited for the border control guard to come back.

It had been two hours and she still hadn't been able to cross into Yamal. Her press pass had meant squat. Her feminine wiles were lost on the officer. Russians were clearly not besotted with redheads like Americans. Her last resort was bribery. It could get her in a lot of trouble, but without a visa, she really had no other choice.

The border control officer came storming back toward her. He no longer had the wad of American dollars clenched in his hand. Did that mean he'd accepted it? He clasped her by the wrist and began dragging her to the office.

Apparently, the bribe had not been enough. Catherine kicked and fought, pleading with the officer to just let her return to Moscow. Her cries fell on deaf ears, and he continued to force her back to the office.

Inside the small room it was no more. In fact, with three pairs of eyes fixed on her it felt colder. Catherine shuddered.

"You are American spy," the clean shaven guard said. It was not a question.

"Perhaps smuggler," the bearded guard countered.

"I'm just a reporter, on environmental issues. I'm no spy," Catherine said.

"You offer bribe. You are hiding something," the guard who had dragged her in said. "We must search you."

"Search me? Don't you need a warrant or something?"

"Take off clothes," the smooth-faced guard said, his eyes scanning her form.

"I most certainly will not," Catherine replied, clutching her coat closer to her body.

"Yes, you will," said the bearded guard with slow purpose drawing his side arm from its holster and pointing it at her stomach.

Catherine's body stiffened. She scanned their hungry faces. There wasn't a flicker of remorse. They were deadly serious. Her eyes welled as she began to shrug out of the jacket sleeves.

The three men stood in front of her, cruel smirks fixed on their lips, a primal fire in their eyes. With each garment that fell to the floor their enjoyment obviously increased. One guard adjusted his crotch. Down to only a bra and panties, Catherine's skin prickled and she shivered uncontrollably.

She hesitated, hoping this would satiate them.

The guard jerked his gun and raised his eyebrows expectantly.

It wasn't enough.

Catherine closed her eyes, a stream of tears flowing across her frozen cheeks.

The bra came away, and she shielded her breasts with one arm.

Catherine held her breath and slid the fingers of her spare hand into the band of her panties to slide them across her hips. She felt a hand clasp her by the arm, but she dare not open her eyes. If she did it would be real.

Then, just like that, he let go. Catherine tumbled to the hard ground, the cold immediately penetrating the flesh of her butt. Above her, the officer stood stiff as a board and next to him, peering down at her with an outstretched hand was a tall broad man in a long, moss-green, thick wool coat.

She clasped his strong hand and pulled herself to her feet.

"Put on your clothes." His accent sounded East Coast.

Catherine wasted no time in redressing herself. All the while the three officers stood to attention, their faces drained of color. The new man remained silent.

"Are you American?" Catherine asked, fastening the buttons of her coat all the way to the top.

"No," the man replied. "But I have lived in America."

"You're here to arrest me?"

"On the contrary, Miss O'Reilly. You can pass through."

"You know who I am?"

He simply nodded. "Follow me." He opened the door, and Catherine shuffled past keeping as a far from him as possible, afraid he might grab her and pull her back inside.

The man turned and barked something in Russian at the three guards. Their eyes widened, fear etched into their faces. Then, the door snapped shut.

"You have transport on the other side? To get where you're going?"

Who was this? Why was he helping? "Ummm, no. I figured I could rent or pay someone to take me."

The man laughed. "I see. I don't think that's entirely possible. And you're not dressed to be going anywhere by sled. Where are you headed?"

"Up to a sinkhole ... somewhere in the north. I have coordinates ..."

He eyed her, then said: "There is a rescue team coming back in a few minutes. I will radio in and ask them to fly you where you need to go."

"Thank you," Catherine said, already shuffling toward the gate and the helipad on the other side. It wasn't wise to look a gift horse in the mouth and she needed to get where she was going—fast. Still, Catherine turned back to him. "Really, thank you for …"

He gave a knowing nod and waved a hand dismissively.

"You never told me your name."

"Vetrov," he said. "Polkovnik SashaVetrov."

CHAPTER SIX

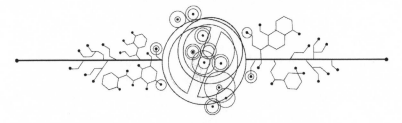

Location: Nenets camp, Yamal Peninsula, Siberia.

A deep, low-lying, fog had set in across the barren landscape. The sky was now darker, the never-ending twilight no longer alive with the aurora, confusing Freya's internal clock. She couldn't sleep. So instead, she stood watch; a sentinel scoping and waiting—though for what, she wasn't sure. Some hidden danger perhaps? Maybe a rescue chopper? The Secretary of State hadn't been in contact since their last conversation. Perhaps she was busy trying to sort something out. Perhaps she was doing nothing at all. Not knowing was the worst part. And Freya's back-up plan, in case the US government wasn't willing to help, hadn't come to fruition. And Jonathan hadn't arrived yet.

Freya pushed back into the warm tent, but it was no more comforting inside. There, curled up in a ball was KJ with K'awin wrapped around him—her blue, iridescent skin sparkling in the firelight. Bundled up next to them was Nikolaj and his Huahuqui—Chernoukh, Russian for *black eared*. This Huahuqui had black gills, not red. Freya didn't like it much as it reminded her too much of Wak. But Minya insisted that it was very affectionate and nothing like the monster the American government had engineered.

The children's and the creatures' breathing was synchronized, their chests rising and falling together. KJ looked peaceful, wrapped in reindeer skin and spooned by K'awin. In fact, he hadn't had a nightmare since being here. For the first time since Freya could remember, her son had slept without incident.

"They're resting," Minya whispered.

Freya nodded and took a seat on the floor, pulling her knees to her chest.

"It will be okay, my friend," Minya said.

Freya sighed. "I just hate this waiting more than anything. It's been too long. We're stuck here like sitting ducks, exposed and vulnerable. I don't like it."

"We are in middle of Yamal Peninsula. No one is here but us. We are safe."

"No one is safe, Minya. We just have the illusion of being safe."

"You sound more like Kelly every day."

Freya exhaled hard. "Maybe he was right to be cagey. To be cynical. Can't trust anyone."

Minya stared long and hard at Freya. "Your moods are becoming worse, my friend. Are you taking—"

"Yes, yes," Freya interjected. "Of course."

Minya remained silent, but held Freya's gaze.

"I'm sorry. You're right. I'm fine, I promise. You're here with me and I'm grateful. I just don't like feeling helpless. We need to get our kids out of here."

"*Da*. This is true."

"So, Nikolaj and Chernoukh, they are okay with each other?" Freya asked.

Minya nodded. "Seem to be. They have not been apart since they bonded. Most of time, children and creatures stay close together. Sometimes they play; sometimes they sit and do nothing.

But there is no harm. Nikolaj is happy. He would tell me otherwise."

Freya nodded, again. Minya was calm about everything as usual. It's why Freya had chosen her, for when the time came. But the fear of losing KJ to K'awin, or worse, a government hell-bent on stealing him and the creature, weighed heavily on her mind. She'd give it one more day, then take matters into her own hands.

There was a shrill scream outside.

Freya leaped to her feet. "What the *fuck* was that?"

Minya shook her head, eyes narrow as she concentrated on listening.

More screaming and clanging of bells, followed by the panicked grunts and squeals of reindeer. Freya reached into her bag and pulled out two black Berettas.

"You said you had no weapons, Freya," Minya exclaimed.

"I lied." Freya tossed a gun to Minya. "It's loaded. Stay here with the boys. If anything comes through this flap except me, kill it."

Outside, Freya crouched down behind a small scrub bush and readied her weapon, gripping it tighter than usual to steady her hand. She studied the scene. Nenets women ran in all directions, hugging their children close to their chests. The Huahuqui followed them, bounding behind on all fours, their gills bobbing with their gait. But still, Freya couldn't see where the danger was.

A bullet whistled past her head. Freya instinctively ducked, then fired two rounds in the direction from which the first shot came. There was no scream. She'd missed. Squatting close to the ground, Freya moved quickly and circled around to what she guessed was the position of her attacker. Then she saw him; laid in the snow, a sniper rifle wedged into his shoulder, the sight tight against his right eye. She crept up behind, but the permafrost crunched under her boots. The man flipped onto his back and swung the rifle around to point it at Freya. She parried the barrel as he fired off a shot. Freya stamped down but missed his head. He kicked her legs out from beneath her and she fell to her back, knocking the wind from her lungs and causing her to drop the Beretta. The man came again, standing over her, the rifle in her face.

A flash of blue and the soldier crashed to the ground. Freya scrambled to her feet.

"Leave my mom alone!" KJ stood some ten feet away, his eyes aglow with a blue fire.

The soldier lay pinned to the snow, K'awin atop him, trapping his arms. K'awin's face was inches from the soldier's as he studied it.

Freya searched the area and found her Beretta. She scooped it up, cocked the hammer, and pointed it at the man's head. Trembling, she squeezed the trigger—but K'awin reared up and slapped the sidearm from her hand. Freya glared at the creature. The man squirmed so K'awin resumed pinning him down.

"Killing is bad, Mommy," KJ said.

"Kelly Junior, what the hell are you doing out here? Minya was supposed to be with you. Get back inside, now!"

"We're here to help, Mommy."

K'awin, pushed down harder on the man's arms and continued to glare at him. Transfixed, the man stared back, his thin eyes as wide as they could stretch. Then he slumped unconscious to the ground. K'awin climbed off him, padded back to KJ's side, and reared up on her hind legs so that she towered over him in a protective stance.

"Freya!" Minya ran toward them.

"Minya, you were supposed to watch him."

"I am sorry, he and Nikolaj awoke. Together, suddenly. Before I could stop them, they ran out of tent."

"Where's Nikolaj?"

As Freya asked the question, Minya's son appeared with his Huahuqui. Chernoukh waddled on his hind legs just like K'awin, scanning the horizon for danger like a meerkat.

"I'm here," Nikolaj said. "What is going on?"

"I don't know. KJ, come here," Freya demanded.

KJ didn't move.

"Kelly Junior, I said come here!"

But Freya's son still didn't budge.

Another bullet whistled by. Both KJ and Nikolaj took off, their Huahuqui in tow. Their mothers chased after them.

Not far ahead, everyone seemed to have gathered. Some of the older children had formed a perimeter with their Huahuqui companions around the Nenets and those children and creatures who were much younger. KJ and Nikolaj joined the boundary, slotting into a position.

"KJ, get back here!" Freya yelled.

KJ ignored her, his eyes burning brightly in the dark. K'awin's eyes glowed just as brilliantly, her gills outstretched as wide as possible. All of the Huahuqui simultaneously let out a deep warble that filled the air.

Four soldiers, dressed in arctic camouflage gear, their rifles high, stepped from the gloom toward the group. Freya and Minya sprinted to the head of the perimeter, putting themselves between the assailants and the children. With weak arms, Freya raised her Beretta and pointed it at the lead soldier's head.

"Back off, or I put a bullet in your skull," she shouted, her breath misting with each word.

"No Mommy, no killing," KJ said, his tone distant, as if the words weren't his.

"Shut up, KJ, not now!" Freya turned back to the advancing soldiers and jerked her sidearm. "I'm not joking, asshole, back off!"

The men kept coming.

Freya tried to squeeze the trigger but her finger wouldn't move. *Oh God, not now*, she thought. Freya frowned, grunted and tried again. Still, her finger wouldn't do as commanded. "KJ, are you doing this?" she yelled over her shoulder.

Panicked, Minya raised her gun to fire but also found that her trigger finger no longer responded.

"No death," Nikolaj said in the same monotone voice.

"Fuck!" Freya screamed in frustration.

A high-pitched *snap* filled the air and the lead soldier slumped to the ground, his brain matter splattered in the snow. The other fighters scattered, firing blindly.

Freya and Minya spun on their heels and launched to the defense of their children, crashing to the permafrost and using their own bodies as shields. More snaps and squeals sounded as one by one the assailants fell lifelessly to the cold ground, their blood staining the frost. The Huahuqui wailed, as if pained by the death of the men.

Then, silence.

Freya unscrewed her eyes. She was alive. Beneath her, KJ panted. Now seemingly released from his trance, his eyes were full of tears. He threw his arms around Freya's neck and hugged her tight. As she squeezed her son, Freya became aware of the weight on her back. K'awin had wrapped her small body around Freya and

KJ. She shot a sideways glance at Minya, who was laid across Nikolaj, Chernoukh enveloping them both.

Slowly, the Huahuqui slid off their wards. Freya shifted her butt to the ground holding her son close. The Nenets and Huahuqui had surrounded them and were all gawking at Freya and KJ. Behind, there was shuffling and murmuring until, eventually, through a gap in the crowd, Jonathan Teller appeared, as tall, broad and good-looking as ever, though he seemed to be hobbling on an injured leg.

Freya sighed. "Jonathan. Thank God."

"Seems like I got here just in time, huh?"

Freya scowled. "Nothing like leaving it to the last minute, Jonathan."

"Better late than never."

The crowd closed in again, chattering to one another. Freya narrowed her eyes and, shakily, raised her gun. "Okay, that's close enough. Back off, people."

"I think they're kinda interested in your son," Jonathan said, studying Freya's hand.

"This isn't a ticketed event, so they can fuck off."

Jonathan raised his hands. "Okay, okay, no need to get defensive. But to be honest, I'm kinda interested, too." He nodded at KJ.

Freya turned to her son. A clean tear through the sleeve of his left arm revealed a deep gouge left by a stray bullet. KJ didn't even seem to notice it.

"Oh Jesus! KJ, are you okay?" But as she pawed at his arm, she realized why the crowd was so intrigued. The wound in KJ's arm was already healing, zipping up from one end to the other, leaving only a slight scar behind that she knew would disappear in a day or two.

Jonathan folded his arms across his chest. "You wanna fill me in?"

Location: Fort Leavenworth, Kansas, USA

The President had acted exactly as Lucy had imagined he would. To be fair, it was exactly as a President should have acted. He was amazed and disgusted with the events since 1945. Appalled at how a sentient creature had been kept like a lab rat, and then fought over like the only ball in a playground. Aghast at the creation of human-Huahuqui chimera. But most of all, he was sorry for the loss of life—American, Chinese and Russian. And it was for this reason he had refused to take affirmative action that would mean invading a country without permission.

"If the Russian government has not given us permission to extradite the Nenets people or the Huahuqui, then America cannot, and will not, invade and take them," he'd said. *"If these people want asylum, they have to ask for it. In the meantime, Lucy, it is your job to begin talks with the Russians on how this will be handled, and how we get our citizens back."*

What had she expected? That he would mount a full-scale rescue mission for one woman and one child, and while they were at it, steal an entire nomadic tribe? Not to mention the Huahuqui. She couldn't call Freya back and tell her there would be no help. Diplomatic relations would take forever and long before any resolve, Freya and every man, woman, and child, would mysteriously disappear. The Huahuqui were too important to the whole world. The time for diplomacy wasn't now.

Lucy needed help. The problem was, she'd shut everything

down after Teotihuacan. Hunted every member of every operation linked to the cloning program and disassembled it piece by piece. Fired the only people who may have understood and had the capability to help. The irony was overwhelming.

Now, there was only a one man she could turn to.

The flight to Missouri was only a couple of hours, and she'd been picked up by a security detail upon landing. This may have been costing American tax dollars, but every life on the planet was at stake. At least, she thought so.

The black sedan hummed along through the town of just thirty-five thousand residents—though that didn't include the prisoners. The area surrounding the town was built on the business of incarceration. The oldest prison where the two men convicted of the Kansas killings were hanged in 1965 over in Lansing. Then, in Fort Leavenworth there was the large civilian federal penitentiary and the Joint Regional Correction Facility—the military's medium security prison. But it was the maximum-security military prison that Lucy was visiting.

The sedan pulled up to the gates and the driver wound down the window in order to identify himself and his passenger to the guard. Lucy duly wound down her own window to show she was truly the only passenger. As she waited, Lucy studied the building. In contrast to the original prison, a huge and imposing complex known as *The Castle* and completed largely by inmates in 1921, the new facility was a small state-of-the-art construction housing only five-hundred prisoners. Set on fifty-one acres of former farmland it was enclosed by two separate fourteen-foot high fences. She could count three, two-tiered triangular-shaped, brown housing units which had windows, but curiously no bars.

Considering this was a maximum-security prison, Lucy found

herself in the interview room all too quickly. Then again, when holding an executive order from the President of the United States, mountains moved. The Commander of the prison, Colonel Martin Gallagher, wasn't to know it was forged.

The keys jangled in the lock and the door swung open. Guided by a Military Police officer, the prisoner she had come to see shuffled into the room—the shackles restricting his movements. He wore the standard brown, heavily starched, uniform and, despite the possibility to choose shoes that might express some individuality as many of the inmates were known to do, military-issue boots polished to a glass-like finish.

The prisoner was forced into the chair on the opposite side of the metal table and his wrist restraints attached to a fixture in front of him. He was going nowhere. Lucy nodded to the officer and glanced at the door. The soldier hesitated then, after scanning his convict, exited and shut the door.

"How have you been?" Lucy asked.

"That's a stupid question," the man said. "I live in a six by nine, sleep on a fucking rock of a bunk next a steel bowl full of my own shit. Still, I get to play a hand of poker or two and a game of ping pong after working every goddamn graveyard shift they can throw at me for the rest of my life. What do you want, Madam Secretary?"

"I need your help."

"You're shit out of luck. Unless you need me to do your laundry? We have some industrial washing machines in here. Even for those big ol' granny panties you have permanently wedged up your ass."

Lucy smiled. "I see prison has had an effect on your vocabulary. Shame you can't utilize your new-found thesaurus with such a well-bred accent."

"Fuck off."

"General Benjamin Lloyd, you are going to help me."

"Which part of *fuck off* wasn't clear?"

Lucy pulled a folder from her bag and dropped it on the metal desk. Opening it for him, she tapped on a satellite photograph of the area: a magnified, if not blurry, image of a Huahuqui sat on permafrost. "It's not over."

Benjamin stared at the photo for a long moment, then raised his head to meet Lucy's gaze. "It is for me."

"Perhaps you should tell that to your goddaughter. She's there. With her son. And the bonding has already begun. With him and the local children."

Benjamin's eyes widened. "Where's there?"

"The Yamal Peninsula, Russian territory."

"Shit. And they're not being extradited?"

Lucy shook her head. "It's a diplomatic nightmare. We can't invade."

"So, the President has ordered a covert op, to get them back? And I'm to advise?"

"No."

"Then what?" he asked.

"In about thirty seconds, the guard is going to walk in here, un-cuff you, and tell you you've been pardoned."

Benjamin studied her. "But I haven't, have I?"

"No."

"That's a pretty ballsy move."

"This isn't one creature anymore. It's a nest. And if we don't act now, the Russians or God knows who, will black-box this faster than we can blink. I can't let that happen. The only way to protect them is to get them somewhere safe. Once they're on US soil, we make it all public. No more black boxes."

"And so, I'm supposed to get a crew, and a plane—"

"Two planes."

"Two planes, collect my goddaughter and an entire village, then bring them back here. All without money, resources or authorized flight routes."

"Kelly Graham managed to steal a plane and get from Peru to Egypt, to India to Siberia without being caught."

The General grunted. "I'll probably get the chair for this, you know."

"And I'll go to federal prison."

"Then what are we waiting for?"

Location: Sinkhole Eight, Yamal Peninsula, Siberia

"What do you think?"

"What? Oh sorry, I wasn't listening." Freya pulled her attention from the *mya* opening.

"He's okay, Freya. There's nothing out there," Teller said.

Freya scowled. "Nothing out there? You mean besides the thirty plus creatures roaming around, eating, drinking, sleeping, and walking with our kids—my kid—twenty-four seven?"

"Does he look in danger?" Teller offered, keeping his tone as calm as possible.

"That depends on what you define as danger."

"Wow, Kelly would be proud."

"What the hell's that supposed to mean?" Freya snapped back.

"Forget it. Look, you can't let this drag you down. The more you fight this, the more you'll push him away. If everything you tell me is true, he—above all the other kids—is going to have the strongest bond. He's different at a genetic level. Like he's switched on to connect with them. Be grateful K'awin seems benign. Have you seen that other one—Ribka? That one will be trouble."

Freya turned and stared out into the tundra where the children played. KJ ran in circles, K'awin chasing him like an excited puppy. And with them were Svetlana and Ribka. Her son and the little Nenets girl, who was approximately the same age, had become best friends over night. They didn't even speak the same language. In fact, they didn't seem to verbally talk to each other at all. Nevertheless, for three days in a row, they were inseparable. KJ never slept more than five or six hours. He went to play with her and her Huahuqui as soon as he woke until late into the evening when he'd come home to eat and then collapse into an exhausted heap.

Svetlana's mother had died looking for her in a storm. The girl had no other relatives. Her Huahuqui—Ribka, a male—was boisterous. Somehow, he seemed older than K'awin. Svetlana didn't speak much Russian but Ribka was a Russian word used by children, meaning 'little fish.' Freya assumed she had named him that for the fact it constantly splashed about in the thin, ice-covered river nearby. It fought and tumbled with Svetlana a lot, like an older brother. KJ was too often caught in the middle—K'awin pulling him out at the last minute to avoid a more serious fall or knock.

"I don't trust any of them," Freya said, finally.

Teller placed a hand on Freya's shoulder and turned her to face him. "You need to concentrate. We need to ensure we're ready. The Secretary couldn't say exactly when we'd be picked up. But it could be any day now."

"Why couldn't she tell us, Jonathan? I don't like this secrecy.

I've lived too much of it. I don't like it."

"Sweetie …"

Freya wrinkled her nose at the pet name.

"Sorry. Look, if she can't tell us there must be a reason. Best guess? It isn't kosher. They've had to mount a rescue off the books. There must have been a political hold up. The Secretary wouldn't chance it. She's a good person. You know that."

Freya stepped away, sat on a reindeer skin, and unholstered her Berettas. Her fingers trembled as she slid them over the barrel.

"You gonna shoot me?" Teller asked. "Might wanna do it in a warmer environment, your fingers are shaking."

"I'm gonna clean them," Freya snapped, then began disassembling one of the sidearms. "I can't just sit here. It's driving me insane."

"Excuse me, Sir."

"Come in, Tony. What's up?"

Tony stepped into the tent and gave a curt nod to Freya. "We got an incoming bird. Looks like they're headed right for us."

"Russian or American?"

"It's not one of ours."

Freya got to her feet and clipped her Beretta back together. "Get the kids inside. Now."

Tony turned to Teller seeking confirmation.

"Get Danny and Glover to gather up the kids, then take up sniper positions around the biggest open field out to the east. If they're landing, that makes the most sense. Freya and I will greet our guests."

"Sir." Tony stepped away and jogged off in the direction of the children.

"Could it be the rescue mission, if it's off the books?" Freya asked.

"Let's go find out." Teller slid a Desert Eagle from his sling bag and locked a round into the chamber.

Freya and Teller pulled their coats around their necks and then marched out of the tent toward the open field. Overhead, a large chopper dropped from the sky, its huge rotors churning up the snow into a blizzard.

"That's a rescue bird," Freya began, "used by the Russians. I didn't think they were allowed near the sinkholes or Nenets camps? I had to schlep it with sleds from a drop point to get here."

"Guess it must be important," Teller yelled over the increasing din.

The helicopter touched down and shut off its engines. The rotors, while still loud, began to slow. The side door clunked open and then slid to the side. From the dark within, a figure climbed awkwardly out and dropped to the permafrost. The slender person, covered head to toe in rescue team gear—coat, goggles, and hat—traipsed toward Freya and Teller.

Freya eyed the person, noting thin jeans and boots not suited for the weather. She slid her palm over her holstered Beretta in readiness.

Teller touched Freya's forearm indicating she should wait, but kept his own weapon in hand.

When the figure stood in front of them, they pulled down their scarf, lifted up their goggles, and pulled back the hood to reveal bright orange curls.

Freya's eyes flared and she clasped her sidearm. "What the *fuck* are *you* doing here? Jonathan, you best get this bitch out of my face, or she'll be eating through a straw for the rest of her life."

"Woah, woah, woah!" Teller said, holstering his sidearm. "No need for that."

"I'm just here—" Catherine began.

Freya stepped to within an inch of the reporter's face. "Say another word, and I swear to God I'll gut you where you stand."

"Freya—" Teller began.

"How did she even know we were here?" Freya yelled. "She's here before the Secretary's rescue? How's that possible? Tell me the Secretary didn't send her." Freya stomped a few paces away, kicked the frost and squeezed the gun back in its holster to alleviate the growing pain in her fingers.

"I told her," Teller said.

"What?" Freya spun to face Jonathan, daggers in her stare.

"So, you're the one …" Catherine said.

"Freya, when we first spoke I had a satellite make a detour over the site. As soon as I saw it I had to act. Images went to the Secretary of State—but I knew she'd have a mountain of red tape to get through. You told me—begged me—to not let this be black-boxed. Now it won't be." He waved at Catherine. "She'll make sure of that."

Freya huffed. He was right, but it didn't mean she had to like it. "You keep away from me and my son, you got it?"

Catherine just nodded.

Freya stormed away, calling for her son.

"Sorry about that, she's a little stressed," Teller said.

"I can imagine," Catherine replied. "Though I only asked her a few questions."

"You hounded her for a year. And you risked exposing her son."

"Exposing him?"

"Forget it. That's a conversation for later. You took your time getting here."

Catherine heaved a sigh. "There was some trouble down at the border in Salekhard. But I had some help getting across. Then the rescue team had to make a detour to find a couple of tourists who'd gone off the beaten track and gotten lost. Cost me a couple days, but they eventually dropped me up here."

"I see," Teller said, searching her face for more than she was saying.

"So, it's true, there's another one? A live one?" Catherine asked, looking over Teller's shoulder.

"Try thirty."

"What?"

Teller nodded. "Yep, a whole nest."

"Woah, where'd they come from?"

"From a sinkhole. Best guess, they've been living under the ice in there—until global warming or something else melted the permafrost and opened it up. They look like they've adapted to the cold. A small community that could be sustained with limited resources."

"That's amazing."

"Freya doesn't think so. They already bonded to the children."

Catherine eyed him. "Is that a good thing?"

"I hope so," Teller said. "I hope so."

"Can I meet them?" she asked.

"Sure. Come on. Just stay away from Freya and KJ. At least for now."

Jonathan and Catherine started toward the camp, hands tucked into their pockets, crunching their way along the frozen ground. Behind them the rescue helicopter lifted off and into the air, disappearing into the wispy gray clouds.

"You say there are thirty … have you been down into the sinkhole? Are there any more?"

Teller stopped in his tracks and turned to face the reporter. That hadn't occurred to any of them.

CHAPTER SEVEN

Location: Tokyo, Japan

"How many?"

"Four," said the voice on the phone.

"So, you still have sixteen."

"Hai, Master Ishii-san."

"Where are the soldiers of the Beast now?"

"With the villagers. Waiting. It was only a small force ... we could have ... I'm sorry, Mas—"

"Un-mastered tactics are the origin of great blunders, Takashi. You will lose a hand for your disobedience. But ... you have confirmed the intelligence. So, I will spare your arm."

"Hai, Master Ishii-san."

"Stay where you are. Watch as the eagle watches. I will find out what is planned by the Beast, then contact you again soon."

"Hai."

"And Takashi ... don't disappoint me. If you fail, you die."

Click. Ishii cut the call.

The information had been confirmed. The system had picked up the satellite imagery. And his men had been sent to find it. The question was: how to utilize the creatures—harness their power, keep it for himself. It was times like this, Ishii needed his Master, Shoko Asahara. He understood the true universe and would know what to do. By combing Indian and Tibetan Buddhism, Hinduism, millennialist philosophies from the Christian's Book of Revelation, and even the writings of Nostradamus, Asahara had found enlightenment beyond any man. His life's mission was to take upon himself the sins of the world, at least before his capture.

Ishii had been enrolled by Asahara himself. A mere teenager, living on the streets of Tokyo, Ishii's real value was seen shining from within. The Lamb of God had taken him to his one-bedroom apartment in the Shibuya ward in 1985.

"Do you want to know the universe as it is, young Ishii?" he'd said, one evening after an intense prayer session. *"How it really is and not what you think you see?"*

Ishii had only nodded, his palms sweaty and his heart racing— no comprehension of the knowledge he was about to receive. He was given a drug, a narcotic-laced square of paper placed on his tongue, to show him the world beyond the physical. Then, he was hung by his feet, doused in water and, using a modified cattle prod, electrocuted on the hour for three straight days. Asahara didn't sleep, ensuring that the procedure continued through each night.

The smell of Ishii's own burning flesh had filled his nostrils and clogged his throat, making him vomit uncontrollably. By the end of day one, he'd emptied his stomach contents and could only dry wretch. One particularly powerful jolt had burned Lichtenberg figures from his right leg, up his torso and across his face, blinding him in one eye. But despite this last injury, God's cosmos opened to Ishii. All the colors, beyond those in the human spectrum, cascaded across his good retina. The world seen as streams of information. Through the dirty windows of the apartment, Ishii spied demons hidden within men, pushing through the walls of their corporeal shell. They were disgusting. Ishii's purpose was clear: to rid the Earth of its fiends.

Together, Asahara and Ishii created publications and lectures that attracted the elite and educated from all over Japan. Four years later, they were a recognized religion. Eventually, Master Asahara revealed his God-given doomsday prophecy: World War III instigated by the United States—*the Beast*, he called them—would destroy the Earth. But he was ignored. Mocked.

It was then that Asahara knew his prophecy was unavoidable. It was their responsibility—his responsibility—to instigate the End Times, before the world was unsalvageable. By taking control and bringing about Armageddon, he would restore Shōhō. Taking life to save the world was justified to prevent accumulating their own bad karma, so proclaimed by *poa*.

Ishii strolled to the door of his humble apartment and put on his brown leather sandals, old and worn. Then, he left and entered the elevator which took him to the underground garage. He sauntered to the dilapidated doors, the soiled windows barely reflecting his long white robe and shoulder length black hair.

A short walk past an array of beat up Subarus and tiny Nissans and Ishii found his car: an armored Mercedes-Benz gifted to them many years ago by a wealthy benefactor. He slid the key into the ignition and fired up the engine. Though old, the car was reliable. It clunked into first gear and then grumbled off the space and out into the night air.

Location: Sinkhole Eight, Yamal Peninsula, Siberia

A frigid wind swept across the tundra, whipping up tiny shards of ice and flinging them into the faces of those who braved the Siberian winter. While only a few miles from camp, the cold stole both energy and enthusiasm for the journey. Only the Irish reporter seemed excited about the destination.

Teller's team, with the Nenets men, took the vanguard. Freya and Minya kept to the back of the human convoy—the women, children, and Huahuqui nearby. At the very rear, Teller and the reporter trailed. They had been talking for the entire excursion from the camp toward the sinkhole.

The whole situation bothered Jonathan. They were too few men to protect everyone they already had, let alone more creatures if there were any. Benjamin Lloyd couldn't get there fast enough.

"So, what's the deal? Why did the Ice Queen go all UFC on me?" Catherine asked Teller.

Jonathan glanced at Freya, who had turned to spy on them for what felt like the thousandth time. "If this thing is going to be open, no black boxes, then you best understand everything," he said.

"Well considering you all made me look like a raving lunatic for even suggesting one of those things existed, and now there's a whole damn nest, I think you owe me an explanation."

"Look," Teller said. "I'll give you as much detail as you need— this whole story will need to be chronicled accurately. And I mean, *accurately*. No sensationalism, you got it? This is going to cost me my career if not put me in federal prison as it is. It needs to be worth it."

Catherine bobbed her head. "Got it."

Teller rubbed his jaw, then took a deep breath. "Okay, here's the short version. The creatures are everything the leak said they were—a sentient race who probably gave humanity what little civility we have, somewhere back in antiquity. They may not speak, or build great monuments, but what they bestowed allowed *us* to do it. They seem to connect with humans, as if it was always supposed to be with us."

The reporter pulled out her note pad and began scribbling.

"Somewhere along the line, we—humans—killed them off. Or we thought we did. In the late 1940s, Chinese scientists found a frozen corpse of one of them in Siberia. When the US government found out, we sent in the military to steal it. The mission got into a bit of trouble on the home stretch and the plane went down in a little town called Roswell."

Catherine laughed. "This is goddamn gold."

"That's a drop in the ocean. For sixty years we studied the corpse without reprimand and, as you know, managed to clone it. In 2012, thanks to another bungled operation, the Chinese found out and all holy hell broke loose."

Catherine's laugh became a snort. "Wow, and I thought the US military were competent. You guys couldn't organize a piss up in a brewery."

Teller stared at her, quizzically.

"Piss up. To get drunk? Never mind."

"You gonna let me finish?" Teller said, his eyebrows raised.

The reporter pantomimed a zip across her lips, then spoke anyway. "So, you cocked up a few missions and annoyed the Chinese and somehow avoided war?"

"As with all things, it was politically complicated. The Chinese government had actually been infiltrated by an ancient cult—the Green and Red Societies—who were hell bent on stealing the creature back and using it to take over the planet. At least after they had destroyed most everything with a global catastrophe."

Catherine snorted, again. "Sounds like a plot to a bad movie."

Teller nodded. "It gets worse. Our government created a

human-Huahuqui hybrid. A Chimera, called Wak. Let's just say that didn't go well. It was only some quick thinking by our Secretary of State and the Chinese Minister of Foreign Affairs—who gave his life—that war was avoided."

Catherine stopped in her tracks and scrunched up her nose. "So, most of that I knew from my digging around. I could just never prove it. Once again, you've said a lot without saying anything, Mr. NSA. It still doesn't tell me why Nilsson is ready to tear me a new arsehole just for asking a few questions."

Teller started walking again, gesturing for the reporter to follow him. He fired a glance at Freya before speaking. "What the reports didn't tell you was there were two civilians involved—heavily involved."

"Now, that's new information. What civilians?"

"One was a guy called, Kelly Graham. An all-round pain in the ass with a James Kirk complex. He got inadvertently caught up in this whole shit storm and bonded to the first creature, K'in. And I mean *bonded*. If you separated them, they both became sick. The second was a friend of his, Victoria McKenzie. She bonded to Wak."

Catherine's scribbling became intense as she struggled to take down the detail.

Teller paused briefly to allow her to catch up. "Victoria began to change, morph into something not quite human. To devolve, if you will. But then, Wak was killed and so Victoria was freed."

"And the guy, Kelly?"

"His bond was different—almost natural. K'in died and so did Kelly, but not until a year after the creature. While Kelly didn't devolve, it did change him at a genetic level. Something we didn't realize until after he'd passed on his genes." He nodded toward the group of children.

Catherine's eyes widened in realization. "Her son. Kelly was the father? I figured he was yours and you two were, ya'know, divorced."

Teller tried not to let that thought take hold. A son. A life, with Freya. He shook it off and said: "Even I didn't know until a few days ago about the different genes. Freya didn't tell anyone for fear of KJ being put in a sterile room and prodded for the rest of his life."

"How does she know KJ has these alternate genes?" Catherine asked without looking up from her pad.

"He has abilities—like the Huahuqui. He can regenerate damaged cells without leaving a scar. He can telepathically connect with other living organisms and, if they're weak enough, control them to a certain extent. At least that's what Freya has told me. Doesn't mean she hasn't kept things back."

The reporter stopped her scribbling to meet Teller's gaze. "Holy shit."

Teller chewed his lip. "Yeah. So, when you went poking around, particularly around her son, you were treading on thin ice. Feel lucky you still have all your teeth. Don't let that wiggle in her walk deceive you. That right there is a wolverine if ever there was one. A female Klingon warrior."

"Oh, Jesus. You're a Star Trek nerd."

Teller just smiled.

Catherine offered a weak smile back. "I'm going to get some shots of them, if that's okay? We need to document they're not harmful, so filming their interactions with the kids is important. I'll stay away from *her*."

"Good idea. But, nothing to your editor 'til I've vetted it."

Catherine gave a curt nod then ran ahead.

"They are still there, my friend. Just as they were an hour ago," Minya said, resting a hand on Freya's shoulder.

Freya turned back to Minya and kept trudging on. "They're pretty cozy, wouldn't you say?"

Minya shook her head. "Men are weak. They will talk to any pretty face. But he is also good man. Maybe he is interrogating her."

"Yeah, but interrogating her *what?*"

The women laughed but stifled it as the reporter jogged past, camera in hand.

"How are you?" Minya asked. "And you know what I'm talking about."

Freya sighed. "Okay, I guess. The cold isn't helping, that's for sure. But the pills are."

Minya nodded. Freya liked that about her. She never pressed too hard. It was enough to ask once and hear the answer.

"Come," Minya said. "We are almost there. Just up ahead, I can see it."

"Jonathan!" Freya called. "Get your ass up here."

Teller trotted up to the front of the group. A few feet ahead lay the sinkhole. More than one-hundred feet wide, the almost perfectly circular puncture in the ground was made of solid rock—as if it had always been there. Inside, the gaping maw was as black as night.

"Looks mysterious in there," Teller said.

"You should know," Freya replied.

"What's that supposed to mean?"

77

"Where the hell were you, Jonathan? It took you forever to get here."

Teller threw his hands up. "Hey, I had to get out of North Korea."

"North Korea? What the hell were you doing there?"

"You know I can't tell you that, sweetie."

Freya scrunched up her nose. "Still. Could've gotten here sooner."

"And you could've told me about KJ, but you didn't. I'm not the only one who likes mysteries."

Freya shot a glance at Minya, then changed the subject. "So, Brainiac, any idea what caused these holes to open up now?"

Teller eyed her, then shrugged. "No one is actually quite sure. I've heard rumors ranging from shale gas explosions to meteorite strikes. The Russian government said scientists suspect the sinkhole 'burst like a bubble' due to gas in the ground—though conspiracy theorists reckon the fossil fuel mining not so far away is to blame."

"And what do you think?" Freya asked, resting her weight on one hip and pulling her ponytail tight.

"If you want to put on your tinfoil hat and join the real nuts, it's also been suggested the sinkholes were caused by the same gas hydrates that have been blamed for the anomalies observed around the Bermuda Triangle." Teller laughed. "But for me, global warming makes the most sense."

"And now we're here. What's the plan?"

"We take a look inside," Teller said. "What if there are more down there?"

"I'm not sure if I want to know," Freya said.

"Freya, look at children." Minya nodded at KJ, Nikolaj and the Nenets youngsters.

The children and the Huahuqui had formed regimental rows, equally spaced apart, moving in perfect unison around the sinkhole, as if probing it. Occasionally, one group from within the troop would seamlessly move to the front, backfilled by those they had replaced. A cacophony of shades of blue that sparkled in the what little daylight there was.

"Remarkable," Teller said quietly.

Freya took two steps closer. "What the hell are they doing? Is KJ—"

"He's fine, Freya. Or I think he is. They're operating like—"

"Hey, have you seen this?" The reporter interrupted as she jogged up to the group and offered a glance at the digital viewfinder in her camera. "They're moving like ants, or bees or something. It's incredible. No one seems to be leading, but they're moving as one." She flicked through several pictures.

"A hive mind," Teller said, rubbing his palms together for warmth. "That might explain a lot."

"A hive mind? That sounds dangerous." Freya rested a hand on the heel of her Beretta.

"No, no not at all. In fact, it's actually theorized to be the epitome of intelligence. Think of each individual like a single neuron in a brain. They achieve a collective wisdom by organizing themselves in a way that even if each one has limited information and limited intelligence, the group as a whole makes a collective consciousness. Bees and locusts do it without telepathy. Now imagine what you can do with it."

"How do you know this stuff?" Freya asked, shaking her head.

"It's part of some of the higher mathematics and war gaming we do at the NSA—particularly when considering linking many computers together to gather intelligence or in understanding radicalized religion-based decision making," Teller replied, before huffing into his hands again. "We humans pride ourselves on being rational thinkers with an intrinsic sense of morality. It holds true across many levels of society, yet collectively, on a global scale, we often make self-destructive decisions resulting in war, pollution, inequality and climate change."

"If we're all so moral, then why bad decisions?" Catherine asked.

Freya exhaled loudly. "I'm really not in the mood for a science lesson."

Teller continued anyway. "It's the *Tragedy of the Commons* problem. Think of it like this: you're a cattle farmer. As an individual farmer, it's wholly rational and moral to capitalize on the size of your herd. But, if *all* farmers do this, the shared pasture gets overrun and is ruined for all. Individuals, who act both morally and rationally at a local level are predisposed to generating immoral results on a larger one."

"So, we're inherently set to make bad decisions as groups, you know, like governments?" Catherine asked, while still scribbling.

"It's more an artefact of *how* we come to those decisions," Teller said, his gaze shifting between the women. "Polling of the masses for a central figure to then execute. It takes time and is imbalanced. If you look at animals that swarm, they form *real-time dynamic systems* that negotiate in synchrony and come together on ideal outcomes. Research has shown, swarming amplifies the intelligence of a species, resulting in *super-organisms* that solve problems and make decisions beyond the capacity of individuals." He looked to the creatures. "If that's how the Huahuqui operate, it makes sense that they are a super–organism, with wisdom and knowledge beyond ours, yet intangible and not necessarily centered around building technology or monuments, etc. We just equate intelligence with such things."

The reporter blew a curl of orange hair from her face. "Wow, that's fascinating and depressing for our own species, but—"

"Where's Freya?" Teller interrupted.

"And Minya, for that matter," Catherine said, scanning the vicinity.

Teller's gaze fell on the two mothers marching toward the swarm of Huahuqui and their children.

"Oh shit, what's she up to now?" Teller said, already starting after her. "Freya, wait up!"

"Come here, Mr. Man," called Freya.

KJ didn't respond, instead he stood regimented next to K'awin, with Svetlana, Ribka, Nikolaj and Chernoukh at his sides.

"*Da, Nikolaj! Davai!*" Minya said, her tone stern.

The children turned to look at each other. The Huahuqui made low warbling sounds and padded on all fours as if nervous. The waddling spread through the group, the creatures' low murmurs becoming louder. Above, the sky darkened, threatening another snowstorm.

KJ turned to his mother, his expression cold and emotionless. "We are not safe. They are coming."

"They? They who?" Freya demanded.

Svetlana and Nikolaj shot a knowing glance at one another and then KJ.

"Yes," said KJ. "You're right. Time to go."

Each Huahuqui stood on their hind legs and grabbed up their companion child, then tucked them into an armpit. The swarm heaved and undulated as one and, in a fluid motion, spilled like ants over the lip of the sinkhole into the dark. Gone.

"No!" Freya screamed. "KJ, come back! KJ!" Her voice echoed off the walls of the sinkhole.

"Nikolaj!" Minya yelled.

The Nenets adults wailed and scrambled to the edge of the pit, peering inside but the dark was impenetrable.

Freya sprinted to the edge but was grabbed by her coat and dragged backward. "Get the fuck off me. KJ is down there!"

"Wait!" Jonathan yelled, before calming himself. "Wait. We have no idea how deep that is, the fall could kill you. And we don't know *what's* down there."

She shook herself free of his grip. "My *son* is down there!"

"I know and we'll go after him. I promise, but we have to do this right."

Freya glared at Jonathan, the hate pouring out.

"Kelly would've gone in. He would've gone in for his son," she said, still staring into Jonathan's eyes.

"And where is he now, Freya? Huh?" Teller snapped. "He's dead. Because he was reckless. You wanna die? Who'll look after KJ when you're gone, huh?"

Freya clenched her jaw and steeled her gaze. "Just get me down there. Now."

Location: Nenets camp, Yamal Peninsula

Four bodies were neatly lined up on the permafrost, covered in worn reindeer skin.

Sasha crouched down to the frozen ground and pulled off his goggles. He drew back the hides and pawed at the men's arctic camouflage gear. The clothing had the markings of the Korean Military, but the men didn't look Korean. He searched the bodies

82

for firearms, but their killers had apparently already taken the weapons. *There must be something.* The Polkovnik shuffled closer to one of the soldiers and pulled at the polar necked garment. Sure enough, across the jugular vein, there it was: an Arabic nine. He quickly checked the other men. Each had the small tattoo. Sometimes behind their ear, sometimes at the nape of their neck. But all four men sported it. They were the same organization he'd been chasing from the orphanage in Moscow. The question was: how was it connected to a Nenets camp in Siberia?

"You were correct, Polkovnik. Boot tracks. Probably US military, walking side by side with Nenets. The tracks move off into the west." The soldier paused, his lips parted as if more was to come but wouldn't.

Sasha raised his eyes to see his subordinate. "The reporter was on to something. She must have met up with an American outfit. What were they doing here?" The last question was spoken quietly, almost to himself.

The Polkovnik scanned the horizon. Beyond the Trekol they had arrived in, the camp was empty—even the reindeer were gone. Yet a few of the *mya* were still there, which meant the Nenets intended to come back. That would suggest a scouting mission, maybe? But why take everyone?

"Sir?"

"You have something else?"

"There are two more set of tracks," the soldier replied.

"Two?"

The soldier bobbed his head. "One seems to be the remainder of … this outfit." He pointed to the corpses. "At least a dozen other men. They stay far enough behind not to be seen, but not so far as to lose the Americans."

Sasha stood, his full height dwarfing the FSB agent. "And the other?"

"I'm not sure, sir."

"What are you talking about? Show me."

The soldier stepped away and led his Polkovnik fifty feet or so to the west.

Sasha duly followed until they came to the fresh tracks. As expected, he could make out the regimented footsteps of American soldiers, the pattern a standard defensive formation. Nenets animal skin boots were also easy to identify, as were the reindeer tracks. He crouched to the ground again. Just as his lieutenant had described, another set of tracks, the faux Korean Military, were not far behind. And then, amongst the impressions of human and reindeer feet, was a very different set of trails. He crept forward and touched the depressed, thin layer of snow.

They were feet, not boots. Some showed signs of only two large toes, while others had four—three finger-like projections and perhaps a thumb. Sometimes only the two-toed tracks were visible, while other times it was all more—as if the animals were changing from running on hind legs to running on all fours. Sasha stayed close to the ground, following the strange trails.

"They move like a herd, or flock, but much faster and with purpose. They never cross. See? There. It's coordinated."

The Polkovnik's team didn't respond. They just watched the colonel at work.

Sasha continued to mutter under his breath. "What kind of animal moves on both two and four limbs? A bear? No, a bear doesn't have two toes ..." He wracked his brain. "What would the US military risk coming into Russian territory for without informing us? What animal could they and our Asian corpses want—"

It wasn't possible. The only creature he knew of, with limbs that could make those tracks, and two powerful nations would fight over, was supposed to be dead. Sasha jumped to his feet and stormed back to his Trekol.

CHAPTER EIGHT

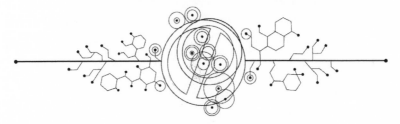

Location: McConnell Air Force Base, Kansas, USA

Four miles southeast of Wichita's central business district, McConnell Air Force Base was now home of the Air Mobility Command's 22nd Air Refueling Wing, Air Force Reserve Command's 931st Air Refueling Group, and the Kansas Air National Guard's 184th Intelligence Wing. In terms of military significance, it wasn't high on anyone's radar, which gave Benjamin room to operate with his fake papers undetected. But, more importantly, it had two other essential features: it was a key KC-46 Pegasus military airplane aerial refueling station, and it was home to a few old allies.

Benjamin had not returned since 2003, when he'd left to lead the K'in cloning program. But, as he scanned the arid land and regiments of soldiers double-timing it in the heavy boots across an unused airstrip, he realized it was here his discontent with the military's, even the USA's, view on how to save the world had begun to unravel. It was the shard in his brain that had influenced everything from that point, including his decisions on the cloning project.

At the turn of the millennium, he had moved Freya, once again, and dropped her into yet another school—this time in Kansas. Close to her senior year in high school she was soon to join the military academy, where he could keep her safe. Like any good daughter, she'd done as she was asked and come with him—though, of course, she had nowhere else to go. But as her time to graduate drew near, and her impending military career became a reality, life on the base had him questioning whether it was the right choice.

Benjamin headed up two functions at McConnell. Both related to America's war on terror following the attack on the twin towers in New York. Operation *Noble Eagle* saw thousands of National Guard and reserve personnel mobilized to perform security missions on military installations, airports and other potential targets. Benjamin's job was to ensure these reserves were trained to a basic standard. Then, of course, there was *Operation Enduring Freedom*. For the most part, it referred to the war in Afghanistan. The hilarious and little-known fact was that it was originally called *Operation Infinite Justice,* but several religions had used similar phrases as descriptions of God, so it was changed to avoid offense to Muslims. The same Muslims who, on October 7 2001, were systematically annihilated by a barrage of indescribably destructive arsenal including carrier-based F-14 Tomcat and F/A-18 Hornet fighters, and Tomahawk cruise missiles, not to mention land-based B-1 Lancer, B-2 Spirit and B-52 Stratofortress bombers. The start of a war lasting more than a decade achieved nothing, but put more terrorists in power.

Freya had not understood the operation, and questioned her entry into a world where so much collateral damage was acceptable—even in the name of peace. But, Benjamin had resolved they were protecting the USA and freedom, and that her joining the military would be the best thing she could do. In retrospect, he was only ensuring her safety. Ultimately, it had cost him everything.

Benjamin approached an open hangar. Inside, Colonel Albert G. Mills, commander of the 22nd Air Refueling Wing, was addressing his men. A robust man in his late fifties with a bristly gray moustache, he carried himself with purpose and authority. His men stood in three perfect and unmoving rows. As Benjamin approached, not even a fleeting glance from the soldiers gave a hint that he'd been noticed, let alone recognized. All the same, Colonel Mills spun on his heel to face Benjamin and immediately saluted.

Benjamin returned the gesture, but quickly fell into informality. "At ease, Albert."

Colonel Mills dropped his salute into an offer of a hearty handshake which was well-received. "Benjamin Lloyd. As I live and breathe. I heard you were at Leavenworth?" Mills's dark brown eyes held concern and even a little suspicion.

"That I was, Albert. Can we take a walk?"

"Absolutely." He dismissed his troops and then beckoned Benjamin to follow him.

The two friends ambled slowly along an empty runway, away from prying ears and eyes. The sun beat down on their heads, both men sweating under their heavy uniforms. Benjamin recounted everything that had happened in the last few years: K'in and Wak, the bonding, the near war with the Chinese. How Russia had come to the rescue. The Green and Red Societies, and the Shan Chu. Benjamin's role in it all, and that of Colonel Roberts. And, of course, the death of Kelly Graham. Now, even after the cover-up, Benjamin's original plan—to expose the Huahuqui to the people—seemed to be the only answer. Crazy as it was.

Colonel Mills studied Benjamin. "There's no way you were getting out of Leavenworth with that rap sheet, Benjamin. What's the deal?"

Benjamin rubbed his unshaven jaw, contemplating his answer. Albert knew everything now, anyway. "The Secretary of State got me out. I have the pardon and reinstatement as General right here in my pocket. Only she knows if it's real or not. As far as we're concerned, it's official."

Albert raised one bushy eyebrow. "That still doesn't mean you have an executive order to mount a rescue mission."

"No, it doesn't," Benjamin confirmed.

The Colonel turned away, staring at the collection of hangars and airplanes at his base. Then, without looking at Benjamin he said: "You know, I remember Freya when she was a young lady. She was a sweet kid. A strong kid. But, she's not a kid anymore, Benjamin, and can make her own decisions. You sure you wanna do this?"

"She's my daughter. Maybe not biologically, but that doesn't mean shit. I'm going back to prison if I'm lucky. Otherwise, it's the chair. If it's the last thing I do, I'm not leaving her there."

Albert turned to his friend again, his square face creased with concern. "And these creatures? The Huahuqui?"

"We can't let them fall into the wrong hands."

"And we're the right hands?" Albert asked, his eyes wide.

The words stuck in Benjamin's throat. "I don't know. I'll figure that out once I get them out of there."

The Colonel sighed. "Let me see those papers."

Benjamin pulled the crumpled sheet from the inside pocket of his tunic and handed it to Albert.

After a few moments of scanning, the Colonel folded it up and handed it back. "So, General Lloyd, how can we assist you? Assuming the Secretary can corroborate these papers are legit."

Benjamin allowed a small smile of relief. "How many Pegasus

do you have fully fueled and ready to go?"

Location: Sinkhole Eight, Yamal Peninsula

The last time Freya had been this worried about KJ, he was lying in a hospital bed.

The monitor had beeped rhythmically with his tiny heartbeat, a blue line pulsing across the black screen. Tubes protruded from his delicate mouth, his long brown hair scattered across the pillow. Blood stained his ripped T-shirt and pants.

He'd been too confident, even at three years old. Controlling Socks had been easy, the cat following his every move, his every command. Playing fetch with a ball, walking the yard wall, literally jumping through hoops. He and that cat practically lived in the garden. Only coming in to eat, then straight back out until the sun disappeared. Freya had become complacent. Using the time to get chores done. And so, on that summer day, she hadn't noticed the coyote come into the backyard until it was too late.

Later, KJ told her he had tried making friends with it, approaching slowly and holding out his hand to calm the beast. Staring into its eyes as he had with Socks and the other small rodents and rabbits that called Connecticut home. But the coyote had its own will, and KJ's power wasn't strong enough. It had bitten right through his little forearm. KJ's scream was heard two houses away.

Freya had sprinted into the yard, kicked the wild dog off, and pumped two shots into its head killing it outright. KJ was bleeding out, and didn't seem to be healing fast enough. Freya had rushed him to the hospital. He'd been hurried through the ER and immediately had his wounds painfully flushed out. KJ cried and struggled until eventually he had to be sedated to ensure the doctors could clean the wounds properly and prevent infection from the bacterial cesspool that was the coyote's mouth. They'd even debated whether surgery was necessary.

But as he lay in his cot, the wounds had begun to slowly heal. At least, slowly for KJ. It was fast enough to arouse interest from the hospital staff who insisted he stay overnight. Freya had to balance KJ's health against exposing him for what he was.

So, she sat in his room and waited. Counting the minutes and checking his wounds, until she felt he was healed enough to be taken home, before the doctors started asking too many questions. Luckily, despite protests from the staff, she'd been able to get him discharged early and he'd survived. She'd risked his life to save it later—and Freya hated herself for it.

"Can't they go any damn faster?" Freya snapped.

"They're going as fast as they can, sweetie," Teller replied.

"Will you stop calling me that?" Freya dangled precariously into the sinkhole, a pocket lamp fixed to her jacket. In one hand she clasped a Beretta, leaving the other to help guide her as she descended into the dark.

The Nenets above strained to hold reindeer sinew ropes that suspended Freya and Teller in the hole. Tony Franco and Gibbs followed, hanging twenty feet above. Slowly and carefully, the team of four were lowered into the void. The poor Siberian daylight was quickly attenuated by the blackness of the sinkhole, so Freya flicked on her headlamp. It barely lit a few feet in front of her. She swung around to illuminate Teller's worried face.

"What's up with you?" she asked.

"Oh, I'm just not a fan of small dark spaces," he replied, swiveling his head to search their surroundings.

"You were the XO of a submarine," Freya said. "And when I met you, it was docked in a cave."

"That had lights. And submarines don't have bats."

Freya sighed. "My hero."

After what felt like an eternity, Freya found purchase. She tentatively rested one foot, then the other. Satisfied whatever she was on was stable, she allowed her full body weight to rest on the shallow slope of icy mud and wet gravel that spiraled down into the void. Her thighs felt weak, and her legs almost buckled beneath her but Freya managed to keep herself upright.

Teller dropped down beside her. "You okay? Have you hurt yourself?"

Freya ignored his question. "It's a ledge or gangway or something. It goes down that way. It's much bigger than the hole itself. I think it's a cave system." She pointed her Beretta into the dark.

Franco and Gibbs set down beside Teller and Freya.

"What now boss?" Franco said. "Do we get more of the boys down here?"

"No, Tony. I'm more afraid of what's up there than what's in here."

"Except bats," Freya said as she untied the makeshift rope and marched off into the dark.

Teller quickly untied himself then yanked on the rope indicating the Nenets should let it drop. It slapped into a muddled heap on the ground next to him. Teller coiled it up and slipped it over his shoulder. As he was about to leave, the cone of light from his lamp fell on a heap in between two jagged rocks. He pulled his Desert Eagle and approached cautiously.

As he drew near, the heap came into focus. It was a Nenets woman, both legs broken—the bones protruding through the skin. Her skin was pallid and her eyes rolled back in her head. If the fall hadn't killed her, the cold and lack of fresh water would have. Teller sighed and holstered his weapon. He then checked one last time for small, flying rodents, and tramped after Freya.

Jonathan clambered and slithered over rocks, through a labyrinth of what avid cavers would call 'squeezes' and 'meanders.' Only the freshly disturbed gravel and wet boot prints offered him guidance—though it was the blind leading the blind. He could only hope Freya's motherly instinct would guide her true. Out of breath, with scuffed palms and knees, Teller ducked under an archway of translucent blue ice and into a massive chamber. At the edge of a ledge overlooking a large body of water, Freya and his men were standing.

Teller sidled up to Freya. "We're not swimming across, that's for sure. We'll freeze before we get ten feet."

"You're assuming there is an across, boss," Tony said.

"Give me a flare, Tony," Freya said, holstering her Beretta and holding out her other hand.

Tony fished around in his combat pants, pulled out a red flare, and slapped it into her palm. Freya popped it on against her thigh and heaved it over the subterranean lake. The water's surface and the dripping cave walls covered in feathers of hoarfrost sparkled like a Russian Tsar's necklace as the flare sailed through the air. It clipped a stalactite and hurtled downward, bouncing off a series of stalagmites, before coming to rest on an icy gravel shore.

"She's got quite an arm," Franco said to Gibbs.

Teller shook his head. "That's got to be fifty feet across. And at least twenty down. We'd need a zip line."

"Then we have to improvise," Freya said, her eyebrows raised expectantly.

"Improvise? With what?" Teller asked, waving his arms around the desolate cave.

"You're the strategist. Think of something," Freya snapped back.

"I'm trying."

The flare fizzled out leaving them in the dark once again.

"Uh, boss? You know, I've done some caving in my time. This place is a bit like Dark Star."

"Dark Star?" Freya asked.

"It's a cave system in Uzbekistan," Tony offered. "I've been in there. Eleven miles of passageways have been identified, all nearly three-thousand feet below the surface. There's even talk of it connecting to neighboring Festivalnaya."

Teller searched the ledge and without looking up said: "What's your point, Tony?"

"This place looks a lot bigger. We can't know how deep this goes, if it's penetrable, or even where the Huahuqui and the kids went. In Dark Star, professionals have put in a series of ropes to aid cavers. There's at least a dozen just at the entrance. In here we got nothing. I don't think we should be going in any farther."

"What's your suggestion—" Teller started.

"Uh, boss." Gibbs nodded to something behind Jonathan.

Freya had pulled her hair tight and was sitting on the edge of the ledge.

"What the hell are you doing?" Teller asked, reaching for her arm.

Freya shook off his grip. "I'm going to find my son."

Jaw clenched, Teller dropped to his haunches to meet Freya's stare. "How?"

"Swim."

"Are you insane? From what I've seen, you're exhausted. Barely able to lift your Beretta half the time."

Freya glared at him. "Look, the lake isn't frozen, which means it's probably salty. Which means I'll be more buoyant. It'll be just above freezing, but if I get to the other side I can warm myself up with a fire or something. Then keep going."

"You'll fucking die and you know it."

"I'm going after KJ."

Teller flared his nostrils. "You're a pain in the ass, you know that?"

"Yeah. I remember telling someone else that once or twice."

"He's dead, Freya," Jonathan reminded her.

"And so will my son be if I don't get to him."

Tony crouched down to the quarrelling couple. "We rope her. If she freezes up mid-way, we can pull her back and warm her up ourselves. In the meantime, Gibbs will go back and see if the Nenets have anything to help—won't you Gibbs?"

"Already on it," Gibbs said, then ducked under the archway and disappeared back the way they came.

"Go with him," Teller said. "I'll deal with this."

Tony nodded and disappeared into the dark after Gibbs.

Teller slipped off the sinew rope and pulled it around Freya's back and under her armpits. He stared deep into her eyes as he expertly tied a knot at her chest. "You sure you wanna do this?"

"He's all I have ..."

"Of Kelly?"

"… in the world," Freya finished.

"Okay, Freya. Let's do this," Teller said.

Freya clambered over the edge and hung on by her fingers. Teller held onto the rope and slowly lowered her down. The drop was short to the shore below. Freya shed the large outer reindeer skin jacket and shivered. She then slipped off her reindeer hide boots and hurled them one after the other as hard as she could over the lake. The satisfying sound of pebbles sliding over each other signified they had found the other side.

Freya looked up to Teller and smirked.

"She really does have a good arm," Teller whispered to himself.

Freya turned to the inky water and held her breath. Then, she closed her eyes and lifted her foot to plunge in.

"Freya!" Jonathan's voice bounced off the cave's walls.

Freya blew out her breath and glared at Teller. "What?" she called up.

"Um, your lamp. You'll need it on the other side. You might wanna toss that over, too."

"Good idea." Freya fumbled with the coat, pulled out the lamp, and hurled it to the other shore. As soon as it hit the other side, it went out. The sound of it skitting across the gravel echoed all around. "Shit. I hope it's not broken," she mumbled.

From the ledge, Teller could only watch her silhouette. He held onto the rope, resisting every instinct to drag her back to his side of the lake. Then, after a full ten minutes of her slowly paddling away, she disappeared into the dark. He couldn't even hear her panting or her strokes in the water anymore.

"C'mon Freya," he whispered. "C'mon. You can do it." He pulled the rope to the point of almost being taut with one hand

and shook the other to reveal his watch. "You got one more minute."

The luminescent hand ticked rhythmically past thirty seconds. Forty-five. Fifty. Teller grabbed the rope with both hands. *Okay, you're coming back.*

A small cone of light shone out from the opposite shore. In the yellow hue sat Freya hugging her knees.

"I-I-I'm o-okay," Freya called through chattering teeth.

Teller sighed loudly. "Jesus, Freya. You know how to make a guy worry. Are you okay?" he called into the dim.

"C-cold," Freya replied, but this time her voice was barely audible.

"Shit. Freya, I need you to slip off the noose and put it on rock or a stalagmite or something, okay?"

Freya didn't respond.

"Did you hear me? I need you to—"

"I h-heard you," Freya wheezed back.

Teller waited and watched Freya disappear from the light. Twenty seconds passed. Had she done it?

"Freya?" he called.

She didn't answer.

Teller gathered up the rope and pulled on it—hard. It didn't budge. She must have tied it off. He searched his side of the lake until he found a jagged rock sticking out from the ledge. Teller quickly tied off his end of the rope, then twanged his makeshift zip line. It seemed taut enough.

With gloved hands, Teller held onto the zip line and then, hand over hand, began to descend to the other side. The rope stretched under his weight and bounced every time he gripped it anew. A violent crack echoed behind. The peg wouldn't hold much longer. He increased his pace, swinging from one hand to the next.

The chamber reverberated with a deafening snap and the rope went loose. Teller plummeted down and splash landed in the shallow water of the other shore. Unfazed by the impact or the cold water, he scrambled on hands and knees across the gravel, following the rope to the tie off point.

Freya wasn't there.

Jonathan unclipped his lamp and held it outward scanning for where to go next. Two gaping holes sat in the rock face. Which one to take?

"Freya!" he yelled into the dark.

There was no answer.

Fuck it. Teller opted for the left one, darting inside. Twenty feet of crawling on his elbows down the hole, he emerged in a blind end the size of a small car. *Goddammit.* He squirmed to make an about face and began his ascent back up the cramped shaft.

Darting into the second tunnel was worse. The passage was barely large enough for him to squeeze through. At several points, he had to nearly dislocate a shoulder just to pass. Then, after forcing his torso through yet another jagged gap, he flopped into a new cavity.

Teller climbed to his feet. The chamber was gargantuan—and light. Clusters of pink minerals gave off an iridescent glow reflected by a thin, but gushing, waterfall that started some thirty feet above and plummeted at least forty feet below the ledge on which he now found himself. Hundreds of natural platforms jutted out from the cave walls, each with its own tunnel leading off farther underground.

As he scanned the chamber, Teller thought of the scheelite cave in South America. The one in which K'in had appeared as an apparition—and Kelly had died. Freya had fought so hard to revive him.

Freya! Teller leapt to his feet and trudged to the brink. He peered over the ledge. There, at the foot of the waterfall were the Huahuqui. Their blue bodies squirmed over each other. Jonathan searched for the best path and then clambered down as fast as he could.

Battered and out of breath, he reached the pebbled bottom. He hobbled over the shifting stones to the writhing mass of Huahuqui and children, who seemed to take note of his advance and break from their scrum. One by one they peeled away to sit a few feet from him, until at the center of the activity, there she was: Freya, curled up in a ball on the ground with KJ and K'awin clasped to her. Her limbs jerked, as if her shivering had become uncontrollable.

Teller rushed over and crashed into the gravel beside them. "Freya!"

A light murmur signaled she was okay. Teller scooped her up in his arms and held her to his chest to keep her warm—but she already was.

"She was cold," KJ said. "We just warmed her up."

"Did you, indeed?"

Freya's spasms subsided. Jonathan studied her, pulling away the wet hair from her face. Even with blue lips and limp hair, she was beautiful. "What are you not telling me, huh?" he whispered.

"She likes you, you know," KJ said.

Teller studied the little boy. The face of a young Kelly Graham stared back. The same eyes. That same half-smile. He was cute as hell now, but something else lingered behind his stare. If Kelly was arrogant, how would his son be—with powers? Teller offered a weak smile before turning back to Freya.

"She'll be okay, we'll protect her," KJ said.

K'awin smacked her lips together and ruffled her bright red gills as if excited. KJ rubbed her nose.

Teller considered the creature, then KJ. "You and K'awin?"

"Me. K'awin. All of us," KJ said, smiling.

All the Huahuqui in the cave shuffled and warbled. As the melodic sound filled the chamber, Jonathan laughed gently and gazed up to the very top of the waterfall. Then, on each of the ledges lining the walls, new Huahuqui appeared and joined the chorus. Teller stared, wide-eyed.

Catherine had been right. There weren't thirty. There were hundreds.

CHAPTER NINE

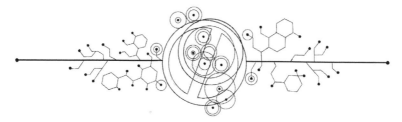

Location: McConnell Air Force Base, Kansas, USA

"What do you mean, I don't have clearance for takeoff? Do you know who I am, son? I have approval from Colonel Mills." Benjamin's face flushed with annoyance.

The young sergeant swallowed hard. "I'm sorry sir, it's Colonel Mills who revoked the order."

"That's impossible."

"I'm sorry, sir," stammered the young officer, his eyes glassy.

"Get out of my way." Benjamin climbed out of the Pegasus cargo hold and stormed out of hangar ten.

He marched across the tarmac, his stride confident, his inner thoughts preparing for the worst. Had he been discovered? Did they know the pardon was fake? Whatever happened, he had to get at least one plane off the base.

Without knocking, Benjamin pushed into Albert's office—a small room with little in the way of decoration save a photograph of the Colonel and his wife that sat on a large wooden desk. The shades were pulled down halfway to block the midday sun.

The Colonel held the phone in one hand, a pen in the other. He eyed Benjamin carefully, then ended his call abruptly and replaced the receiver.

"What the hell is going on, Albert?" Benjamin demanded. "Some field sergeant just told me I'm grounded."

The colonel nodded. "I gave the order."

"You know I don't have time to waste."

Albert sighed. "I just got a call, Benjamin. They said your pardon isn't legit and that you're a fugitive from Leavenworth."

"What? A call from whom?"

"Actually, it was anonymous. Not that it changes anything."

Benjamin placed his palms on the desk and leaned into the Colonel, speaking calmly but firmly. "You're going to trust an anonymous tip over me?"

"No. I trust Washington. I'm going to call the Secretary myself. But until I can confirm it, you can't go anywhere. It was one thing having your word and the document. But to get a call like that? I can't ignore it."

General Lloyd stood straight, contemplating his next sentence. "Let me ask you something, Albert. Why an anonymous tip? If I'm a fugitive, why aren't the military police tearing up your runways? Don't you think this might be connected to my leaving for Yamal? Someone doesn't want me to get to Freya and the Huahuqui."

"Maybe it's connected, and maybe it isn't. But this is my base and I'm not letting a single plane off a runway until I've spoken to the Secretary."

Benjamin balled his fists. "And? Have you called?"

"I was trying when you barged in."

"I don't have time for this shit, Albert. Freya needs me."

The colonel shook his head, solemnly. "I'm sorry, Benjamin. I can't until I know."

Benjamin slammed his fists down on the table, sending papers flying and pens rattling to the floor. "You're letting me fly. That's an order, Colonel!"

"And I told you, not until I've spoken to the Secretary. You have no authority."

"This is bullshit, Albert. You always were a bureaucratic old fuck." Benjamin turned on his heel to storm out, but was immediately met by two military police officers.

"You need to come with us, sir," the taller of the two men said.

"Son, you best get out of my way or when I'm done you'll be demoted to barrel boy and I'll see to it you get fucked every day for a year."

The men didn't move.

"Confine him to quarters," the colonel said.

Location: Washington DC, USA

Lucy paced her office. He was late.

The last few days had been a flurry of activity to set up the framework granting the Nenets children and Huahuqui asylum once they had found their way into the USA—legally or not. Meetings upon meetings in a convoluted process involving the Office of Refugee Resettlement, the Department of Health and Human Services, the Bureau of Population, Refugees and Migration and of course the Bureau of Citizenship and Immigration Services of the Department of Homeland Security. Despite offering asylum to people the world over, actually achieving it seemed almost impossible. For a nation made up of immigrants, many fleeing persecution over the past few hundred years, the number now actually admitted was the lowest it had ever been.

But the Huahuqui were not just refugees. If the General had

been right all along, they were possibly the answer to human suffering. Of course, trying to explain what the Huahuqui were to a bunch of bureaucrats was proving difficult.

All of it hinged on one man: Steve Chang. One of the president's more controversial postings, Steve was a bit of a poster child—a descendant of Chinese immigrants heading up the CIS. Steve handled the criticism with grace. He was a good guy and always listened to Lucy when she asked, often acting as a sounding board when she was confronted with a tough decision. But she wasn't looking for a sounding board today. Today, she needed him to back her. It was no small request.

Lucy checked her watch again. Twenty minutes past the hour. She stepped to her desk and picked up the phone to dial his number.

"Hey, sorry I'm late." Steven stepped into her office, out of breath.

"No problem," Lucy lied, putting the phone down. "Did you run?"

"Sure, I hate to be late. And it's you, Lucy. What man could keep you waiting?"

Lucy smiled. "That's a whole other story. Take a seat. So, what do you have for me?"

Steve sat in the guest chair opposite Lucy, who settled onto her soft leather chesterfield.

"It's complicated," he said. "They may not qualify for asylum. The children or the Huahuqui."

"What, why?" Lucy frowned.

"They're not refugees, Lucy. Yamal peninsula is not a war zone, and the children are not under threat that we know of. The Nenets have lived a peaceful life under Russian rule for a long time. And the Huahuqui—well, we can't even ascertain what they are and if they're even sentient, let alone if Yamal is or isn't the place they're supposed to be."

Lucy leaned back in her chair and crossed her arms. "Trust me, they're sentient."

"Well, if you could find any information on the program you described? Anything that shows they are not an indigenous species to the Eurasian continent? Anything that shows they're intelligent?"

Lucy's diligence in ensuring the military could never repeat the cloning program had backfired. No one knew about it. The scientists could back her up, but without physical evidence no one would care. No one would believe General Lloyd—now an escaped convict. She was screwed.

"Lucy?" Steve sat with wide, expectant eyes.

"If I could get you something—something to prove it—do we have options?"

Steve pulled at his face with both hands and sucked in a breath. "Maybe. If they were already here—and I don't even want to ask how you're going to achieve that, Lucy—but if they were here, then we could file a *priority two* case for groups designated by virtue of their circumstances and apparent need for resettlement." His voice dropped to a whisper, as if speaking to himself. "We could do it as a package. If the children are bonded, they are part and parcel with the Huahuqui. Of course, we'd have to show detrimental effect upon separation …"

"You're rambling again, Steve."

Steve snapped back to the conversation. "Sorry. There might be a way. But you have to get me that evidence." He stood up to leave. "I'll make some calls. Oh, and you realize, the CDC will get involved."

Lucy knitted her eyebrows, half listening to Steve, half thinking on where to find what she needed. "The CDC?" she asked.

"Sure. They're animals, Lucy. Maybe intelligent animals, but the CDC will want them quarantined. Can't say I'd argue with their rationale."

The Secretary nodded. "Sure, CDC."

Then it hit her. The CDC. There might be some evidence after all.

Location: Sinkhole Eight, Yamal Peninsula, Siberia

In the pink hue of the cavern's glowing crystals, Freya sat on a rock observing her son. KJ splashed around, knee deep, in the shallow lagoon at the base of the waterfall. Despite being told numerous times to get out, he inevitably followed K'awin in—the frigid water never seeming to bother him. Instead, he giggled and chased the creature. Of course, Svetlana and Ribka were never far behind. The little Nenets girl and her Huahuqui.

Other than using their proximity to specific children, Freya had learned to distinguish between some of the creatures. K'awin was slightly rounder than the rest, her limbs softer. Her very movements were graceful, springing and pouncing like a kitten—albeit, a very large kitten. Ribka on the other hand, boisterous and almost clumsy. With a dark blue stripe that ran from the tip of his nose, down his spine and into the ventral fin on his tail, he lumbered about much like a teenage boy—purposefully splashing the others.

And then there was Chernoukh. The only Huahuqui with black gills, he was also the largest that had bonded to the kids. He and Nikolaj sat on a higher rock observing the other Huahuqui and children. Much as the eldest offspring in a family would, Chernoukh refrained from play, only intervening when he deemed it was getting out of control. A quick hop down to deliver a firm, but harmless, bite on the back leg of the offending Huahuqui before climbing back to the pedestal.

High above them all, were the very largest creatures. Freya could only assume they were the adults. They hadn't come down from their perches yet. Perhaps afraid of Teller and Freya, though they had no qualms about leaving the younglings alone with them.

"Hey." Teller plonked himself down on the ground next to Freya.

Freya just nodded, not removing her gaze from KJ.

"KJ's okay."

"Is he? Have you seen him?" Freya pointed to her son. "It's getting stronger."

"What is?" Teller asked.

"The bond. Look, he's going blond at the roots. He's changing, Jonathan."

Teller nodded solemnly. "Maybe it's an adaptation to cold. Maybe KJ is taking on Huahuqui characteristics. Some hamsters go white in winter."

"Is that supposed to make me feel better?"

"No. Yes. Maybe? Just try and stay calm. Tony'll be back soon, and we can hopefully leave."

"Not soon enough, Jonathan. Where the fuck is he? It's been hours."

"The caves down here aren't exactly easy to navigate. They may have gotten lost."

Freya didn't respond.

Teller picked up a pebble and tossed it into the lake, watching it skip across the surface several times before plopping out of sight. "How long do you think they've been down here?"

"The Huahuqui? How would I know?" Freya snapped. "What difference does it make?"

Jonathan sighed. "What's going on with you?"

"What are you talking about?"

Teller touched her arm to draw her gaze to his. "You. You used to have life and curiosity in those big green eyes of yours. Now all I see is …"

"Is?" she demanded, her eyes wide, lips pursed.

"Fear."

"Of course, I'm afraid." Freya jerked her arm away and continued to watch her baby boy. "Do you not remember what was going on at Paradise Ranch or Dulce Base? If the government found out about KJ's powers, they'd take him away and stick needles in him for the rest of his life. Now, I have to worry about him and *these* things." She waved a hand at the Huahuqui.

"I'd never let that happen to KJ, you know that. And as for *these* things, if anything written in your report is true, then being with them might be the best thing that ever happened to him. But it's more than that. I've seen you pop pills. You've got the shakes. Are you using? Is it the stress? Tell me."

Freya turned to Jonathan, incredulity etched into her face. "You were never around to help. How are you going to be there for us? It took you *how long* to get to us when I did call you?"

"Hey." Teller climbed to his feet. "That's not fair. I tried to stick around. You pushed me away. And you're avoiding the question. Last time, Freya. What's going on?"

"Huntington's," said a voice from above.

"Minya!" Freya snapped, eyes wide, turning to the direction of the voice. "What the hell?"

"Huntington's?" Teller repeated.

"*Da*," Minya said.

Freya's heart beat fiercely in her chest. "What the hell are you doing, Minya?"

"He needed to know. It puts everyone at risk, my friend. Especially KJ. It becomes worse, no?"

"The mood swings, the tremors. Of course," Jonathan said, staring at Freya. "Freya, why didn't you tell me? I could've helped."

Freya didn't answer.

"How long? Before full neural degeneration?" Teller asked.

Freya sighed and turned to Teller. "Feeling as ever, I see. I don't know. Ten years, tops. Maybe sooner. I'll lose control of my limbs, thrashing out until eventually I'm a big jabbering mess. Is that what you wanna hear?"

"I'm sorry, I didn't mean ..." Teller sighed, searching her face. "That's why you risked bringing him—KJ—because you couldn't wait ..."

"It would be too far gone later," Freya said, her voice steady, firm. "I'd never make the journey. And I couldn't let him do it alone." She turned away and swallowed the lump in her throat, her gaze fixed on her son.

Minya stepped beside Freya and put a hand on her shoulder. "I'm sorry, my friend, but he had to be told."

"I guess," Freya said, then wiped her face and turned back to Jonathan. "Do *not* tell KJ. He doesn't know. Promise me."

"What're you going to tell him? When? He's going to have to watch his mother ..."

"I will help her," Minya interjected. "And then take Kelly

Junior. This was always plan."

Teller stood in silence, apparently trying to absorb the information, his brow creased in concern and disbelief. Finally, he said: "How did you not know? It's genetic—"

"My parents died in a car crash when I was a kid, remember?" Freya said. "*Obviously*, neither showed any symptoms that were noticed."

The cave fell deathly silent.

Uncomfortable with the revelation and the quietness, Freya changed the subject. "How did you get down here, Minya? I didn't even hear you come in or climb down."

"Too busy arguing with Mr. Teller, it seems. But I had help," Minya replied.

Freya and Teller shot a glance up to the ledge expecting to see Tony or Gibbs standing there. Instead, another familiar face peered back at them.

Freya squinted. "Vetrov?"

CHAPTER TEN

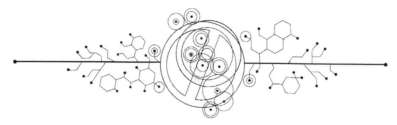

Location: Washington DC, USA.

Lucy wandered the garden of the Korean War memorial. Frost clung to the tiny blades of grass that still resisted the winter cold and tree branches waved lazily in the frigid breeze. She shivered and pulled the soft cashmere scarf tighter around her neck. Normally, the park was empty and she was able to think alone while meandering through the small shrubbery, pondering the statues honoring the near four-million Americans who had fought in one of the fiercest conflicts in modern history.

But not today.

Today, there were groups of foreign tourists being led by overly-eager guides holding little colored flags. The crowds shuffled and chatted to each other in their native tongue. Most toyed with their smart phones, or took photographs of themselves in frivolous poses in front of statues. Perhaps they didn't appreciate the importance of the site. Perhaps they just didn't care. Their freedom, the freedom of any nation, was often owed to men whose names they would never know. Just like they would never know about the Huahuqui, unless she could save them. But she'd sealed their doom years ago.

In an hour she would see Steve, but she didn't have anything for him. All she could do now was play the political game she hated to play: tie things up in red tape. Get the Huahuqui and the children here. Stow them away somewhere safe, probably Alaska, and then fight it out. It may take years, but as long as it was a public battle, no black-boxed agency could undermine her and take the creatures for themselves.

The secretary stuffed her hands into the pockets of her poppy-red trench coat and meandered away from the crowd. Her cell phone vibrated. She pulled it from her pocket: one new message. Lucy opened the app and tapped on the icon. It was Steve.

May have good news, but will need your evidence of sentience. I'm on my way. Come now.

Finally, something had moved. Now she just needed her contact to come through. Lucy typed a quick note back then slipped the phone into her pocket.

Across the garden, the man she had been waiting for approached. His familiar broad, bald head shining in the winter sun. He marched toward her, his stride wide and angry. Lucy produced a soft smile that vaguely hid her disdain for him.

"What's so important that you feel the need to drag me all the way up here?" he demanded.

"It's a pleasure to see you again, Colonel Robertson."

"Cut the bullshit, Madam Secretary. Why am I here?"

"Our little problem is back."

"I wasn't aware there was a problem, let alone it being, *ours,*" the Colonel said, scanning his surroundings.

"We're quite alone, Colonel. I'm not here to cause you any problems. Actually, I need your help." It stung to even admit that, but he may be the only person who would have answers.

"Why the fuck would I help you? You almost killed me. And I had to step down from heading up the CDC."

"The Huahuqui aren't gone."

His eyes narrowed.

Lucy pulled the satellite photograph from the inner pocket of her coat and handed it to the Colonel. "It's not one. There's at least thirty. They were living under the ice in Siberia. A sinkhole blew open and now they're free. They've bonded to the children of a local Nenets tribe—and at least one American child. Benjamin Lloyd's goddaughter's son."

The colonel gave it a cursory glance, then handed it back. "And? Why does this concern me?"

Lucy stuffed the photo back into her coat. "Because, we need to grant them asylum or refugee status—but to do that, I need to prove they're sentient. You might be the only person left who has any records. Perhaps something on a personal drive? I confiscated and destroyed everything at Paradise Ranch and Dulce Base."

"Personal drive?" the colonel exclaimed. "How stupid do you think I am? Look, you made this bed, now you have to lie in it. There are consequences for everything. Your little one-woman mission to shut down my operation, and the years of research of Professor Alexander, and even that nut job Lloyd, has backfired. Should've kept your nose out of what you didn't understand." He gave an almost satisfied smirk, then turned and walked away.

Lucy stood in a daze. He was her last hope. It didn't matter what mountains Steven had managed to move, without proof these creatures were intelligent, she was screwed. No, *they* were screwed—and the Earth with them.

The crowd of tourists became louder. The secretary watched with mild irritation. The bustle rapidly escalated into a fully panicked stampede. Frozen to the spot, the secretary watched as the herd of foreigners sprinted toward her, chased by a white-paneled van spewing a cloud of green-brown gas. One by one, the tourists dropped to the floor hacking and coughing, their limbs tight in spasm, as the nerve gas took hold. The van careened through the crowd, smacking into tourists who had made it far enough away to escape the gas. They were immediately crushed under its tires.

Lucy instinctively jumped to the side and hit the grass as the vehicle sped past. She lifted her head from the dirt and tried to take note of the number plate, but her eyes stung and her lungs burned. She coughed hard, fighting for oxygen, but it was no use. Enveloped in a cloud of gas, her limbs stiffened until she lay outstretched, wide eyed, on the ground, unable to move.

In the grass, just out of reach, Lucy's cell phone began to ring.

Location: McConnell Air Force Base, Kansas, USA

"It just went to voicemail, Benjamin. She's not answering," Albert said.

The General stood fast in the tiny office, contemplating what to do next. If something had happened to the Secretary, his alibi was about to be blown and he'd never make it to Siberia.

"Benjamin, did you hear me?" Albert pressed.

"I heard you. She's the Secretary of State. A busy woman, wouldn't you agree?"

"I imagine so, but so far I've been unable to confirm your release status. Normally, I'd have you thrown in the brig. But we're friends. If the Secretary can confirm it, then we're ready to go. Otherwise, you're grounded."

Benjamin eyed his long-time friend. There was no way to convince him otherwise. He could bend rules, but break them?

Unlikely. Time was running out.

"Take him back to the barracks. House arrest is fine for now," the Colonel said to the lone military police officer standing by the door.

The military police officer nodded and turned to Benjamin. Before the young man could take another step, the General struck him in the throat. The MP stumbled around, unable to cry for help.

"Benjamin!" Albert yelled. "What the fuck!"

The General pulled the sidearm from the MP's holster and pistol whipped him. The soldier fell unconscious to the floor. Benjamin then pointed the weapon at Albert.

"I'm sorry, but I don't have time for this," Benjamin said. "Make the call. Clear two Pegasus for takeoff."

"You know I'm not going to do that Benjamin. And you're not going to shoot me."

"Albert, you and I have been friends for a long time." Benjamin stepped around the desk. "And you know Freya means more to me than life. You also know, if I say I'll do something, I'll do it." The General stared long and hard into Albert's glassy eyes.

"You're not going to let this drop, are you?"

"Would you?"

Albert shrugged. "I don't have family. I wouldn't know."

"Trust me, you wouldn't." Benjamin pressed the barrel of the gun against the Colonel's head. "Make. The. Call."

The Colonel sighed, and with the cold metal muzzle pressed against his temple, he picked up the phone and dialed. "Yes, this is Colonel Mills. The order has been confirmed. Scramble two Pegasus for takeoff, under command of General Lloyd. Priority one." He replaced the receiver.

"Thank you, Albert."

"Don't thank me ye—"

Benjamin struck his friend across the back of the head, sending the man sprawling unconscious into the desk. He then dragged the limp body of the young officer to the Colonel and handcuffed them together using the desk leg as an anchor. A quick search provided some tape that he wrapped multiple times around the men's heads and mouths so they were stuck together and unable to speak. A last taping of their ankles and he was satisfied. It wouldn't hold them forever, but hopefully long enough for him to take the planes.

The bright sunshine burned Benjamin's retinas as he headed for the hangars. As he approached, he could make out the bustle of activity inside as two crews prepped and fueled the planes. He sucked in a deep breath, and stormed in with as much authority as he could muster.

"Where're we on the final preparations, boys?" he bellowed.

"Almost done sir," called one of the crew. "We have your co-pilot here and your flight pilot for the second bird, but we're waiting on another cleared first officer."

"Where the hell is he?"

"She sir, but she had to be brought in from home. No one left on the roster for active duty."

The General grunted. "This is a goddamn work hours thing, isn't it?"

"Everyone maxed out their hours, sir. We had to bring someone in," the crewman replied. "She'll be ten minutes, tops."

"Fuck me. Where is the FP for my second bird?"

"Captain Fleming. He's in the next hangar."

Benjamin stormed out and into the hangar next door. "Captain Fleming?" he called out.

"Sir!" A young man answered and saluted the General.

They all looked young to him these days. The pilot was probably thirty years old. Benjamin struggled to remember what it was like to be that age. Instead, his thoughts were filled with Freya.

"I'm General Lloyd. You're under my command for this mission, son."

"Yes, sir," replied the pilot.

"This is no ordinary mission. We're going into foreign territory to rescue American citizens. It has been authorized by the Secretary of State herself." Benjamin pulled his fake pardon with the White House seal on it from his jacket pocket and flashed it at the pilot, before quickly stuffing it away again. "Once we're airborne, it's radio silence with home. If we're caught, we're on our own. We change frequency to communicate with each other, but that's it. You don't deviate. Do you understand?"

"Yes, sir!" the pilot said.

Benjamin had lucked out. A good and eager airman who followed orders. "Good. And deactivate the transponder. Hop to it, son."

With that, Benjamin turned about face and marched back to his Pegasus.

"Ready, sir. And the first officer just arrived," the lead crewman said.

"Excellent, let's get these birds off the ground." Benjamin saluted his crewman and then stomped up the main cargo ramp into the Pegasus. He slammed on the close button as he passed it and marched straight to the cockpit. He climbed into the pilot seat and began flicking switches. "What's your name, son?" he said without looking up.

"Lang," the co-pilot said.

"Lang, we are about to pull off the rescue of American citizens from hostile territory. Can I count on you?"

"Yes, sir," replied the man.

"Good. Then we're gonna get on fine. Prepare for taxi. We take the lead. Bird two will follow."

The ground crew scattered as Benjamin pressed the thrust levers that edged the Pegasus from the hangar. He maneuvered the jet onto the runway and then contacted the tower.

"Bird one, you are clear for takeoff," came the voice over the headset.

"Roger that," Benjamin confirmed. "Set take-off power."

"Power set," replied Lang.

The Pegasus began to move, slowly at first, but then accelerating faster and faster toward the end of the runway.

"Eighty knots," the co-pilot said.

"Confirmed, eighty knots. V one," Benjamin said, letting go of the thrust levers. "Rotate."

The nose of the jet began to raise.

"Positive rate," the co-pilot confirmed.

"Roger that. Gear up."

Lang positioned the gear lever to the up position. "V2. Transition."

Benjamin adjusted the nose again. "Climb power."

"Power set, sir."

The Pegasus climbed and climbed until Benjamin was satisfied they had reached the correct height and speed. "Flaps five … flaps one … flaps up."

"Flaps up, roger," Lang repeated.

The General called to the other jet. "Bird two, this is bird one, have you cleared the runway? Over."

Static.

Benjamin's breathing quickened. Had they been grounded? Had Albert gotten free? That could mean there would be fighters scrambled any minute. He'd be shot down over the base before they were allowed to reach civilian airspace or pass over a populated area. "Bird two, this is bird one, have you cleared the runway? *Over*."

More static.

Dammit. "Bird two, this is—"

"*This is bird two,*" came a female voice of the first officer. "*We have cleared the runway. We had a bit of a delay. We're right behind you, sir. Over.*"

Benjamin sighed with relief. "Switching frequencies. Radio silence now in operation. And kill the transponder. Let's get our people. Over."

CHAPTER ELEVEN

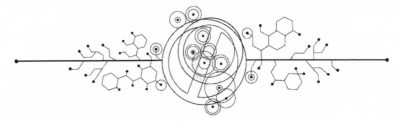

Location: Sinkhole Eight, Yamal Peninsula, Siberia

Catherine sat on the ledge at the entrance to the chamber, observing the odd scene. Teller, who seemed to be the *de facto* leader of this ragtag band of soldiers, children and strange creatures, had advised that the majority stay underground where it was safe. The cavern was difficult to find let alone mount an attack upon. Above ground, a handful of his crew kept guard and waited for the rescue that every passing hour felt less likely.

So, they waited. The children played and giggled, splashing around in the cool water at the foot of the waterfall, the Huahuqui chasing them like happy puppies. Bathed in the soft glow of crystals lining the cave, the scene was almost idyllic. Almost.

While the Nenets families appeared at ease with the Huahuqui, and even helped to catch a few of the fish that swam in the underground lake—and must have formed the diet of the creatures—the soldiers remained distant. As Catherine watched the men, it wasn't clear if they chose to remain vigilant and disconnected, or if they just wanted to stay away from the strange blue, giant axolotl-like animals. Perhaps Teller had warned them of the perils of bonding. Perhaps the Huahuqui chose not to bond themselves to men of war.

Catherine picked up her Nikon camera and focused the

telephoto lens on KJ and his mother. Freya had decided she didn't like his hair two different colors and so now sat with him between her legs and, using a large serrated knife she'd borrowed from Tony, was chopping away the chocolate ends leaving behind a much shorter blond tousle. K'awin, as KJ called his personal Huahuqui, lay at his feet curled up in a ball.

Another Huahuqui came into the shot. Catherine refocused to sharpen the image. It was the same one she'd seen earlier. An apparently unbonded Huahuqui had been sniffing around Freya and KJ. At first, Catherine had thought it was interested in the boy. Everyone seemed focused on him. The children and the creatures followed him around as if he were a tiny general. But, the more she observed, the more Catherine came to realize this particular animal, the one with the darker blue marks across its snout, was trying to approach Freya. Freya constantly shooed it away.

Catherine squeezed the button. *Click.*

"You have a death wish?" Teller plonked himself down next to Catherine.

"I'm just taking a few photos and notes. Anyway, I'm not in her face."

Teller laughed softly. "Trust me, she can feel you observing her. She's probably calculated how to whip a pebble at your camera and crack the lens without even looking."

"I'm a reporter. I'm reporting. It's what I do. And in this case, it might even save her kid's life."

"She'll see that eventually. She's just scared right now."

Catherine shrugged. "Guess you have to be a parent to understand. Tell you what, though, if anything you've told me about these creatures is true—how they seem to give the people they bond with a feeling of calm—she might do well to let that one closer."

"Ah you mean Freckles."

"Freckles?"

"Yeah, that's what I've called that one. It seems to have taken a liking to Freya. I've been watching it."

Catherine laughed. "That's the best you could come up with? Freckles?"

"I'm a strategist, not a novelist. That's your job." Teller smiled.

"Journalist," Catherine said.

"Potato, po-*tah*-toh."

They laughed.

"Agent Teller." Sasha stood over Catherine and Jonathan, his huge frame even more intimidating when observed from the ground.

"What's up, Vetrov?"

"We have to talk."

Catherine narrowed her eyes.

Jonathan shot her a glance before speaking. "If you're worried about the reporter, don't be. You and I know what's going on here. We need this chronicled properly. Neither the Russian nor the US government can come out of this looking bad. She's going to report the truth."

The Russian colonel studied her with untrusting eyes, then dropped to his haunches and lowered his voice. "I'm not worried about the reporter. How do you think she got into Yamal without a visa? I let her in."

"You?" Teller asked, his voice full of suspicion.

Catherine hadn't mentioned it up to now. The tension was already palpable when Vetrov showed up in the first place. Pick your battles, her grandmother had always told her.

"The sinkholes are not news," Vetrov continued. "It was in my interest to see where she was going and to follow her. Didn't think it would lead me to you."

"And who did you expect her to lead you to?" Teller asked.

"That's what I need to talk to you about. You have a problem. Intelligence has told me there has been an attack in Washington. Sarin gas. Looks like the Koreans are being blamed."

Teller sighed and shook his head. "Shit, that's not good. Any dead?"

"Five. Many in the hospital. They hit tourists. Your Secretary of State was among them."

"Fuck." Teller rubbed his face. "She's the only one moving to help us. Without her, we're on our own."

"What about this General Lloyd? The one coming to get us?" Catherine asked.

"General Lloyd?" Sasha probed. "I thought he was at Leavenworth?"

"He was. Seems you FSB boys don't know everything." Teller gave a wry smirk. "It's a long story. He's supposed to come get us—backed by the Secretary. Now she's out of action. Do we know her condition?"

"No, not definitively," Sasha replied, then seemed to hesitate.

Catherine put her camera down and shuffled around to meet the Polkovnik's gaze. "Spit it out colonel, what are you not telling us?"

Sasha once again hesitated before deciding to speak. "I don't think it was the Koreans."

Catherine watched Teller eye the man carefully.

"Now what would make you think that?" Teller asked, his tone almost accusatory.

"I thought your reporter friend had a lead on a group of terrorists I tracked from St. Petersburg to here. I think they are Japanese. A defunct cult called Aum Shinrikyo who have risen up again."

Teller screwed up his face in confusion. "Aum? They were disbanded years ago. Why would they raise their heads now? And why try and frame the Koreans? They liked people knowing what they did."

"Who's Aum?" Freya stood above all three of them, staring down with distrusting eyes. Even Jonathan didn't seem to escape her scrutiny. "What's going on?"

Teller sighed. "There was some kind of terrorist attack in Washington. Seems the Korean's are being blamed, but Sasha here thinks it's a defunct cult called Aum Shinrikyo. They're the end of the world nut jobs responsible for the Tokyo sarin attacks in the 90s."

Catherine chewed her lip, deciding whether to say anything. "The secretary was caught in the attack. She's in hospital."

Freya glared at Teller. "Is she alright?"

"'Fraid so. That doesn't mean Benjamin isn't on his way."

"It's doesn't mean he *is*, either," Freya snapped back. "Colonel, can you get us out of here?"

Sasha rose to meet Freya's worried stare and smoothed down his uniform. "I have no orders from Moscow to do anything, right now. Besides, my small team came by Trekol. There simply isn't the room to move all of you."

"Fuck Moscow!" Freya shouted, inches from the Russian's face. "Can you not get a team in here? You're the closest military operation we have."

Catherine watched the exchange, the Russian Colonel's

patience running thin.

"I don't make any moves without more information, Ms. Nilsson," Sasha said, his voice calm.

Freya exploded again. "You want to talk about more information? All you've told us since you arrived is that you tracked some soldiers to Yamal, and then to us. Why are you even here, Vetrov?"

Teller jumped to his feet. "Okay, okay, I think we need to calm down. Sasha, you wanna fill us in a little more? For transparency's sake?"

The Polkovnik muttered something under his breath in Russian before speaking up. "As I told you, I tracked a terrorist group here from Moscow. I believe them to be Aum Shinrikyo, though they seemed to do their best to disguise themselves as Korean military."

Teller nodded. "That actually makes more sense than you think. I'd tracked a potential threat to North Korea. They were dressed up like military, too, but something felt off. Then we took out the a-holes who ambushed Freya and the kids back at the camp. They were playing dress up, too. You're saying they're all Aum?"

Sasha gave a curt nod. "Perhaps."

Teller scratched his strong jaw thoughtfully, then said: "Did you note a symbol tattooed on the guys you were chasing, Vetrov?"

The Polkovnik stared at Teller for a moment.

Catherine sat quietly, observing the constant game of chess between the two men. Each not truly trusting the other.

"The number nine," The FSB colonel said, finally.

Jonathan nodded slowly, emphasizing he was connecting the dots in his head. "Same here," he said. "Whoever they are, we're dealing with the same guys."

"And I think they are building an army. Or rather, growing one," Sasha interjected. "Several orphanages in Russia have been taken over in the last few years. We suspected an organization was grooming the children to be soldiers. This latest evidence would suggest it was Aum."

"An orphanage?" Catherine was now also on her feet, scribbling in her notepad.

Freya shot the reporter another cutting glance for apparently having the audacity to speak, then turned her attention back to Teller and Vetrov. "What's that got to do with the Huahuqui? How did *they* know to come here?"

Teller paced again. "If they're building an army, what better army than one attached to Huahuqui. A super army."

Freya shook her head. "That's a leap. This sinkhole opened up not long ago. No one knew the Huahuqui were even here."

Again, Sasha nodded. "But once they did find out, it wouldn't take them long to make the same conclusion. So, they sent in a team to take the creatures. The same team you killed and left back at the camp—though, from the tracks I saw, you didn't kill them all."

"We figured there were more," Teller said. "So, they attack Washington, perhaps in an attempt to stop any kind of rescue mission, and blame the Koreans to keep us busy, while they steal the Huahuqui?"

Catherine wasn't sure whom Teller was asking.

Freya scrunched up her nose. "Wait. So now a Japanese cult, who was already building some kind of army, got wind of the Huahuqui and decided they wanted them? And somehow found out about the Secretary's rescue plan for us? There's too many coincidences. There's gotta be a mole."

"I don't like any of this. Something feels off." Teller paced back and forth on the stony ground, glancing at the children and the Huahuqui in the water below. "This doesn't feel like Aum, right? And why blame the North Koreans. Most extremist cells *want* you to know it was them. They *claim* attacks. What do they gain from hiding and dragging North Korea into it?"

"I do not know," Sasha replied. "But they were taking Russian children. My children. And this I cannot allow. I will find out more, and stop them."

"I've got serious nutflies," Freya said.

"What?" said Teller, Sasha, and Catherine in unison.

"Oh." Freya blushed a little. "Something Kelly used to say."

Catherine watched Teller, the hurt in his eyes almost palpable.

"Okay," Teller began. "We need to confirm somehow that General Lloyd is still coming. And that Lucy is alive and able to help us get asylum once in the US. And tell Washington to hold off on nuking North Korea."

Sasha bobbed his head. "Let me do it through Moscow. If you have a mole in Washington, you don't know what you can or can't trust."

"And we're supposed to trust you?" Freya asked, her tone accusatory. "I'm going to find my son. And Minya and Nikolaj for that matter."

"I'll go to the surface and brief the boys to be on the lookout for the rest of the Aum team," Jonathan said.

Catherine was left alone with her thoughts. It was as if she were stuck in the middle of a movie—conspiracies and government secrets she had only read about in mystery novels. Even the deep-seated political and financial games she'd witnessed following the

Deepwater Horizon incident didn't compare. This was the big leagues, and everyone's life was at stake.

Location: Tokyo, Japan

Ishii sat on the hardwood floor of his tiny Tokyo flat, legs crossed, hands placed lightly together. He'd taken this posture, initiated steady breathing, and focused his mind a thousand times. But today he was unable to focus on the present, to sink into his prayers. The words passed his lips, but they didn't have meaning.

"OM Ami-dehva re," he repeated. The verse was hollow.

Ishii broke from his struggling trance, climbed to his bare feet, and smoothed down his long white robe. He glided across the apartment and picked up the pail of water that sat next to a child's paddling pool in the center of the room. He then poured it over the naked woman, bound with thin ropes that cut into her white flesh, and suspended upside down from the ceiling. The woman wailed through her gag. Ishii cocked his head to meet the petrified gaze of his latest recruit. Tears streaked from the corners of the woman's eyes as she shook her head and sobbed.

"You wish that I remove your gag?"

The woman nodded with fervor.

Ishii stared at his captive for a beat, then tugged on the cloth, releasing it from the woman's mouth. Saliva dribbled from her chapped lips, and ran down her cheek and onto her temple. Ishii dabbed it away with a handkerchief like a doting mother, and brushed away her long dark hair.

"It is better now, Aiko?" Ishii asked.

She nodded slowly.

"Good," Ishii said as he stepped to the only sideboard in the room and collected the long metal pole.

The woman began to whimper again, a stream of urine running down her torso and across her chin.

"It might be that you are not open to the universe, Aiko. It has been four days yet you have not reached enlightenment. Perhaps, we need to break your physical being to allow it to accept the universe?"

Aiko cried out again in protest.

Ishii jabbed the cattle prod into Aiko's soaking torso. Blue arcs of electrons fizzled from the prod and crackled across her skin. Her body smoked and stiffened with involuntary seizure as she chomped down, cleaving off her own tongue. Through a clenched jaw she gurgled a blood-filled scream. Ishii relinquished his torture and the woman went limp.

Down on his haunches, Ishii met the wet gaze of Aiko. "You will not miss your tongue. Only through silence can we hear our world crying out to be saved."

The woman sobbed, warm, salty, red liquid now running into her eyes.

"The system confirmed it, you know. A covert rescue has been mounted for the Americans and the creatures. That means our window of opportunity is limited."

Aiko didn't respond.

"Why am I telling you this? You cannot even reach enlightenment."

The woman choked on her own coagulating blood.

Ishii pulled his cell phone from the pocket of his robe and hit redial.

"Hai, Master Ishii-san?" The voice on the phone said.

"We need to move now. A rescue will come soon. Kill the Beast and capture the creatures. I will initiate the attack as planned." Ishii raised his voice as the wails of his captive intensified. He placed a single finger to the blood-covered lips of Aiko. The woman's howls became whimpers.

Aiko's forehead exploded, splattering Ishii with brain and bone.

Ishii reeled backward, fell to the floor and dropped the cattle prod and his phone.

Smoke drifted from the bullet hole in the woman's head. Ishii's gaze was then drawn to the silhouette of a tall man standing in the doorway to the apartment. The killer closed the door and approached Ishii, who scrambled back against the sideboard, still clutching the cattle prod.

"Master Ishii-san? Master Ishii-san!" came the voice from the cell phone on the floor.

Ishii scrambled to his feet, stepped to the side board, and grabbed the katana from its ornamental cradle.

The large man, with cold black eyes, wearing a dark green jumpsuit and hefty boots, collected up the cattle prod and came at Ishii.

The Aum Shinrikyo leader unsheathed his sword and held it high. He threw away the *sayo* and, with a flurry of slices and thrusts, attacked. Each attempt was parried away with the cattle prod. Ishii rushed forward again. He roared, advancing with his strong foot, the blade striking the prod over and over. The ringing of metal on metal filled the apartment.

Ishii raised the katana above his head with both hands to deliver a strong blow. The assassin kicked him square in the chest. Ishii tumbled backward, released his blade, and crashed to the floor. The large man dropped down to Ishii's eye level. Without a word, he set down the cattle prod, pulled a satellite phone from a pocket on his leg, then pushed dial and held it up. All the while his silenced Glock was pointed at Ishii.

Ishii stared wide eyed at the satellite phone.

The call connected.

"I don't tolerate insubordination, Ishii," came a deep, digitized, but calm voice from the speaker.

"Insubordination?" yelled Ishii, defiantly.

"I gave you the location to investigate, Ishii, not to take any other action."

"There was no time," Ishii spluttered. "You hide behind desks and push pieces around a chessboard. Manipulating what you want to make a few dollars. You are blinded by money, believing it to be the ultimate power. But the frog in the well knows not of the great ocean. My men and I could wield the power."

"That's what the Sagane said, Ishii. Now he's dead. And the creatures were thought lost. You say I play chess. Perhaps you are correct. And that would make you a pawn. One I will now sacrifice."

"Wait! You can have the creatures; I would have given them to you. We can still do as planned. The world can still be ours!" Ishii whined.

"Mine, Ishii. The world will be mine. And of course, the plan is still in motion. I just don't need you to carry it out. Cut off the head of a hydra and another grows back. Someone will take your place. Someone more ... subservient."

"Aum Shinrikyo is mi—"

The large man fired a single slug into Ishii's head, who slumped to the parquet. Thick red blood pooled around his head. A whisper of smoke floated from the barrel of the suppressed Glock G26. The killer then slid the gun back inside his jumpsuit, collected the cell phone from the floor, and held it up to the satellite phone.

"Takashi," the voice said.

"Where is Master Ishii?" replied Takashi.

"Dead. You lead Aum now. At least under my supervision."

Takashi didn't answer.

"I take your silence is acceptance. I had to change the target of our sarin attack. The American's were planning a rescue mission. Their primary source of help is now ... unavailable. You must take the creatures immediately and hide. I will send a team to collect you. Do not fail."

There was a long pause before Takashi simply said: *"Hai."*

The assassin ended the call on both devices. He stood, dropped Ishii's phone to the floor, and stomped on it, then scanned the room and left as silently as he'd entered.

CHAPTER TWELVE

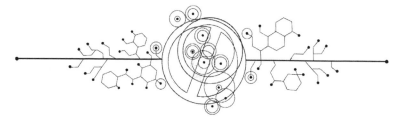

Location: Sinkhole Eight, Yamal Peninsula, Siberia

Out of breath, Tony Franco burst into the cave. "Sir, we got two incoming birds!"

"Friendly?" asked Teller, rising to his feet.

"It's General Lloyd!" he said. "And another pilot."

"Benjamin …" Freya closed her eyes and sighed. *He came.* "Okay, we need to gather up the children and the Huahuqui and get the hell out of here."

"Okay, chop, chop, people, this isn't a drill!" yelled Teller, his voice reverberating around the chamber.

Freya sprang into action and leapt down from her elevated position, calling for KJ. He didn't respond. Annoyed, Freya scrambled down to the lake at the bottom of the waterfall. Sure enough, there was KJ, playing in the spray with K'awin, Svetlana and Ribka. They frolicked and splashed, chasing each other in circles.

"KJ!" Freya said through a clenched jaw. "I told you to come here!"

Again, her son paid no heed, continuing his game.

Freya's nostrils flared and her eyes widened. She stomped into the water, grabbed her son by the elbow, and marched back out onto the pebbled shore—KJ in tow and complaining. Freya dropped down to meet his defiant stare.

"What did I say, Kelly Junior? Hmm? You have to listen to me. We need to go now. Benjamin is here to rescue us. We need to move."

KJ stared at his mother, his eyes welling with tears, and began to sniff. "I'm sorry, Mommy. I was only playing."

"Now's not the time, KJ. We have to move."

"He's five, Freya," came Teller's voice from behind.

Freya rose to her feet and spun to face him in one smooth, angry movement. "This isn't a goddamn game. If he wants to see six, we have to go."

Teller remained calm and offered a weak smile. "He knows. He's a smart kid."

"Smart won't keep him alive—I will! Let's go, Mr. Man." Freya grabbed for KJ's hand but he shied away and retreated until he and K'awin were standing together.

KJ placed his hand on the animal's head, who in turn nuzzled his palm.

Freya was losing him, and losing him fast. How to compete with the creature? Freya knew the feeling, the completeness of being bonded. For a five-year old it must have been like a drug. Freya needed to separate them.

"I'm sorry, Mr. Man," Freya said, stepping forward and crouching down. "We need to go, okay?"

"I wanna stay here with K'awin!" KJ whined.

Freya heaved a sigh. No matter his intelligence, he was still five years old. And like any other five-year old, tantrums were part of the package.

"Kelly Junior. You should listen to your mother." Minya's voice was calm but firm. "K'awin will come with us. They all will."

Freya turned to see her Siberian friend standing with her son and Chernoukh. A warrior maiden with two odd bodyguards, framed in a pink glow of crystal light. It was hard not to admire the woman. She was the perfect choice, for when Freya was no longer capable. A lump formed in her throat again, but she swallowed it away. Now wasn't the time for self-pity.

"Come, KJ. Let's go. I'll even race you," Nikolaj offered.

KJ's face lit up and he launched into a sprint, quickly followed by K'awin. Nikolaj gave a two-second head start before chasing after them, his own Huahuqui galloping behind, its black gills wafting with its gait. Then, exploding from the water came Svetlana and Ribka. The little girl clung to the creature's neck as it bounced from rock to rock and then scaled the cavern wall to the ledge at the entrance—beating both boys to the punch. The little girl smirked with satisfaction and then disappeared under the archway and into the maze of tunnels.

KJ hesitated at the top of the ledge and gave Freya a hopeful look.

Freya sighed and nodded. "Go, and find Gibbs. Stay with him."

She'd barely finished her sentence and KJ was already gone, Nikolaj hot on his heels. K'awin and Chernoukh raced after them.

A light nudge at her knee broke Freya's concentration. She looked down to find the little Huahuqui—Freckles Teller called it—at her side, eager to join in the fun. Apparently *with* Freya. All Freya could think of was how Kelly had described the bond with K'in. Losing himself a little. His pain, his focus. She had felt a little of the warmth, the contentedness, merely through contact with K'in. It was intoxicating. And like any drug, dangerous. She couldn't afford to lose focus; not now.

Freya shifted her weight to one hip. "Not a goddamn chance." She then tightened her ponytail, checked her Berettas were secure in their holsters, and tramped after her son.

Teller sighed and patted the sad little animal on the head. "Sorry, Freckles. Give her time."

Two enormous Pegasus aircraft sat on the permafrost, just feet from the mouth of the sinkhole. The engines whirred, deafening Freya as she pulled herself over the rocky rim into the open. She quickly scanned for KJ. He and K'awin sat, mouths agape, staring at the gigantic flying machines. Far too close to the engines for Freya's liking.

"I told you to find Gibbs. Get away from there, KJ!" Freya yelled, but her voice was drowned by the two Pratt & Whitney PW4062 turbofan engines that powered each jet.

A strong pair of old hands scooped KJ up and into an even stronger embrace against a hard chest. Benjamin Lloyd held onto the little boy and marched toward Freya.

"I believe this one is yours?" he said, without breaking his stride.

Freya took her son and held him close. "Benjamin, you came." She threw a spare arm around her godfather, making a KJ sandwich between them. "I'm so glad you're here."

Benjamin squeezed her, more tightly than Freya could remember. But all too quickly he let go and stared in her eyes. It was as if she was a kid once again, about to be reprimanded.

"What the hell are you doing out here, Freya? And with KJ?" Benjamin yelled, but half his words were stolen by the constant rumble of the engines.

"It's a long story!" She yelled back. "We need to get out of here. Out of Siberia and to a place to refuel. Then back to the States."

Benjamin nodded in earnest. "Let's go. I don't like the look of this weather. Get everyone on board."

Teller jogged up beside Freya and saluted the General. "Sir."

The General saluted back, then offered his hand to Jonathan. "Good to see you, son. Freya's lucky you were here."

"Of course, sir." Jonathan shook the General's hand with a firm grip.

"Do we have time for this?" Freya asked, her eyes wide.

"She's right," Teller agreed. "Let's get a move on."

Freya wasted no time in taking KJ to the cargo hold of the nearest Pegasus. She clanged up the ramp and sat him down in one of the few seats bolted to the wall. She then placed the harness across his chest and clicked it into its locked position. K'awin bounded in behind, and padded up to KJ. She plonked herself down next to him, like a loyal dog awaiting her next command. Freya stared at the creature, studying her huge blue eyes. K'awin stared back, cocked her head quizzically and smacked her tiny lips together.

Freya scrunched up her nose, pushing away any affection she may have for the animal simply because it reminded her of K'in— and Kelly. "You two, don't move," she ordered. "I'm going to load the others in here. Got it?"

KJ saluted his mother. "Affirmative."

Freya kissed KJ on the forehead, took one final hesitant look at K'awin, then stormed down the metal ramp to gather the others. On her way down, she passed Svetlana and Ribka who were already making their way inside. Freya kept her focus on the small girl and her Huahuqui until she had to round the side of the jet.

Outside the sky had darkened and a storm was closing in. Snow laden clouds hung heavy in the air and the wind began flinging stones it had gathered against the sides of the planes. At the mouth of the sinkhole, Benjamin Lloyd was standing an inch from Sasha Vetrov's face. Neither said anything. Jonathan was apparently trying, and failing, to placate whatever situation was brewing.

"What's the hold up?" Freya yelled over the din, her hair whipping about her face as she approached the men. "We gotta move!"

"You think I'm going to trust a Ruskie? Who knows what he's up to," Benjamin yelled over his shoulder without breaking his stare off with the Russian.

"He's with us, Benjamin. He helped us before," Teller said.

"Son, never trust a Russian. They're only looking out for number one," the General said.

Freya grabbed Benjamin by the shoulder and shouted over the engine noise. "We don't have time for this, Ben! He won't even have to come with us, all right? His team came with a Trekol. Even if he did report to Moscow, they'd have to get here. We can leave *now*."

Freya felt another nudge at her knee. It was Freckles. The strange little animal shifted its weight from left to right, a look of almost worry on its face. Freya shooed it away again by pushing it off with her boot. "Go away."

A high-pitched squeal pierced Freya's ears. She instinctively dived for cover. The ground was cold and hard, the frost biting at her hands and cheeks. Chaos erupted. The Nenets ran in all directions, their Huahuqui chasing after them. Jonathan's soldiers took defensive positions behind the landing gear of the Pegasus. Through the snow that puffed up with munition strike, she couldn't see Sasha.

Two more squeals, followed by the patter of bullets raining on metal.

Hands clasped over her ears, Freya chanced a look between her elbows to see Benjamin and Jonathan also on the ground. Jonathan gave her a knowing nod, then stood and ran for the sinkhole. The permafrost exploded at his heels as the assailants peppered his trail with bullets. Teller chased down the panicked people and creatures like a border collie rounding up sheep. He chivvied them toward the planes' cargo hold. The creatures quickly understood, grabbed up their children, and darted into the two planes.

"We gotta go!" Freya yelled to Benjamin.

He nodded, one eye screwed shut as another bullet whistled past his head. "You make for the nearest Pegasus, I'll take the other."

Freya acknowledged the plan, took three deep breaths then sprang to her feet and launched into a sprint. Flying over the permafrost she dared not look back, focusing only on the jet with KJ inside.

A few of the Huahuqui had gathered outside of KJ's plane and formed a semi-circle around the ramp—their Nenets children beside them. They stared blankly into the bluster of snow that increasingly obscured visibility. Freya pushed past and ran up the ramp, but stopped halfway to look back. *What the hell are they doing?* She tramped back down and yelled at them.

"C'mon, get inside! What are you doing?"

Another bullet squealed off the metal work. Freya ducked.

Benjamin waving from the ramp of the other plane caught her eye. He was ordering her inside.

"They won't move!" She yelled into the storm.

The General's gesticulating became angrier. He *really* wanted her inside.

Jonathan practically crashed into the group of Huahuqui. He clambered to his feet, wiped the sleet from his face, then clanged up the ramp to Freya. "We got to get them inside!"

"I know!"

"I'll do it, you get to the cockpit. We need to go!"

Freya turned tail and sprinted for the cockpit. She passed KJ, who was thankfully still strapped in. Without stopping she called out to him. "Stay put Mr. Man. We're leaving."

To her surprise, another pilot already sat in the co-pilot's chair.

"Captain Fraser," said the man.

"Nilsson," she fired back, climbing into the seat. "Let's get this bird off the ground."

The pilot nodded and assisted Freya in preparing for take-off. They flicked switches and checked systems. A constant patter of ammunition on the hull made it hard to concentrate. Freya peered through the windshield. "Where's Minya? And Nikolaj? I can't see them."

The pilot shrugged, apparently unaware to whom she was referring, and continued to prepare the aviation system as quickly as he could.

Freya yelled back from the cockpit into the cargo hold. "Jonathan, have you seen Minya?"

"I am here, my friend." Minya stepped into the control center. "We both are."

Freya sighed, grabbed for her friend's hand and gave it a quick squeeze. "Is Nikolaj okay?"

"He is fine. The other creatures followed him and Chernoukh into cargo hold."

"Great! Then let's get a move on."

Through the windshield and the snowstorm, Freya squinted to see into the cockpit of the other plane. Benjamin was inside. He gave the thumbs up, then slipped on the headset. Freya did the same.

"Let's go, Freya. They're all inside," Benjamin said.

"Affirmative!" Freya muffled the microphone with one hand, then yelled over her shoulder. "Jonathan! Are you in, we have to go!"

Teller rushed into the doorway and clung onto the frame. "Have you seen, Catherine?"

"Who?" Freya snapped without looking back.

"The reporter, Freya. Catherine!"

She shook her head, and continued to flick switches. "Benjamin?" she called into the headset. "You have an Irish girl on your bird? Red hair. Annoying face."

"That's a negative, Freya. She's not with us. We have half of the creatures and the locals. A few of Teller's team. That's it."

Freya shook her head again. "She's not over there."

Teller slammed his fist on the bulkhead. "Goddammit! I'll go find her."

"You will not!" Freya snapped, turning to glare at Teller. "We need to go!"

"We're not leaving her behind. She's a civilian."

"Wasn't it you who told me once the needs of the many outweigh the needs of the few?" Freya shouted.

Teller's face softened. "Wasn't it you who told me to think with my heart not with my head. She's a person, Freya. I'll go get her. You leave, I'll hitch a ride with the Russians."

"You're leaving us?" Freya's voice cracked.

"Tony is in the back and Gibbs is on Benjamin's plane. You don't need me here. But we do need to find out who these bastards are. Cut them off at the source. If we can't trust Washington, then we're on our own and have to do it ourselves. I'll get Catherine and do some recon. I'll be back. I always come back."

Jonathan's gaze lingered, but then he was gone.

Freya clenched her jaw, then turned back to business. "Let's get the hell out of here."

She flicked the switch to initiate the long procedure of ramp closure, but began to move the humongous plane already—pulling around to a strip of permafrost that would allow her enough room to take off. As the plane rotated, more of the battlefield came into view. Soldiers in Korean Military gear speckled the white ground, their guns raised high, firing at Benjamin's Pegasus.

One soldier caught her eye. He was knelt on one knee with a tube pointed at the plane.

"Oh God no!" Freya's eyes widened in realization. She grabbed at her microphone. "Move it Benjamin, his got an RP—"

The rocket exploded from the muzzle of the launcher on the soldier's shoulder. Freya could only watch as it flew through the air in slow motion toward her godfather and jet full of children and Huahuqui. She caught a final glimpse of Benjamin struggling to maneuver the plane, before the warhead penetrated his windshield and exploded into a ball of fire that engulfed the cockpit. The Pegasus's hull buckled and the engines caught fire. The fuel ignited and a second larger explosion tore the plane in two, vaporizing everything and everyone inside.

"No!" Freya screamed in horror. She was unable to move, unable to pilot any longer. She stared at the burning pieces of fuselage, her mouth open.

Freya numbly watched a lone soldier walk up to the RPG-wielding man, put a gun to his head and pull the trigger. Blood sprayed from his face and he slumped to the ground. The soldier then turned to her plane and opened fire. The remaining assailants resumed their onslaught.

Freya sprang into action, her cheeks wet with tears, and pulled on the yoke to turn the plane. She lined it up with the long stretch of permafrost and pressed the accelerator. The engines roared and the plane jerked powerfully forward. Freya growled loudly as they reached the end of the useable terrain and pulled as hard as she could on the yoke to lift the Pegasus.

With considerable effort, it began to lift.

In the back of her mind, Freya could make out the fading sound of bullet patter against the hull and distant clunk as the ramp closed. Then, only the hum of the engines filled her ears and mind.

Sasha stood panting in the cargo hold as the ramp finally clunked shut. He slumped against the bulkhead and coughed out the ash from his lungs. An unconscious, barely breathing, red-headed reporter lay at his feet. He steadied himself with one arm as the Pegasus lifted higher into the air. From within the dark, one-hundred pairs of eyes stared at him; Huahuqui, children, and soldiers.

Tony Franco pushed his way to the front of the crowd. "Where's Teller. He went after the reporter."

Sasha shook his head, still coughing. "I have no idea."

CHAPTER THIRTEEN

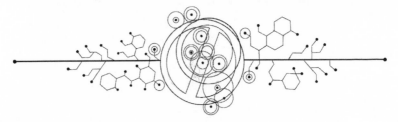

Location: Sinkhole Eight, Yamal Peninsula, Siberia

The wreckage of the Pegasus burned brightly against the gray sky, an orange beacon amidst the bleak tundra. Takashi faced the inferno, the heat washing over him with each gust of wind that passed. He had failed, and failure meant death. He didn't even need to call to know the outcome. He and his men would be killed. An assassin, a missile, a staged accident. However it would happen, it was inevitable. Begging for another chance would be futile. And what could he do about it? Takashi studied the orange flames as they licked at the blackened corpse of the American jet. What power did he have?

Then, the thought ignited in the back of his mind and spread into his consciousness. He could take away the Nine Veils' toy, that's what he could do. If he was to be murdered for his efforts, why should the Doyen be allowed his prize? They were likely the only ones in the field and able to track the plane. He, Aum, had time to catch up to them and kill every last one of them.

Takashi turned on his heel and marched across the permafrost. Without stopping, he kicked the corpse of Hamada, the man who had made the fatal blunder and destroyed the Pegasus. "Idiot," Takashi said.

A short stocky man ran up to Takashi and gave a deep bow. "What do we do now, Takashi-san?"

"We follow them," he said.

"The Puma's range isn't long enough," the short man said.

"They're not going far in that. It came from the USA. Fuel will be low. Go prep the Puma now."

The man bowed and scurried off to find the others.

Takashi calmed his breathing and attempted to focus his mind. He would be some time behind the Beast. His own chopper, the Puma, was back at the Nenets camp. But how many places could his enemy go? No fuel. No resources. A covert rescue mission meant nobody else was coming for them. Their only friend, a Russian. And where would a Russian go with a military plane to feel safe? There was likely only one place.

A fresh explosion shattered Takashi's train of thought. He spun to see a pillar of black smoke rising from the wreckage. From under a sheet of buckled fuselage, a charcoaled man, his clothes still alight, crawled across the permafrost. The man's muffled moans were barely audible above the snapping and crackling of the flames. Takashi grabbed the pistol from Hamada's dead body, took aim and fired a single kill shot to his enemy's head. The man slumped to the ground. Takashi's nostrils flared and his chest heaved as he thought of vengeance—against the Beast and the Nine Veils.

Location: Pegasus aircraft, Russian airspace

Above the snow-laden cloud line, the sky was clear and blue. Moving southward also meant the sun could finally begin to dip below the horizon. For the first time in many days, Freya would be able to sleep in comforting darkness. At least in theory. Instead, her chest felt hollow and her mind was lost in a thick fog.

Benjamin was dead.

She should be mourning everyone on that plane. Gibbs. The Nenets children. Even the Huahuqui. But the searing pain of losing her Godfather swallowed all else. Sure she'd been at him for his role in the Huahuqui program. For lying to her about it for so long. Even for his crazy plan to give K'in back to the world. But he raised her when her parents died. As close as she would ever know to a father, Benjamin had kept her by his side since she was nine years old. Every scraped knee. Every teenage tantrum. Every cheating boyfriend. He had been there. Because of him, she was strong. But, right now, she didn't feel it.

With Benjamin at Leavenworth, he was at least still alive. She could be mad, but go back whenever she wanted to see him. Now, because she had dragged her son halfway around the world into a war zone, he'd broken out of prison and flown to Siberia to rescue her.

And rescue her he did.

Freya slid off her headset, nodded to the pilot, and stumbled out of the cockpit into the cargo hold. Her head swam and her stomach roiled. She braced herself against the wall, but her legs gave way and she crumpled to the floor in a defeated heap. She patted herself, searching for the bottle of pills, but it was nowhere to be found. "Shit," she said and put her shaking hands over her face.

KJ's small arms slid around his mother's neck, and he climbed onto her lap. Without saying a word, he placed his head on her shoulder and squeezed.

Freya burst into tears and hugged her son as tightly as she could. KJ hugged her even tighter.

"Don't be sad, Mommy."

She opened her mouth to speak, but only a blub came out. Freya sobbed uncontrollably.

The patter of delicate feet drew closer. K'awin cautiously approached, first nuzzling at Freya's side with her snout, and then inch by inch she sidled up until she too had wrapped herself around mother and son. Freya didn't open her eyes, but her sobbing died down into a whimper. Other Huahuqui trundled slowly over. Freckles was the first to arrive, her huge cobalt eyes wet with concern. She too wrapped herself around Freya and KJ. Then another creature, and another, until all that was visible was the top of Freya and KJ's heads under a mass of blue sparkling Huahuqui.

The pain didn't subside, but suddenly Freya didn't feel so alone. She'd experienced a similar sensation when touching K'in, but this—this was something else—something more. The power of K'in multiplied. The ultimate empathy. She felt their pain, too, at the loss of the other Huahuqui and the Nenets children. Their collective anguish was shared, diluted, among each other. And so, together, it was somehow bearable.

Freya pulled her son away from her shoulder and stared deep into his eyes. The same blue fire his father had danced within. "I love you, Kelly Junior. You know that, right? You're my Mr. Man. Now and forever."

KJ nodded. "I know. I love you as well, Mommy."

The Huahuqui slowly backed away, shuffling off one another to reveal Freya and KJ. Only Freckles stayed nearby, hovering at Freya's side. As Freya began to pry herself from the floor, a shadow passed overhead. She glanced up to see Sasha Vetrov and the reporter standing over her.

Freya got to her feet and glowered—her old confidence and hatred for Catherine rising to the surface. "What the hell? You're here? Where's Jonathan? He left to look for you."

"Me?" Sasha asked, a frown creased into his forehead.

"Not you, *her*." Freya nodded at the reporter.

"He did? I didn't need anyone to come after me. I can look after myself." Catherine attempted to sound confident, but guilt had drained the blood from her face.

"Jonathan Teller is a resourceful man," Sasha said. "He will be okay. My men will take care of him."

Freya scowled. "Vetrov, I've never really trusted you. I have zero idea whose side you're really on. Right now, I can't kick you off this plane, and I can't go back for Jonathan. We have to get to a safe place."

"And where would safe be, Miss Nilsson?" Sasha asked, one eyebrow raised.

He was right. There was nowhere to go. If Washington had a mole, and the Secretary was out of action, then who did she have to return to? Not to mention she was now probably considered a co-conspirator in Benjamin's escape, party to the grand theft of government property and trespassing through Russian Airspace without clearance.

It was a mess.

"Franco? Tony? Is Tony in here?" Freya asked.

Tony stepped through the crowd, careful not to tread on the children. "Ma'am. The boss is gonna be okay. He's hardcore."

Freya offered a weak smile. "I'm sorry about Gibbs and your other men."

Tony became solemn and gripped the rifle slung across his chest. "Me too."

"Do you have any buddies in this region, Tony? Any small or obscure military base we could land and refuel?"

Tony shook his head. "We're caught between the Middle East and Russia right now. Which on one hand gives us a little more latitude. If we fly over the EU then NATO is going to be all over us. So, your mole in Washington will know what's going on."

"Or we get shot out of the sky by a Russian Sukoi," Freya snapped firing a glance at Sasha. "We are in enemy skies with nowhere to go."

"Mommy, what's a Sukoi?"

Freya ruffled KJ's short, now very blond hair, and spoke without looking at him. "It's a plane, sweetie."

"Oh," KJ said, then rubbed his tummy. "Mommy, I'm hungry."

That made Freya look down. KJ was right. Now that she thought about it, the pit of her own stomach began to grumble. They hadn't eaten in a long time. The likelihood on there being food on the plane was next to none. "We'll have to land somewhere and get some. I know you're hungry."

I just don't know where. Or when.

K'awin cocked her head one way then the other, as if listening to the conversation. She stared at Freya, then at KJ, and back again. Then, having seemingly made up her mind, the pudgy little Huahuqui stepped forward and began hacking a cough. Once, twice, three times. And then it came. A slew of stomach acid and half-digested fish slopped onto the floor from K'awin's mouth. She took a couple of steps back and looked up, apparently proud of her offering.

KJ squealed and backed away. Freya fought the urge to vomit. The stench was incredible.

"Jesus, that stinks," said Catherine, covering her face with her arm.

"I don't see you offering anything better," Freya said.

Catherine sighed. "You want me to throw up for your kid?"

"Ladies, ladies," Sasha interjected. "We don't have time for this."

Freya huffed and pulled her ponytail tight. She'd have time to grieve later. Right now, they had to survive. "We need to get out of this airspace. Somewhere over international water, somewhere neutral."

"Neutral ..." the reporter said, almost to herself.

"Did you say something?" Freya bored a hole in the woman with her stare.

"Neutral. We need to take them somewhere neutral."

"So?" Freya barked.

"Antarctica."

Freya clenched her jaw. "What are you talking about?"

"The Antarctic Treaty," Sasha said, his tone almost enthusiastic.

The reporter nodded.

Freya knew what the Antarctic Treaty was. Signed in Washington in 1959 by twelve countries. By 2017, fifty-three parties had joined. Since no native human population was known to reside on Antarctica, the treaty was installed to establish freedom of scientific investigation and simultaneously ban military activity on the continent. The idea had been to ensure, in the interests of all humankind, that Antarctica shall forever continue to be used only for peaceful purposes and not become the scene of international discord. Whether Freya wanted to admit it or not, it was a good idea.

Still ...

"The Huahuqui are adapted to the cold, and no one can touch

them there. It's perfect." Catherine blew a lock of curly orange hair from her face and crossed her arms.

"We're still over Russian airspace," Freya said. "How Benjamin came in without being spotted is a miracle. I doubt we have much time."

"I doubt it, too," Sasha agreed.

The pilot called through the doorway, "Miss, Nilsson?"

Freya turned and entered the cockpit, wiping any last tears from her face. "Let me guess ... Russian air force?"

"We have a couple of jets approaching fast. From how they're moving, I think they're MIGs."

"You gonna help us, Vetrov?" Freya asked, having turned back into the cargo hold.

Sasha seemed to study Freya, then her son who looked up with eyes like saucers. Finally, he scanned the Huahuqui and Nenets people huddled together, apparently considering his options. Then, he simply nodded. "I'll do better than that. I'll get you to Antarctica. Set the destination to Kyrgyzstan. And give me the radio."

Location: Washington DC

A light, rhythmic peeping sound penetrated the darkness. Lucy concentrated on it. The sound was annoying. And the more annoyed she became, the faster the pace of the sound became—until, eventually it was so rapid, Lucy jolted awake. Her heart beat fast in time with the peeping. A heart monitor. Where the hell was she? A hospital. This was a hospital.

Lucy sat up to take in her surroundings, but her head spun and her stomach roiled. She quickly lay back down to quell the nausea and blinked until her pixelated vision once again returned to normal.

"You're lucky to be alive, Lucy," said a familiar voice.

She turned slowly to see the President at her bedside.

"What were you doing in the memorial gardens?"

"Meeting someone," Lucy croaked.

"Steven Chang?" he pressed.

Lucy bobbed her head. "Uh huh, have you heard from him?"

"Actually, no," the president replied. "He had a note in his diary that he would see you. But he's not answering his phone. Would your meeting have anything to do with the escape of General Lloyd?"

Lucy's stomach cramped again, but she didn't respond.

The President pulled a piece of paper from his jacket and handed it to her. Lucy reached out a weak hand and took it.

"What's this?" she asked.

"That is an executive order, pardoning General Benjamin Lloyd and reinstating his military authority," the President replied, his gaze firmly fixed on her. "It's funny, Lucy, I don't remember signing that."

Lucy coughed and propped herself up. "I didn't have a choice. Someone had to go and rescue them. The red tape was killing us."

"You realize this is treason, right? That could carry the death penalty."

"I had to do something. This is bigger than me. Than all of us."

The President seemed to study her for a few moments. "Well, he stole two Pegasus planes and went to Siberia. Except now, at least one of them has been destroyed. Blown up. The Russians are pissed we were even there. I've had the Kremlin up my ass. They say the bodies of Korean soldiers were found there. They want to know why we and a bunch of Korean soldiers were in their territory."

Lucy stared wide eyed. A plane had been destroyed? "Do we know if the Huahuqui made it out, or the children, or—"

"There were no bodies in the wreckage. Everything was burned. But did you hear what I said? Korean soldiers were found there. You know who attacked you in the gardens? Koreans. We have a big problem on our hands, Lucy. Why the hell are the Koreans involved?"

Lucy shook her head. "I don't know."

"Look, Lucy. I'm keeping you out of prison, until a hearing at least. Right now, I need your help. I need you on your feet. We've got to deal with this Korean situation, placate the Russians, and you need to tell me where that other Pegasus plane is going."

Lucy turned her head away and stared at the wall. One plane destroyed. No clue as to how many Huahuqui survived. Now the Koreans were after them, and Russia was on the warpath. To make matters worse, Lucy had no idea where the other plane was headed. It was a mess.

"I don't know where it's headed, and that's the truth," Lucy said, rolling back to meet the President's gaze. "They haven't been in contact. Considering they were attacked, they might suspect their location was given away. Maybe they've lost faith in us."

The President seemed to think for a moment, rubbing his temples. "We need to get on top of it. This gas attack might be enough to convince the Kremlin we aren't in collusion with North Korea, but it still doesn't explain to them why we were there in the first place, Lucy."

"There are people, inside Russian headquarters who know all about the Huahuqui. They actually helped us last time around. I need to speak to one of their FSB colonels, A Sasha ... Vit ... Vet ... something." Lucy's voice trailed off as she struggled to remember the name of the Russian intelligence agent who had helped Jonathan Teller track, and eventually kill, the Shan Chu.

"Vetrov? Aleksandr Vetrov?" The President said.

"Yes, that sounds right," Lucy replied, propping herself up on her elbows. "How did you know that?"

"Your office has been receiving calls from Moscow, with instructions that they will talk only to you. A message from Polkovnik Aleksandr Vladimirovich Vetrov."

Lucy nearly fell from her bed. Vetrov had called. He knew something. Something that could help. She swung her legs out of bed and put her bare feet on the cold floor. Her stomach convulsed and her head spun with nausea but she fought it back, clinging to the bed frame for support.

"What're you doing? Wait for a nurse," the President said.

"If I'm going to prison, then I want to do *what* I can *while* I can. Help me up, I need to call Moscow."

CHAPTER FOURTEEN

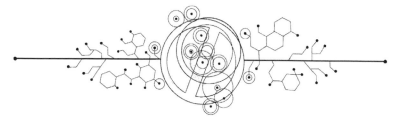

Location: Somewhere in Poland.

The satellite phone hummed its dialing tone. Three, four, five minutes. Teller pulled it from his ear to check the connection. Full signal. It was the fifth time he'd tried and it was so damn frustrating. He'd watched Benjamin's plane explode and Freya's Pegasus barely make it off the permafrost. He had to know she was okay.

Answer dammit. He rapped the phone against his knee as if brute force was the answer to the technical problem.

Apparently, it was. The call connected.

"Da?" came a woman's voice.

"Minya? Is that you?" Jonathan asked.

"Da! Mr. Teller?"

"Yes, it's Jonathan. Put Freya on, will you?"

There was a light ruffling sound as the phone exchanged hands.

"Jonathan?"

"Yeah, it's me."

"Thank God you're alive!"

"I couldn't find Catherine ..." *Not sure why that's the first thing out of my mouth*, thought Teller.

"It's okay, she's here with us. Vetrov dragged her onto my plane. Where are you?"

"Somewhere in Poland," Jonathan said, checking the view through the filthy car window again. "Vetrov's guys dropped me at the border and I hitchhiked. Keeping a low profile, you know? I'm headed to London. I have a friend there who might be able to help. But I can't risk telling him I'm coming."

"Okay, that's good. We're on our way to Antarctica."

Jonathan's forehead creased. His unshaven Polish driver glanced at him. Teller turned away to gain privacy.

Freya would have a reason for that. Such an odd, and yet specific destination. So remote and ... "The treaty," he said once it came to him. "Very clever."

"Yes, Vetrov agreed to take us, but it'll be a convoluted route. We'll refuel in Kyrgyzstan, then on to Somalia. From there, it's land transport to Mozambique, then somehow make it to Madagascar, and finally, La Reunion to travel to Antarctica."

Jonathan's frown shifted into an expression of worry. "That's insane."

"You have a better idea? We have to keep a low profile, too. I'll call you when we land, okay?"

"Sure." Jonathan pulled the phone away to end the call, but then lifted it to his ear again. "Freya ... I'm sorry. About Benjamin."

There was a lasting silence, before Freya spoke—her voice cracking a little. *"Me too,"* was all she said, then cut off the call.

She was hurt. She always went quiet when she was really hurt. Jonathan knew that much. It's just how she'd reacted the last time they'd seen each other. KJ had been a toddler. A tiny little version of Kelly Graham, crashing into everything and going where angels, and other children, feared to tread. The little guy just seemed to lack a self-preservation instinct. It was difficult to watch him and not think on where—or whom—he would end up. Freya had hid his powers from Jonathan. After everything, she didn't truly trust him. Not like she did Kelly. It was impossible to compete with a ghost. With the idea of Kelly Graham—even if it was misguided. So, Jonathan left.

Perhaps he shouldn't have. Not then. And certainly not now.

Teller sighed and stared out of the grimy passenger window, trying to block the stench of vodka on the breath of his Polish Samaritan. The man was friendly enough, but Teller was wary of his driving ability. A slight swerve every now and then made Teller grab for the inner handle—which, coincidentally had been ripped off the dilapidated vehicle long ago. Probably by another nervous passenger.

The drab Polish landscape whipped by as Teller and his driver hammered along the A4 Autostrada. Part of the European route E40, it ran east west from southern Poland to the German border. Teller had chosen this route as it bypassed Warsaw, Opole, Gliwice, Katowice, and Krokav. He was unlikely to be seen, or stopped.

Since he didn't read Polish, Teller relied on the landscape to communicate their location. In the distance, through the driver's side window, he could see a mountain range. A green beacon in the otherwise gray landscape, the sierra appeared to be lush with spruce and other coniferous trees. He surmised they must be the Carpathian Mountains. The range mostly lay in Romania and was the backdrop for the famed Dracula stories. For Teller, they represented the call of the wild. Its siren song was strong. To run with the bear and lynx that hid within the forests. At this moment, it was almost easy to see why Kelly Graham had the habit of dropping off the grid to live alone in his makeshift hut. Almost.

Teller checked his watch for the thousandth time since his journey began. Traveling incognito was too slow. But if he couldn't trust Washington, then this was the only way. He had to reach London. Reach MI5—and Stuart Jones. He and Stu had been friends for a long time, and had an almost amusing respectful distrust of one another. Stu had always watched the NSA, and Teller kept an eye on MI5. If there was a mole in Washington, Stu would know.

He thought about offering to drive for a while, but figured his attempt at communication would be futile. He'd barely managed to agree on the fact they were both headed west. Teller was to be dropped off in Germany. Instead, he shifted lower in the old leather seat and closed his eyes to sleep.

Location: Kant airbase, Kyrgyzstan

It had been a long time since Sasha had been in Kyrgyzstan, let alone Kant airbase.

Located just twelve or so miles south of Kant, in the Ysyk-Ata District of Chuy Oblast, the base had been set up by the Soviet regime in the 1940s. During World War II, nearly two-thousand Soviet military pilots were trained there. But when the Soviet Union collapsed, control of the air base had been officially transferred to Kyrgyzstan.

The keyword being, *officially*.

In accordance with a bilateral agreement between Russia and Kyrgyzstan, signed in 2003, the air base actually hosted Russian Air Force units. Then, in 2012, Kyrgyzstan agreed to lease the base to Russia for at least fifteen years. In return, the Russian government reduced the Kyrgyz debt by five-hundred-million dollars.

Mother Russia never truly let go of her children.

Bringing American soldiers, Nenets children, and of course nearly fifty giant axolotl-like creatures to the base was a massive risk. But the FSB still held a lot of power. Sasha was well known among his peers within the FSB and the military. His reputation untainted, his devotion to his country unquestioned. Until now. Sasha doubted his own motivation.

The Polkovnik stared at the Huahuqui and the children in the cargo hold of the Pegasus as its wheels touched the runway tarmac. He braced himself against the sudden jolt as the brakes were applied. Freya called something to him from the cockpit, but Sasha wasn't really listening.

Why risk it? Why risk everything he had fought for? Was it for the protection of Russia's interests? If they took control of the Huahuqui, that would likely only bring a storm of political hell upon his president and his nation. Terrorist attacks, or even covert insurrections were probable. But in his heart, this wasn't the reason.

A small child sat on the floor, perhaps four years old. Her Huahuqui companion wrapped around her to keep her safe. She stared at Sasha with big, brown, wet eyes. Their gaze locked. It wasn't clear if what he was feeling was truly his own heart, or that of the child through her newfound telepathic ability, but something inside him connected the children with his own days as an orphan. Most of those in his orphanage had died. Or gone into organized crime. Sasha had been lucky enough to escape.

He loved his country more than his own life. But perhaps not more than the lives of millions of Russian orphans that were probably being groomed for some kind of mercenary army. He was protecting Russia, even if she didn't know it.

"Vetrov? Did you hear me?" Freya was staring at him.

"What?" he snapped, irritated at her interruption.

"You're up. Ground control is radioing us. Looks like a security contingent is on the way. We've been told to wait here. They need to secure the area. Thirty minutes." Freya's green eyes flashed with adrenaline. "What were you daydreaming about?"

"I don't daydream. I was thinking, piecing this together."

"And what did you come up with?" Franco asked, pushing his way to the front of the crowd of Nenets.

"I was chasing Aum, but I don't think they're behind it. Grooming orphans? It just seems beyond them. They're too small-minded. And too self-righteous and petulant. This kind of planning takes patience and cunning. A long-term vision." Sasha squinted his eyes in further thought.

"So, they're a puppet. A puppet used to confuse us. Make us chase them and even the Koreans?" Freya asked.

"*Da*," Sasha agreed. "I have a theory, but ..." His voice trailed off.

"But?" Freya said. "But what? Any idea is better than no idea. And if we can tip off Jonathan, he might be able to track the source."

The Polkovnik eyed the Americans and then Minya. The woman stared back with her usual stony expression. Yet, in her almond shaped eyes he was sure he saw a glimmer of understanding. Trusting Americans was just not something Russians—or Siberians—did easily. Especially if you had any involvement with the military or Mother Russia's security. The Americans were the antithesis of everything he was taught to believe. Living there, undercover as a sleeper agent near Langley, acting as one of them, had been painful. Yet, Minya's wordless communication was clear: this wasn't about Russia or America. It was about everyone. Actually, it was about the next generation. The Huahuqui represented something bigger than political boundaries.

"The Nine Veils," Sasha said.

"You're going to have to be more specific, Vetrov," Freya snapped. "Jonathan isn't here to figure out your riddles, and I'm too damn tired for this shit."

Sasha swallowed away his irritation. "When I was a sleeper agent in the USA, living in Maryland, I was told to investigate an up and coming cult; The Nine Veils. Nothing really came of it and eventually the intelligence mission was called off."

"You think they're behind it? Who were they?" Tony piped up from the crowd.

Freya checked her watch and then threw Sasha a sharp look: *get on with it.*

"It was a small cult, comprising conspiracy theory fanatics," Sasha continued. "They'd meet up and discuss how they would be part of the ruling class when the world ended. But it never seemed more than that. Unless of course, I only saw a small chapter. A fragment of a larger organization."

"What would make you think some backwater hicks could be behind any of this?" Freya asked, still glancing at her watch.

"Their theory suggests there to be eight or nine barriers to human understanding of everything," Sasha said. "Some argue passing through all the veils is the true path to God, while others say it could represent the route to enlightenment. The first veil is to understand that humans have been conditioned to accept that government officials and network media personalities are the primary voices of authority. Passing the second and third, means you can explore self-governing and comprehend that the resources of the world are controlled by extremely wealthy and powerful families. Piercing the fourth means you believe in the Illuminati, Freemasons, and other secret societies. These societies use symbols and perform ceremonies that perpetuate the generational transfers of arcane knowledge that is used to keep the ordinary people in political, economic and spiritual bondage to the oldest bloodlines on earth."

Freya pulled on her ponytail again. "Is this going somewhere?"

Sasha hurried his explanation. "This is where it becomes … strange. Passing the fifth and sixth veil means you accept that the secret societies are so far advanced technologically that time travel and interstellar communications are possible, and that dragons and lizards and aliens we thought were fictional, are not only real, but the actual controlling forces behind the secret societies uncovered in the fourth veil …"

Tony scoffed. "We don't have time for this."

"No, wait," Minya said. "Think about it. If a cult believes this, true or not, they may consider Huahuqui to be controlling force behind all things. Very good reason to want them."

Sasha waited for Freya's response. Her eyes searched Minya and then him.

"Plausible," Freya said finally. "Go on, but hurry up."

"Moving past the seventh veil means seeing the very fabric of time and the universes as simply numbers. If you can do that, you can control it. The eighth means revealing the true face of God."

"And the ninth?" Freya pressed.

"If you pass the ninth, you're essentially equal to God, seeing everything as he sees it." Sasha gave an awkward smile. He was barely Christian orthodox. Such notions were pure nonsense.

Freya scrunched up her nose. "And what makes you think it's them pulling strings?"

"A hunch," Sasha replied without thinking.

"A hunch? A fucking hunch?" Freya all but shouted, her eyes wide.

To Sasha's surprise, Minya jumped to his defense. "Think about it, my friend," she said. "A cult that believes the rich can control and manipulate. Whoever it is has been able to fund and manipulate an old Japanese terrorist group, and make their activities look like the Koreans. They chase the Huahuqui multiple times now. And ..." Minya tapped her neck with her index finger. "They all have a tattoo of the number nine."

Freya didn't appear convinced.

KJ tugged at her jeans. "Any idea is better than no idea, Mommy," he said.

Freya's expression softened. She ran her hand over his round cheeks and gave his chin a squeeze before turning back to Sasha.

"It's a starting point," she said. "I'll call Jonathan."

A rap on the hull of the plane quieted everyone, the stillness filling the cargo hold.

Sasha nodded to Freya.

She stepped over to the release button and hammered it with her fist, her gaze still fixed on Sasha. "I hope you're not going to fuck us, Vetrov."

Sasha didn't bother responding. Instead, he turned to the slowly opening cargo ramp.

A shard of bright Kyrgyz light pierced the hold, accompanied by a blast of cold, dry air. The Huahuqui seemed to complain with quiet warbles, all the while shuffling on their webbed feet. The Children huddled closer to their companions, as if to defend them.

The ramp clanged to a halt. A round man in sand-colored fatigues, accompanied by two soldiers, marched toward them. The sound of boots on metal rang loud.

Sasha pulled up the collar of his coat around his thick neck and walked calmly toward the Kyrgyz officer. The rotund man, clean shaven, with his head covered in a thick fur hat with flaps that protected his ears, stared without a word at Sasha.

The Polkovnik could feel Freya and the entire cargo hold staring at the back of his head.

The Kyrgyz officer peered over Sasha's shoulder. His eyes registered the Americans. Then the children and finally the Huahuqui, but gave away no sense of astonishment or fear.

The silence in the cargo hold was deafening.

A full two minutes passed, with Sasha simply staring into the narrow eyes of the Kyrgyz.

"In trouble again, Vetrov?" the man said, finally.

Sasha heard Freya suck in a confused breath. He could hold his composure no longer, allowing a full-blown smile to break across his square face. He threw open his arms and gave a strong manly hug to his long-time friend. "Zhyrgal!"

The man returned the manly embrace, patting Sasha firmly on the back.

"Vetrov, do I ask?"

Sasha pulled back. "No. Best not to ask. We just need to refuel, and then be on our way. If you can spare the fuel—"

"And food!" KJ piped up.

Sasha glanced behind, amused at the boldness of Freya's son. "And food," he added, turning back to Zhrygal. "And maybe keep our airspace clear as we leave."

"Anything for Polkovnik Sasha Vetrov of the FSB. Where are

you headed?"

Sasha hesitated, before giving a half answer. "Somalia."

CHAPTER FIFTEEN

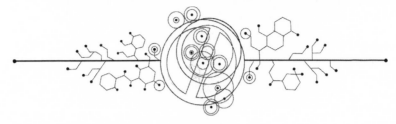

Location: Polish–German border

Teller waved goodbye to his driver, who sped off then promptly turned 180-degrees and headed back toward Poland. Teller had paid the man a little extra to actually take him a few kilometers over the border into Germany. The Schengen Agreement in the European Union was a wonderful thing, with few cars being inspected—especially those that made the journey frequently, which his driver apparently did. This meant Teller was able to make it into Germany with his sidearm.

He trudged along the highway, hands tucked into his pockets, braced against the frigid wind. This far south there were fewer cars to hitchhike but one would pass soon. It was a long process, but he couldn't afford to use public transport, and there was certainly no opportunity to fly. Right now, he had to lay low and make his way west.

The wind bit at his cheeks and stung his eyes. But Teller hardly noticed, lost in thought—contemplating the last conversation with Freya when she'd landed in Kyrgyzstan. They used the satellite phone sparingly and so far, the NSA hadn't figured out what they were doing—the link to the satellite was still active. Still, the latest intel had him worried. Vetrov had told Freya his thoughts on who may have been funding Aum—a little known cult called the Nine

Veils. It bothered Jonathan that he knew nothing of them. There were thousands of conspiracy theory nut job groups around the world. But if they were that sophisticated, and that covert, having a mole in Washington may not be out of their reach. Teller shook his head in frustration. Vetrov was making a giant leap—but it was the only lead they had. Teller would ask his contact at MI5.

A beat-up BMW, probably first manufactured in the 1980s, hurtled past.

Jonathan instinctively threw out an arm to signal his need of a lift. The car continued to tear off into the developing snowstorm. Teller cursed his luck for not paying attention, and with his injured calf burning, powered forward, hungry and tired.

No more than half a mile ahead, Teller saw two red hazy lights—the tail lights of a car parked at the side of the motorway. As he trudged farther, the car came into focus behind the wall of falling snow. It seemed to be the same BMW that had passed him earlier. Had they stopped for him? He picked up his pace until eventually he reached the passenger side window of the car. It was steamed up, obscuring the occupants.

Teller rapped on the glass.

In a jerky movement, the window wound down to reveal a clean-shaven man in his mid-thirties leaning across the passenger seat and, with considerable effort, manually operating the mechanism.

"*Guten nacht. Kann ich ihnen helfen?*" the man said.

Teller scratched his head. "Oh, damn. I don't remember my German well. *Um, Ich muss nach Frankreich gehen.*"

"American?" the man said, with a thick Bavarian accent.

"Ah, yeah. Exactly. I'm just trying to get to France."

"The train would be faster, *doch?*" the man asked, his cold gray eyes conveying no sympathy for Teller's predicament.

"You think you could give me a ride, just to where you're going?"

The German studied Teller suspiciously. "What is your name, American?"

"Teller. Jonathan Teller."

The driver seemed to accept his name as some kind of affirmation Teller was not a serial killer, and simply clicked open the passenger side door.

Teller stamped off the snow from his boots and climbed in. The car smelled old, and like cigarettes, but at least it was warm. He rubbed his hands together and patted his arms for warmth, before pulling the seatbelt across and locking it into place. "You didn't tell me your name."

"Heinz," the man replied, checking his left blind spot to pull out.

"Is that first or la—"

As the man twisted to see over his left shoulder Teller caught a glimpse of a tattoo behind his ear. Small, and hidden away. But there. The number nine. Teller grabbed for his gun, but a searing pain around his neck stole his breath.

Heinz continued to drive, while someone hidden in the backseat strangled Teller from behind. Teller flailed and dug with his fingers at the garrote wire cutting into his trachea.

"You are a wanted man, Mr. Teller," Heinz said without looking away from the road. "A high price on your head it seems."

Teller could hardly focus on the man's words, his own life's breath cut off and his heart hammering. In a moment of clarity, he searched for his Beretta, pulled it from the holster and, with his vision darkening, swung it left firing off six shots. The blasts were ear-piercing. Glass shattered. Unable to see, Jonathan's only confirmation he'd hit his target was the lurch of the vehicle as the driver lost control. The car swerved and skidded and then came to an organ-crushing halt. The garrote around Teller's neck slackened, glass broke somewhere, and everything went dark.

His eyes slowly opened, but still Teller couldn't see well. Night had fallen. He must have lost consciousness. Teller rubbed the worn skin on his neck where the garrote had cut in. Within the gloom he made out two bodies to his left. One was the driver with three bullet holes having oozed blood. The other was his attacker. The impact had thrown the man forward and into the windshield, his bloodied head, covered in snow, poking through the hole in the broken glass.

With a groan of pain, Teller climbed out of the BMW. Snowflakes tumbled slowly all around, coating the dark motorway in a thin fluffy white layer. The car had crashed into a tree, but didn't seem too damaged. Still rubbing his neck, Teller walked to the front of the BMW. The air around his attacker's mouth was misting. He was still breathing.

Teller grabbed him by the hair. "Hey, asshole! Who are you? Who do you work for, huh?"

"*Nein ... Kopf ... schmerz ...*" the man's words were slurred.

"I don't speak German, dickhead. What's your name? Who do you work for?" Teller shook the man to try to wake him.

"F-Frosting ..." the man replied, blood drooling from his lips and onto the hood.

"Frosting? Is that a name? A place?"

The man was bleeding out and wouldn't be any use. Teller

stepped back, and then fired a kill shot into his assailant's skull. Then, his head still woozy, Teller climbed back into the car and began a brief inspection of the vehicle and the men's pockets. Lint. Cigarettes. A cell phone. Teller fished it out and clicked the home button. Password protected. *Maybe finger print?* He grabbed the hand of the dead driver, breathed on his thumb to make it a little warmer and slightly moist then pressed it to the sensor on the phone.

It pinged into life.

Teller dropped the man's wrist and began searching through the phone's files. It was clean. Too clean. No messages. No emails. No call history in or out. He quickly changed the security setting to a passcode, stuffed it into his coat and resumed his search.

As he pulled on the driver's worn leather jacket, he noticed a small red button pinned underneath the lapel. He pulled it off and stared at it. The small metal badge was emblazoned with a red star and a Heckler & Koch MP5 submachine gun. Teller shook his head. *First Aum Shinrikyo now the Red Faction Army?* Both defunct terrorist groups. Both with members tattooed with the number nine. There was perhaps more credibility to Vetrov's theory after all.

It took nearly thirty minutes, but Teller managed to haul the bodies from the vehicle and dump them out of sight by the side of the motorway. He then swapped his own clothes for some of those on the dead men, patched up the hole in windshield with a piece of card he found in the trunk and sped off into the night.

Location: Baledogle, Somalia

This was going to be a rough landing at best.

Not because the runway of the abandoned Cold-War era air force base at Baledogle, in Lower Shabelle's dusty region, was in complete disrepair. Not because Freya was exhausted and could barely focus on the instruments in the cockpit. Not even because of her Huntington's. But because the chance of being shot out of the sky was very real. Baledogle was not as desolate as it seemed. While not officially acknowledged by the US, Freya knew the base was a covert operation for terrorist counter strikes—primarily using drones. If memory served, nearly forty staff still operated in the shadows of the sun-blasted facility. And because they were covert, they weren't answering her constant hails.

There was no way to know how they were going to respond. She was banking on not being shot down as that might draw more attention than they would want. However, once on the ground, there was nothing to stop the covert team from executing all of them. Or handing them over to Washington. She couldn't decide which was worse.

"Baledogle base, this is Pegasus one," Freya repeated. "We have a mayday situation and need permission to land. Over."

Static wash.

The co-pilot shook his head.

"Anything?" Catherine asked, hanging through the doorway.

"Does it look like it?" Freya snapped, without turning around.

The red-headed woman exhaled loudly.

Freya turned her head just enough to see the reporter from the corner of her eye. "Unless you have something useful to say, shut the fuck up and get out of my face."

Catherine opened her mouth to speak, but didn't. Instead, Minya touched her shoulder and gestured that she should leave the cockpit. The reporter shook her head and shuffled away.

"My friend, we cannot fight amongst ourselves."

"She's a hindrance, Minya. What use is she—really? At some point, she's gonna slow us down or get shot, and we'll have to spend time rescuing her. I'm not risking KJ like that." Saying his name out loud triggered a pang of worry. "Is he okay?"

Minya bobbed her head. "*Da.* He is with Nikolaj, K'awin and Chernoukh. Eating the *paloo, manty* and *lagmann* from Vetrov's friend. Even the Huahuqui seem to eat the *lagmann.*"

Freya gave a weak smile. At least KJ was okay—for now. The guilt of exposing KJ to such danger sent a wave of nausea through Freya's stomach. She should never have let Minya convince her.

"We've circled twice, Miss Nilsson. We need to sit this bird down," the co-pilot said.

Freya checked the fuel gauge. He was right. They couldn't wait any longer. And there was nowhere else to set down. Landing in the open would mean certain death. Targeted attacks on anything and everyone by the Islamist armed group Al-Shabaab, utilizing suicide bombings and IEDs, still ravaged Somalia. Being shot by the Americans was preferable to being beheaded by militants.

"Best take a seat, Minya. We're gonna put down," Freya said.

The Siberian nodded in acknowledgement and disappeared into the cargo hold.

"Baledogle base, be advised we are coming in hot. Touchdown in less than ten. Over." Freya tried to sound authoritative, yet the words seemed to stick in her throat. *They wouldn't execute children, right?* she thought.

Freya's stomach lurched as the Pegasus began a steep descent. Through the cockpit window, she kept her eyes peeled for signs of incoming missiles or gun fire, movement on the ground—anything. But there was nothing. The wheels of the jet touched down on the hard, sunbaked, broken tarmac; the tires and suspension bouncing with the impact. The Pegasus shuddered and shook, even swerving a little as Freya and the co-pilot tried to stay the course on the shifting red soil that coated the dilapidated runway.

Finally, the Pegasus came to a hard stop.

The occupants of the plane remained silent, no one moving. The children clung to their Huahuqui and the remainder of Teller's men raised their rifles in readiness, but stood fast. Freya removed the headset and eased herself from the chair and out of the cockpit. She unclipped her Beretta and threw a commanding glance at Tony Franco. Tony nodded his acknowledgement, and signaled to his men to be ready. Minya corralled the Nenets and Huahuqui as far into the corner of the cargo hold as possible.

"Ready?" Freya whispered.

"I can only hope your American friends are as accommodating as my Kyrgyz friends," replied Sasha, his face deadpan.

Freya tightened her lips in silent agreement, then hit the cargo ramp release button.

Freckles broke from the crowd and padded up to Freya. It nuzzled at her boot. Freya looked down, confused, and shooed it away. The creature, almost despondent, shuffled away back to the children and sat deflated next to K'awin.

The ramp squealing open drew Freya's attention back to the task at hand. The doorway took an age to come to its final position. Once it had stopped, Freya took the vanguard with Tony, Sasha, and the remaining soldiers fanning out in a defensive position.

Outside, the heat was oppressive. Freya squinted in the blinding white of day, unable to focus on any threat should it spring from the heat haze. She stepped forward, swinging her

Beretta left and right. After a few moments, her eyes adjusted to the searing light.

The red soil was dry and dusty. The tarmac badly cracked and crumbling. Some fifty feet away was a collection of buildings including the hangars, a command center and control tower—though all appeared completely dilapidated. To the right was a collection of Humvees. From a cursory glance, they appeared to Freya to be M1114 models, developed after Operation Restore Hope in Somalia. This was a good thing. They had powerful turbocharged engines and a strengthened suspension system, but most importantly, a fully armored passenger area protected by hardened steel and bullet-resistant glass. They would be ideal to transport the children and Huahuqui.

If they could get to them.

Cautiously, Freya took another couple of steps. Still quiet. Was the US contingent still there?

A faint buzzing reached Freya's ears. She froze and concentrated on the noise. She fired a questioning glance at Tony. He pointed up and made a circling motion with his finger. Freya's eyes widened.

A Reaper drone.

"Down, everybody down!" Freya screamed.

They hit the ground, covering their heads.

The small unmanned hunter killer screamed past.

Freya leapt to her feet. "Make for the control center, don't stop until you get there!" The closer they were to the main building the less chance there was of the Reaper dropping a Hellfire missile on them.

The team sprinted for the control center as the Reaper made another pass, this time lower than before.

"What's it doing?" Freya shouted to Tony as she ran toward the battered building.

"I don't know!" he yelled back.

As they approached the stairs to the barb wire-encircled command center, its yellowed walls reflecting the unbearable sun, the doors above swung open and a flood of soldiers in desert combat gear flooded out, their firearms held high. They barked orders that overlapped one another.

Freya held her Beretta steady, taking aim at each one as they took place on the elevated platform. Snipers rose from the brush at the side of the building, their faces rubbed in the same red soil, their fatigues covered in thick wads of dried branches.

"Stand down!" The commanding officer screamed. "Throw your weapons down, and get on the ground. Now!"

Freya stood fast, Tony and his men forming a protective circle around her and Sasha.

"I'm an American!" Freya yelled back. "We need your help!"

"I said down! Now!" the man barked back.

She had no choice. Freya released her grip on the Beretta and let it dangle by the trigger guard from her finger. She then raised her hands into the air. Tony and his men followed suit.

"We have children on the plane," Freya started. "We need help."

Several of the base soldiers stepped forward, tore the guns from their hands, and shoved down hard on their shoulders, forcing them to their knees.

"I'm Tony Franco with the NSA. Part of Jonathan Teller's team," Tony protested as he was kicked on the back of the knee to accelerate his compliance.

"I don't give a shit who you are, son," the commanding officer spat back. He then indicated to the Pegasus and four of his men sprinted off to the plane's ramp.

Freya eyed him. While he seemed in complete control, he also appeared nervous, constantly scanning the horizon. The Reaper made yet another pass. Something else was going on. "I'm Freya Nilsson," she said finally. "Formerly with the US Army, covert operation, based out of Paradise Ranch. We don't have time. Please—"

"Sir, you'll wanna see this!" one of the soldiers called back from the ramp to the Pegasus cargo hold. "You're not gonna believe this shit."

The commander stared at his officer and then at Freya. "What's in the hold?"

"I told you. Children! We need your—"

The Reaper made a third pass, drowning out Freya's words. Then, as it climbed to bank and come back, it exploded. Freya instinctively covered her head as pieces of fuselage fell from the sky and a ball of fire metal plummeted to the ground and crashed on the other side of the command center.

Rapid fire from machine guns and the roar of multiple engines sounded not too far away.

"Al-Shabaab!" one of the base soldiers cried.

Priorities changed, and the base team sprang into action leaving only a few to guard Freya and her team. The others ran in the direction of the oncoming vehicles.

"Get them inside. Now!" the commander yelled.

A soldier grabbed Freya's shoulder. Without thinking, she seized him by the forearm, tucked her shoulder into his armpit and yanked down. He flipped head over heels and landed on his back. Freya twisted his arm and dislocated it. The man yelped. Tony had already sensed her purpose and snatched the rifle from his guard before shoving the butt into his nose—blood spraying everywhere.

Freya fired a few warning shots at the upper platform to give some cover, then ran for the Pegasus. Tony and his team brought up the rear. The base soldiers seemed preoccupied with the incoming assailants, so Freya took the initiative. She clanged up the ramp and burst into the cargo hold.

"We've got to move, now! Some kind of insurgency. We have to make it to the Humvees across from the runway. They're armored. We'll be safe inside. Got it?"

Only Minya nodded.

Freya realized the Nenets and Huahuqui had no idea what she was saying.

Minya relayed the message in Russian and the Nenets nodded sheepishly.

Freya grabbed up KJ in her arms. "You're with me, Mr. Man. Let's go."

Tony blocked Freya's path and dumped his weapon on the floor.

"What are you doing. Tony?" Freya asked, out of patience.

"Boss's orders," Tony replied with a faint smile.

"Jonathan?"

Tony unclipped his ballistic chest armor and pulled on the straps so they were as loose as they could be. He then slipped it over Freya's head so that the back and front plates made a sandwich of her and KJ, protecting their vital organs.

"Boss would kill me if you got shot," he said with a weak grin.

Freya smiled briefly. It was heavy, and awkward, but better than nothing. She shifted KJ onto her front. "Hold on, Mr. Man."

KJ clung to her, squeezing his eyes closed.

Now ready, Tony picked up his weapon. His remaining men took up the rear so the Nenets and Huahuqui were protected. Then, on the final signal from Freya, they raced out of the Pegasus. Locked onto the Humvees as their destination, the strange caravan of people and creatures ran as fast they could.

Though perhaps less than one-hundred feet away, the journey felt epic. Red soil puffed up in dust clouds as munitions peppered their trail. Freya scanned the horizon. An open jeep carrying four attackers and a crudely mounted rail gun careened through the barricade of base soldiers and tore along the tarmac toward them. They yelped and whooped, brandishing blood-stained machetes. Freya raised her Beretta to fire, but KJ grabbed her arm.

"No, Mommy, it's a kid," KJ whispered in that same tone he had back in Yamal.

She had only paused for a second, but it was enough for the attackers to fire off several more rounds.

Tony yelped and fell to the side as a bullet pierced his now uncovered chest. Freya glanced behind, torn between making it to the Humvees and going back for him. But she had KJ, she couldn't chance it. So she kept pace, running for the armored vehicles.

"We have to go back, Mommy," KJ said, his eyes now wide open and almost glowing.

Freya slammed into the side of one of the Humvees and dropped to her haunches, keeping her head low. Behind them more gunfire snapped. "We have to move, KJ. Even if it's just you and me."

"What about Minya and Nikolaj?" KJ asked, his tone that of a scolding grandparent much wiser than Freya. "And K'awin."

Freya peeked over the hood of the Humvee. There, where Tony had gone down, the Huahuqui and their Nenets children had gathered in a protective circle. Three jeeps had pulled up and the dark-skinned assailants had climbed out, their rifles and melee weapons held high.

KJ had been right. They were nothing but children. Perhaps fourteen years at most.

KJ scrambled down from his mother's chest, and before she could catch him, he'd slipped out from under the Kevlar vest and was already tearing toward the huddle of Huahuqui. Freya immediately launched into a sprint after him, and just as she was about to grab the back of his shirt, K'awin bounded up. The creature seamlessly skidded underneath KJ, scooped him up onto her back then dashed back to the scrum of Huahuqui.

"No! KJ!"

Freya froze to the spot. Under the blazing sun, a wave of dizziness and nausea enveloped her. KJ, the Huahuqui, and their children were trapped between the insurgents and the slowly approaching base soldiers who had regained their composure.

Why did they not kill the insurgents? "Just shoot them, dammit!"

Nobody readied their weapons.

"Fuck it. I'll do it." Freya raised her Beretta to fire, but just as at the sinkhole in Yamal she was unable to pull the trigger. "Not again!"

On the back of K'awin, KJ moved to the front of the crowd. Nikolaj, Chernoukh, Svetlana, and Ribka, sidled up either side of him like bodyguards. The eyes of all three burned an intense blue. "No more," KJ said, his voice deep and metallic.

A blue haze began to glow around the group.

"KJ, you have to stop this. We need to leave!" Freya yelled, frozen to the spot.

KJ turned slowly to Freya, his eyes aglow, his face solemn. K'awin shook her head, her gills fluffing in the breeze. "They can learn. They all can learn. Killing is wrong."

This wasn't going to work. Something had to convince him. What would make him move? What would make the Huahuqui move? The Huahuqui ...

"KJ, listen to me," Freya said softly, but firmly. "K'awin is from a cold place, from Siberia. She will die out here in the desert. She'll dry out. Remember daddy's special friend? K'in? He almost died from the same thing. We need to get them to water. To somewhere safe. You don't want K'awin to die, do you?"

Her son frowned just a little. Her words must have registered.

"C'mon, KJ. You need to let the soldiers deal with ... them." She nodded at the African militants. "Give the soldiers their control back."

The blue haze surrounding KJ and his friends began to fade, the resolve in his face waning. "They're just children, Mommy. Like me," he said in his own voice now.

"I know. It's okay. These nice men will just send them home—and they'll let us on our way." Freya turned to the commander who stood transfixed. "Won't you?"

The Commander slowly nodded.

"See? Let's go."

A final glance at the soldiers and then the child militants, then KJ seemed to release his hold. The blue haze dissipated completely.

A teenage militant snarled and raised his rifle to fire. Two sharp snaps pierced the thick air and the boy slumped to the ground in seemingly slow motion. The red dust blew up in clouds and blood poured from his temple, pooling around his face.

Smoke wafted from the barrel of the gun held by one of the US soldiers.

Freya's gaze pulled slowly from the child soldier to her son, now lying limp across K'awin's back. A red streak pouring down the creature's side.

"No!" screamed Freya.

Chaos erupted as the US soldiers dropped into formation and opened fire. A crimson mist filled the air as the front line of teenagers were mowed down by a spray of ammunition. Their comrades returned the favor, a bloody exchange of munitions ensuing.

Freya charged to her son, oblivious to the danger, and tore him from K'awin's back. The creature yelped as KJ's small body slid off, revealing a large wound in its side. Thick blood ebbed from the bullet wound. K'awin toppled over, her breathing labored. Freya dropped to her knees and searched her son's body. No wounds. Nothing. The Huahuqui had taken the hit.

"I'm sorry," she whispered to K'awin.

The creature lifted her head and stared at Freya with sad wet eyes.

"We have to go." Freya slipped the Kevlar vest over KJ and clamped him to her chest. She then shifted to her feet in a crouched position, ready to run.

"Tony!" she yelled over the din of fire. "Minya, Nikolaj!"

"Yeah," came a pained reply from Tony.

"We're here," Minya yelled back.

"Can you run?"

Tony hacked another cough. "Yeah."

"*Da!*" Minya shouted.

"Good, then fucking run!" Freya launched into a sprint heading straight for the Humvees—leaving K'awin behind.

The Huahuqui turned as one; a hundred pairs of eyes watching Freya tear away. Then, as if they had all thought the same thing at once, they raced after her like a swarm of ants. Chernoukh, with Nikolaj still on his back, grabbed up Minya without stopping and charged on ahead. Ribka followed suit, and with considerably more effort, lifted the wounded Tony onto her back with Svetlana. Then, followed by the last of Tony's men, they galloped after the rest.

Freya slammed into the nearest Humvee and began searching for a way in. It was locked. She yanked on the handles and banged on the armored glass. There was no way in.

"Fuck!" she screamed, then sprinted to the next vehicle.

It too, was locked.

Freya screamed in frustration. "Fuck you!"

Tony almost fell from Ribka's back against the Humvee door next to her. "We need the keys," he wheezed.

A lone militant charged at them from between two of the armored trucks, his machete held high.

Freya fumbled to find her Beretta with her son in her arms.

The boy soldier's head exploded, splattering Freya and Tony in blood and brain.

Behind him stood the base Commander, his Glock in one hand and K'awin slumped across his shoulders.

Freya stared at him.

He slid his sidearm back into its holster, fished into his pocket, and pulled out a set of keys. "You'll need these."

Freya climbed to her feet, still clutching KJ, and cautiously reached out to take them. "Why?"

The commander smiled. "You could've told me who you were Ms. Nilsson."

"Do I know you?"

"No. But I know you—or at least a friend of yours. Kelly Graham?"

Freya's head spun and her stomach cramped. *Did he really just say that?* "Kelly?"

Another bullet whistled by, forcing everyone to crouch back down.

"Yeah, he got into a bit of trouble out here with the locals. We helped him out. He then took it upon himself to find me a girl, who now happens to be my wife." The commander laughed. "He's a crazy fucker. Makes the boys here laugh a lot. He'd drop by the barracks in Mogadishu whenever he was in town. He contacted me a few years back on his way to Africa—Egypt actually. Said a pretty young thing called Freya had got him in some shit—and something about a big axolotl named K'in." He nodded at the Huahuqui. "When I saw these things, I knew it could only be you."

The Commander's words melted into white noise. Freya's heart thumped against her ribcage. Even from the grave, Kelly was still saving her.

"Where're you headed?" the commander asked.

Freya tried to focus on him. She saw him as a man, rather than a soldier. He was ruggedly handsome, his jaw strong and unshaven. His hair cropped close. Deep brown eyes searching her face for an answer. Yes, he was the kind of man Kelly would have called a friend.

"Mozambique."

"Okay, we'll get you that far. Once my boys are done with these assholes." He looked at KJ. "The kid all right?"

Freya glanced at KJ, then nodded, her mind still half in a fog.

The rattle of gunfire subsided as the insurgents sped off into the desert, leaving their dead to stain the tarmac red. The remainder of the base soldiers sauntered up to the Humvees, their rifles slung over one shoulder. Their commander slid K'awin from his shoulders and laid the creature carefully on the ground, then straightened.

Freya followed his ascent until he became only a shadow against the bright sun. He began firing orders at his men. Something about med kits and removing bullets.

"I'm Commander Matthew Lauder," he said.

"Sorry?" Freya replied.

"Me. I'm Matt." He eyed her carefully. "Miss Nilsson, are you okay? Are all your people accounted for?"

Freya snapped to attention and scanned the area. Minya stood with Nikolaj and Chernoukh near the first Humvee in the lot. The Siberian woman gave a small, but relieved smile. Tony was stretched out on the ground, being tended to by his men. He coughed once and gave the thumbs up. Her gaze moved across to the other Huahuqui and Nenets. Svetlana and Ribka were at the front like some sort of child leaders.

"Vetrov …" Freya said, her brow creasing. "Where's Sasha?" She climbed to her feet again.

She saw him in the distance. He was crouched down and inspecting the dead bodies of the Al-Shabaab militants. She clasped KJ to her chest and stomped off to the Russian. He looked up at her then back at the body. Without saying a word, Sasha grabbed the dead man's chin and turned his head to one side revealing a large tattoo on his neck. A tattoo of the number nine.

CHAPTER SIXTEEN

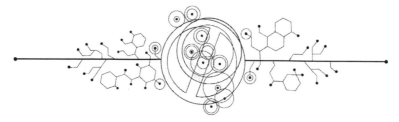

Location: somewhere in Mozambique

The armored Humvees hurtled along the jagged coastline. Catherine's insides jiggled as the vehicle rumbled over the uneven, dusty roads that sometimes ran close enough to the ocean that the unspoiled white sand beaches could be seen from the slot in the door that was supposed to pass for a window.

Catherine was crammed inside the insufferably hot metallic box with Freya, KJ, K'awin, Svetlana, and Ribka—who had refused to leave KJ's side—and Sasha. Their new friend, Commander Matthew Lauder, was driving. She had been surprised that Minya, Nikolaj, and Tony had not traveled in the same vehicle, but Minya had thought it best to spread everyone about, in case the worst happened. Of course, it was even stranger that she had been allowed to ride with Freya. The woman kept firing scathing glances every so often.

So, Catherine kept to herself and scribbled in her notepad—even sketched a little, as she couldn't risk taking pictures with Freya only a few feet away. At this point, Catherine was capturing the last couple of days and trying to pull together the crazy story into something cohesive—particularly around the group, or cult, or whatever they were pulling the strings at the top. The Nine Veils, as Sasha called them, had managed to fund and articulate Aum

Shinrikyo operating out of Russia, Korea, and now even the USA, to attack the Secretary of State. At the same time, a militant group in Somalia had known exactly where they were to attack. How had that been coordinated?

Of course, Teller's call in the morning had added yet more complexity. His report indicated he'd been the target of assassination by the long since defunct Red Army Faction—a West German far-left militant group originally active in the 1970s. They were famous for a series of bombings, assassinations, kidnappings, bank robberies, and shoot-outs with police over the course of thirty years. She'd done a piece on them in 2015 when there seemed to be a resurgence, but the third-generation members were quickly laughed at for bungling the robbery of an armored truck. The truck's onboard computer system had locked down and even the drivers couldn't open it. The three assailants, caught on camera, had to get back into their car and drive away empty handed.

What was the link between Aum, Al-Shabaab, and the Red Army? They were all defunct. Most were active in the latter half of the twentieth century. Did the Nine Veils have a thing for nostalgia?

"What are you scribbling there?"

Catherine chewed on her pen and slowly raised her head to see Freya's scowl. "I'm just trying to piece things together. Aum, Al-Shabaab, the Red Army. How the Nine Veils, or whomever they are, have been able to use them to attack us wherever we are."

"You're a journalist," Freya snapped back. "Not a military strategist."

"You'd be amazed what we put together and figure out, Ms. Nilsson. The media is a powerful thing." Catherine went back to scribbling.

Sasha let out a quiet chuckle.

"Something funny, Vetrov?" Freya asked.

Catherine looked up again to see Freya's angry stare now fixed on the Russian.

"She's right is all. The media can be a lot more powerful than any government."

"You want to talk about election rigging?" Freya fired back.

The Russian colonel held up his hands and clamped his lips together to show he'd say no more.

"You know," Catherine started. "What if there isn't a mole in Washington. What if it's not someone on the inside. What if the Nine Veils, or whoever the guy is at the top, has another way to monitor us and communicate with these terrorist cells."

Freya huffed. "Some kind of sophisticated virus in a computer system? Bugging the offices of every government? We haven't even told Lucy where we are. Just Jonathan. And if the NSA were bothering to listen to the satellite phone calls, we'd have been picked up by allied forces by now."

Sasha nodded. "I have to agree with Nilsson, the FSB would be aware of such advanced listening technology. Hell, it would probably be ours."

"Exactly my point," Catherine said. "What if it's not advanced?"

"What the hell are you talking about?" Freya snapped back.

Catherine turned over a leaf of paper, shuffled between Freya and Sasha and began scribbling so they could see. KJ and Svetlana hung off Freya's knees, apparently also curious as to what she was talking about.

"You said when Teller called, the German guy said something about Frosting."

"Yeah so?" Freya demanded.

"Ever heard of project ECHELON?" The reporter asked.

"Of course," Freya replied. "An old surveillance program set up in the sixties, right?"

Catherine bobbed her head. "Right. In 2015, two internal NSA newsletters from January 2011 and July 2012 were published as part of the Snowden-revelations by the website, *The Intercept*. They confirmed that ECHELON was part of an umbrella program codenamed FROSTING, which was established by the NSA in 1966 to collect and process data from communications satellites. FROSTING had two sub-programs: TRANSIENT, for intercepting Soviet satellite transmissions, and ECHELON, for intercepting Intelsat satellite transmissions. My newspaper was all over the story."

"We were already aware of ECHELON during the cold war," Sasha said. "The NSA in combination with similar agencies in other countries monitored a large portion of the world's transmitted civilian telephone, fax, and data traffic. It was superseded by PRISM and XKeyscore, as the world became digital."

"I know," Catherine said. "But ECHELON is automated. Probably only looked at if it throws something up. If they were piggybacking on it, they might be able to follow our moves when we speak with Teller. We're using a satellite phone. They're vulnerable."

Freya snorted in derision. "Sat phones are encrypted."

"Actually," Sasha interjected. "All modern satellite phone networks utilize one of two proprietary encryption algorithms. Both are vulnerable to cipher-text only attacks. Satellite phones are not recommended for high-security applications."

"Then why the hell would Jonathan use it as a secret line just for me?" Freya blurted out.

There was a silence in the car following the revelation.

Catherine felt the need to break the tension. "Teller's team would be using flagged words all the time. If the NSA constantly had to screen his or his team's calls, and all those of the US military and government agencies, they'd have no time. They focus on civilians and suspects. And there's a lot to screen. We make a billion calls in the UK each year alone."

Freya's eyes narrowed as she seemed to process the information. Catherine figured an ex-military woman would know this. But she'd been away for five years with her son. Perhaps her priorities had changed.

"So you think this puppet master cult is using an old global surveillance system to track us?" Freya asked.

"Maybe," Catherine said, setting her pen down. "It's a possibility, right? And whoever these guys are, they have a penchant for nostalgia. With newer systems like PRISM, who's going to watch ECHELON? I'll bet it's running in the background without much maintenance. They only have to piggyback on it."

"If you're right, then whoever they are they already know where we're going. Do we change the plan?" Sasha asked.

Freya screwed up her nose. "What's the point? We have nowhere else to go. We stick to the plan, and fight them off. We haven't indicated how we're getting to Antarctica. We don't need to tell Jonathan our route. That should buy us some time. We'll let him know our theory on ECHELON. Perhaps he can confirm or refute it. And maybe if they're listening they'll figure they're caught and shut it down." Freya paused and studied Catherine. "Not bad, for a reporter."

Catherine simply took the backhanded compliment and sat back in her spot. If she was wrong, any chance of gaining Freya's trust would evaporate. If she was right, they were probably screwed anyway.

The deceptively quiet seaport of Quelamine came into view. Formerly owned by the Portuguese, the city was the administrative capital, and the largest town, of the Zambezia Province. While most people would have no idea where it actually was in the world, like Freya, many people knew about it due to the famous explorer David Livingstone. Quelamine was the end point of his famous west-to-east crossing of south-central Africa in 1856.

As the Humvees grumbled along, Freya observed the strange town through the slot in her door. For such an important city, Quelamine was small with a ratty sensibility. Besides Livingstone, the only westerners that now passed through the area were backpackers using it as a convenient waystation when jockeying between northern and southern Mozambique, or heading for the border with Malawi. They passed through the tight downtown grid and exited into an area of dense jungle that encircled the delta.

"Hey, Lauder. We're not stopping?" Freya asked.

"We need to stay out of sight, and your aquatic friends here are not exactly discreet. They look like they could use a little water, too. We'll stop in a clearing at the edge of the Bons Sinais," he called back without taking his eyes from the road. "We're about one hundred klicks north of the Zambezi River."

Freya nodded, sat back in her seat, and clasped her hands together, fighting the uncontrollable urge to fling her arms out. Without her meds, it was getting worse. *Think about something else,* she thought. Freya studied her sleeping son who lay on the floor of the Humvee, snuggled up with Svetlana—their Huahuqui, K'awin and Ribka wrapped around them. The creatures were asleep, and appeared comfortable, although their gills were flushed of color and their skin dry.

As much as she hated it, KJ was becoming closer and closer to K'awin, and Svetlana for that matter. They barely spoke, apart from a few words of Aymara, yet their bond seemed unbreakable. She felt as if she was losing him. It was a battle she would never win. Not while K'awin was alive. Killing the creature wasn't an option. The world needed the Huahuqui. But why *her* son? Why not someone else? The conflict tore at her heart. Saving the world compared with saving her son. These things never went well. People who saved the world were called martyrs for a reason. Perhaps if she were to connect to KJ through K'awin. If she could be part of it, she could help steer him to safety and to a path that wouldn't lead him to—the thought was unbearable.

Freya held her hand above K'awin's head and let it hover there, shaking slightly.

"He still loves you, you know," Catherine said.

Freya snatched her hand away. "Of course he does."

"That's not how I meant it. The Huahuqui won't take away what you have. He's your son."

"How the fuck would you know? Have you ever been bonded to one? Do you have kids?"

"No." Catherine moved a lock of her hair behind her ear.

"Then, you might want to keep your opinion to yourself."

"Let me ask you this: when Kelly was bonded to K'in, was it exclusive? Did his bond with that Huahuqui preclude all other feelings for other people?"

It was odd to hear a stranger say his name. Freya's stomach knotted. "He didn't have feelings for anyone else."

"I would say the little boy laid at your feet tells a different story. One thing you learn in journalism: judge a person by their actions, not their words."

Freya studied the mismatched eyes of the reporter. The woman held Freya's gaze, then smiled softly before returning to her scribbling. As much as Freya disliked Catherine, her argument was difficult to refute—Kelly's bond with K'in had opened his heart. Without it, he would probably never have admitted to his feelings for Freya. And KJ would never have existed. Was fighting the bond with K'awin wrong? Could it actually help them as a family?

K'awin slowly opened her eyes and looked up at Freya, as if she had been listening to Freya's inner monologue. The animal cocked her head, blinking slowly like a cat showing affection for an owner. Freya carefully stretched out a hand and lowered it to the creature's head. K'awin responded in kind and pushed her snout forward to meet Freya's fingers. The familiar warmth spread from the tips of Freya's fingers along her arm and into her chest. Radiating outward, it filled her being. Warmth. Contentment—and KJ. Freya, could feel her son. He was happy, and felt safe.

Tears welled in Freya's eyes. Every mother felt an inexplicable bond with their child—the person that grew inside them. The connection with K'awin amplified that feeling a thousand-fold. Finally, she understood.

CHAPTER SEVENTEEN

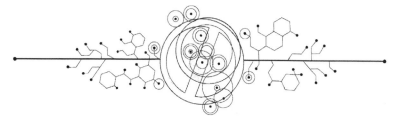

Location: Bad Aibling, Germany

Jonathan had changed direction. Now, he was headed north. The last, and final, transmission from Freya had him convinced— there was a higher force at play here, and they were likely using ECHELON to co-ordinate their attacks. Bad Aibling Station, the largest listening post outside Britain and the USA, in northern Germany, would have the answers. He hadn't told Freya his destination, and she hadn't told him her current location. Until the enemy's access to ECHELON was revoked, they couldn't say much more. Perhaps even mentioning ECHELON on the sat phone would drive the enemy to cut ties already; but still, if they left any traces, it may lead him to them.

Bad Aibling Station, BAS as it was referred to, was a satellite tracking station created by Western allies in 1947 and originally run by the NSA. That was until the early 2000s when public outrage over U.S. surveillance operations in Europe meant that control was transferred to the German intelligence agency *Bundesnachrichtendienst*—at least officially. A group of NSA operatives still worked there in a small building referred to as the *Tin Can*.

The entrance to BAS was unassuming. Low, white walls, and a single arm-barrier blocking the entrance. An almost comical curved sign hung above advertising the location: BAD AIBLING

STATION. Bright yellow lighting illuminated the guardhouse. Teller pulled up to the gate in the beat-up BMW and wound down his window.

An older-looking guard appeared. *"Ja? Kann ich ihnen helfen?"*

It would have been so much easier if he spoke German. "My name is Jonathan Teller. I'm with NSA, based in Washington."

"Ausweiss," said the guard.

"Huh?"

"Identification," he repeated in heavily German-accented English.

"Sure." Teller pulled his ID from the jacket he stole from the Red Army assailant and handed it to the guard.

The soldier stared at the official document, then at Teller, before handing it back. "Who are you visiting?"

Jonathan had not thought that through. Who was he visiting? He knew no one at this base. His only hope was to take a stab at it and hope that the German's weren't taking too much note of who from the NSA was there. "Vasquez." He had no idea where that name came from. Vasquez? Couldn't he think of a more American name?

As Jonathan mentally kicked himself, the guard stepped back inside to make a call. Two minutes passed. Three. Teller shifted the car into reverse, ready to make his escape.

The guard reappeared. "No clearance. Go away, or you will be arrested."

"God dammit." There was no use in arguing. He'd have to find another way in. Sneak in.

Teller closed the window, shifted the old gear stick into reverse and revved the engine—which almost drowned out the phone ringing in the booth. The guard disappeared. Teller continued to struggle with the ancient clutch, almost stalling the car several times as he eased it away from the barrier.

There was a harsh knocking on the window. Teller stopped reversing and wound down the glass.

"All the way to the end of the compound," the guard said. "Last building. Covered in metal." He grunted, turned away and glanced at a closed circuit camera above before disappearing inside the booth.

The barrier raised.

Jonathan didn't question his fortune and instead slipped the car into first gear and shuddered onto the base, past the ten-foot fencing adorned with rows of barbed wire.

In the dark of night, the green fields in which BAS was situated appeared as murky blue mounds that stretched back to the silhouette of a mountain range set against the purple night sky. At first glance, it would seem the perfect place to have a covert listening base—notwithstanding the giant satellite dishes and dozens of white, golf-ball-like polygonal structures of various sizes that dotted the landscape.

Teller drove past them all until he reached an elongated building with a white roof, clad in metal sheets, at the end of the complex. A man was waiting in the shadows at the entrance. Teller pulled up, killed the engine, and stepped out. Still unable to see the man's face, Teller decided not to approach.

"I'm Teller," Jonathan said.

"Vasquez," the man replied in a thick Texan accent. "Follow me."

Jonathan smirked, checked that his Beretta was holstered, then followed the man into the Tin Can. He passed through several doors and eventually into a small room with multiple desks and at least twenty men working at computers.

The man who had identified himself as Vasquez sat down at a desk at the back of the room and offered Teller the chair opposite. Jonathan sat down.

"You're not really called Vasquez are you?" Teller asked.

"No, I'm First Lieutenant Ramirez. You were close, though," the man replied, though his expression did not convey joviality.

Teller allowed a little laugh. "And there I was thinking I was way off base."

"So, Captain Jonathan Teller, former XO in the United States Navy Submarine Division, now NSA Special Forces anti-terrorism unit—what brings you to Bad Aibling? Washington says you were last seen in North Korea and have been off the grid apart from a few sat phone transmissions from Russia, Poland and Germany." Ramirez's dark eyes studied Teller.

Jonathan shifted in his seat. He wasn't used to being the least informed person in the room. "I think we have a mole, or at least a piggy backer using our own tech against us."

"Us *who*, Captain Teller?"

"Now there's a question. What's your clearance, Ramirez?"

Ramirez raised a single eyebrow and then waved to his surroundings.

"Good point," Teller said. "Look, you and I both know that in order to protect the interests of the USA, we don't report every little thing we find and we certainly don't clear everything with the Oval Office unless absolutely necessary."

The Lieutenant nodded in agreement. "I'm sure you can figure that's why you're given the freedom to move about all free like, even when a US Pegasus that shouldn't be in Siberia explodes right there on the peninsula."

"You heard about that, huh?" Teller said, sheepishly.

"We're a stone's throw from Russia. Yeah, we heard 'bout that. What ain't clear is what's goin' on. We know you're movin' people. We know the Secretary of State sanctioned the release of a prisoner from Leavenworth who then stole two planes to mount a rescue of his goddaughter and some locals. What we don't know is what the *Huahuqui* is. A code name? Every lead I chase just ends up being a frog hole. Whatever it is, it was wiped from existence. Not even Top Secret. Gone. You wanna fill me in?"

Teller rubbed his chin. "Not really, but I'm not sure I have a choice."

Teller recounted the last few years, again. Like a rehearsed bedtime story, he left no detail out explaining everything from how the original clone came to be, the near war with the Chinese, the weaponized virus in California, the Green and Red Societies, the Nine Veils, and the attacks by defunct terrorist groups. Most importantly he was careful to describe the fate of Kelly Graham and now Freya and KJ, as well as the plan to move the Huahuqui and the Nenets to Antarctica.

Ramirez sat for a few moments, wide eyed. From the look on his face, he hadn't expected anything Jonathan had told him. That spoke volumes about a man whose sole job was information gathering. The Lieutenant pulled at the skin on his face and breathed out slowly.

"Ya'll have been busy," Ramirez said eventually.

"You could say that."

"And you think they—the Nine Veils—are usin' ECHELON to track your communications and movements? And mobilizin' terrorist cells that are movin' more or less under our radar to attack you?"

Teller scratched his head and heaved a sigh. "It sounds dumb when you say it out loud."

"You'd be surprised what we come across in our surveillance. This sounds quite plausible."

"So what do we do?" Teller asked.

"Well, we don't use ECHELON here anymore. It was superseded. But I'll tell you who does—Menwith."

"In England?"

"Yep. But those British boys are a cagey lot. No USA personnel at Menwith to pally up with."

Teller smiled. "I got a guy. I'll need to make a call to the Embankment in London. But he'll help me."

"Okay, good."

"What are you going to do? In fact, why help me at all?" Teller asked, suddenly feeling this was all a little too easy.

"We are the NSA Captain Teller," Ramirez said. "From what you tell me, this is a matter of national security. Wastin' my time holdin' you here and worryin' the chain of command isn't going to help. Right now, we have some leverage while the Secretary of State still has a job. You get to Menwith and get me proof that ECHELON is being piggybacked, and we'll set up an official investigation. Let me call the Secretary. We can use a system ECHELON can't see."

"No, let me," Teller said. "She'll trust me. But I have another favor to ask."

"Oh?"

"You boys think you can get me to Menwith?"

Ramirez smiled and nodded.

Location: Bon Sinais Delta, Mozambique

Just as Lauder had said, there was a clearing in the jungle on the bank of the Bon Sinais, far enough from Quelamine's tight downtown grid to be secluded, but not so distant that help wasn't far away should something bad happen. The Nenets children and their Huahuqui sat calmly at the edge of the slow-moving river, half submerged to keep cool. The change in temperature was clearly a shock to both the creatures and the Nenets. They were a long way from Siberia. The Nenets parents stayed nearby, but were now stripped down to almost nothing and lazing in the shade of the trees. With no reindeer to herd, there was little else for them to do.

Freya had demanded KJ stay near, but like most five-year olds, he hadn't listened. Starting off a good twenty feet from the others, he had edged his way closer and closer—Freya shifting with him—until, against her wishes he was with all the other kids. Close to Svetlana, in particular.

The little Nenets girl was actually quite pretty. Freya hadn't really paid attention before. Too focused on the little girl's boisterous companion, Ribka, to notice. Svetlana's hair was long and black, and hadn't changed to blonde like KJs. But her eyes had become the same cobalt blue. Her heart-shaped face and wide, dimpled, smile was sweet and yet almost too mature for her age. It triggered an unexpected emotion in Freya: jealousy. Freya had figured she'd have until KJ was at least fourteen to begin worrying about girls. He was only five. Yet, already he seemed to be flirting, constantly following her and bringing her flowers he'd picked from the nearby grassy area.

KJ came splashing over, holding Sveltlana's hand. Freya swished her own bare feet in the cool river water, and took another bite of the *frango à zambeziana* in coconut sauce that Lauder had bought for everyone during a quick stop in Quelamine. She concentrated on how it tasted, creamy and sweet—anything to distract from her childish thoughts.

"Have you met Svetlana before, Mommy?" KJ asked, a huge grin on his face.

"I have indeed, Mr. Man," Freya replied and gave her best fake smile.

Svetlana cocked her head and stared with her brow knotted for a moment. "Why does she call you Mr. Man, Kelly Junior?" she said.

Freya almost choked on her chicken-based dish. "Um, did you, did—did she just speak English?"

"Sure," KJ replied.

"How?" said another voice from above.

It was the reporter, notebook in hand, and her telephoto lens camera hanging about her neck.

KJ shrugged. "Ribka taught her, I think. Like K'awin taught me that other language we speak sometimes. It's like a secret language." He covered his mouth with both hands and whispered that last part.

"You mean Aymara?" Freya asked.

Her son nodded. "*Jumalaykuw kutiniskix*," he said, his voice now distant and his gaze unfocused.

Freya grabbed him by the arms and shook him out of his trance. "Where did you hear that? Where!"

"What seems to be problem?" Minya asked.

"He … he's speaking that language again. The one Kelly did … at the end. He even repeated the same words." Freya's whole body shook.

Minya dropped to her haunches, put a comforting hand on

Freya's shoulder, and then turned to KJ. "You should go play now. Take Nikolaj with you, and Svetlana."

KJ nodded and grabbed Svetlana by the hand before splashing back toward the other children yelling for Nikolaj to come join them. Svetlana glanced back at Freya and waved.

"Bye, Kelly Junior's mom!" she said.

"Did you hear that?" Freya almost squawked.

Minya's usually calm and stony expression had cracked ever so slightly, her eyes narrowed to study the Nenets girl.

"KJ said the Huahuqui taught them," Catherine piped up.

Freya and Minya turned to face the reporter with the same deliberate, irritated, slowness.

"Just sayin'," Catherine said, then trudged away looking defeated.

"She is not mother. She does not understand," Minya said.

Freya just shook her head.

A rustle in the bushes across the slender river drew Freya's attention. She leaped up, drew her Beretta, and pointed it in the direction of the disturbance. Minya climbed to her feet and watched the bushes intently.

The plants rustled again.

"Lauder, eyes up!" Freya called.

Matt stomped over, his hand readied on his holstered sidearm. "What we got?"

Freya nodded at the other river bank, then shot Tony a sideways glance. He acknowledged the unspoken request and made his way to KJ and the children, scanning their perimeter.

Lauder slid out his Glock and indicated to his men to follow him. They edged forward, guns high, searching the jungle plant life for movement. A child, a girl with dark skin, dressed in only a brightly covered sheet burst through then froze to the spot, staring at the soldiers who had fixed their sights on her.

Freya sighed. Lauder cursed under his breath and ordered his men to stand down. "*Kamwaamba!*" he called out.

Freya shot a confused look at Lauder.

"They're Batonga," he said without looking at her. "A few of the tribes got displaced after the dam was built at Kariba. They tend to wonder around Zambia and Mozambique. *Kamwaamba!*"

The large leaved plants rustled and a few tribes people stepped out. Dressed in brightly colored makeshift robes and wearing huge bead necklaces, they looked cautious but curious. None were carrying weapons.

Lauder holstered his Glock, and shooed his men away. "*Mwapona buti?*" he called to them. "*Kunywa muyandanzi?*"

For Freya, it was like watching Kelly talking to the locals all over again. "What did you say to him?"

"I asked if they're okay. If they want a drink. Most of the time they just want water—but some have grown a liking for diet coke. They get it off the tourists."

The Tongans ignored Lauder and were instead fixated on the Huahuqui who had all turned to face the new arrivals.

"*Nyami Nyami,*" said one of the Tongan men.

Others joined in. "*Nyami Nyami!*" they chanted.

Freya raised her Beretta again. "What's going on?"

"They believe Huahuqui are river gods," Minya said. "*Nyami Nyami.* A dragon-like creature believed to control all life on the Zambezi River. You can see why they may think this." She waved a hand at the creatures.

Freya had to admit, from a distance the Huahuqui did appear dragon-like, if not in a traditional Chinese dragon kind of way. "Is this a good or a bad thing?"

"It is good. They believe *Nyami Nyami* protects them," Minya replied.

Lauder nodded. "I heard about this dragon god. There's a famous local legend about it. The tribes around here tell that when the Kariba Dam project displaced the Batonga people who were living in the Zambezi Valley they protested, saying *Nyami Nyami* wouldn't allow the dam to be built. A year after the project started, a severe flood killed several workers and destroyed the partially built dam." He pulled a toothpick from his pocket and placed it in the corner of his mouth. "For three days, the families of the workers waited for the remains to be recovered. The Batonga elders said only a sacrifice would placate *Nyami Nyami*. Legend has it, a calf was slaughtered and dumped in the water. The next day, the bodies of the workers were found in its place."

Freya screwed up her nose. "I still don't see how this is a good thing."

"If they think we're with *Nyami Nyami* then we're safe," Matt said. "Another set of eyes that know this jungle better than anyone. In fact, this gives me the opportunity to go into town. You said you needed a few boats, right? You're trying to get to La Reunion?"

Freya kept one eye on the Batonga people edging closer to Huahuqui. "Yeah, we were going to go via Madagascar ... somehow."

Lauder shook his head. "No transport from Madagascar to La Reunion. You're better off taking a boat from here."

"I still don't get why you're helping me, Lauder. What's in it for you?"

Matt offered a soft smile. "Call it Karma. We're black boxed here taking out terrorists more or less at our own discretion. If we get caught, we're disowned by the powers that be. Can't have it tied back to Washington. So, we got a little more freedom to move. Kelly did me a solid. And from his garbled message, what you two were doing was pretty important. So, I'm returning the favor. Five years later, you got a bunch of kids with you and some big ol' amphibians. What kinda man lets them get hurt, huh?"

Freya studied his dark features. He reminded her of Kelly so much. Brave and just a little reckless. "You could get court martialed."

Lauder just laughed. "You think people are chomping at the bit to take my place in this shit hole? We'll be fine." He turned to walk to a Humvee, but then spun on his heel to face Freya again. "By the way, when is that crazy bastard coming? Not like him to leave his lady and, I'm guessing his son, out to dry." He nodded to KJ still splashing about in the water with Svetlana, K'awin, and Ribka.

The knot in Freya's stomach returned and her throat dried up as if to prevent her from speaking the words. She clamped her trembling fingers together. "He's dead," she said softly.

Lauder seemed to take a moment to absorb the information. "Did he die a hero?"

Freya almost choked on suppressed tears. "Yeah. He did."

Matt nodded, respectfully. "Good." He turned back to the Humvee. "I'll be back in a couple of hours. The boys will watch you. Oh, and ask the Batonga about the Eboka shrub—*miracle wood.* It'll help with those DTs."

Freya glanced at her hands and then back to Matt, but he was already in the Humvee and pulling away.

Location: Washington DC, USA

Lucy sat in the modified Boeing 737, waiting for the call.

Frankly, it was hard to believe she was in this situation again. Five years ago, she had been struggling to avoid war with China. Now it was the Koreans. With China, she'd had an ally in their Minister. In this situation, she doubted that would be the case.

While the outside world may have seen the North Korean threat as somewhat of a joke, Lucy and the US government took the country and its political party seriously. National propaganda, through *Rodong Sinmun*—the chief newspaper and mouthpiece of Central Committee of the Worker's Party of Korea—regularly made threats against South Korea, Japan, and the USA. They were almost always nuclear. Constant missile testing kept the public aware of their capabilities, but it was the lesser known advances that were bothersome.

In recent years, North Korea had fired solid-fuel missiles from submarines and land. That was a problem for any of their enemies. Land-based missiles with solid propellants could be readied for launch much faster, long before satellites or drones spotted them. A strike could come and no one would know.

Yet, it was this very fact—a preponderance with nuclear arsenal—that gave Lucy hope. They wouldn't bother with a gas attack. A strange communication from the FSB had suggested there was someone else at play. Choosing North Korea as the scapegoat in a sarin gas attack was only a means to tie up resources and keep her, and the Ministry of Foreign Affairs, busy. Now, Jonathan Teller had confirmed as much. Calling from Bad Aibling, he'd filled her in as best he could. They should *all* be looking for the Nine Veils—controlling multiple terrorist factions and using

North Korea as a smokescreen where possible. They were the real target. But, first things first: managing Pak Yong-Ho, their Minister of Foreign Affairs, a prickly man at best and a devout supporter of his President, though whether his devotion was genuine or coerced was never clear, and never would be.

The phone on Lucy's desk began to ring. She breathed out slowly, pushed a lock of blond hair behind her ear, and picked up the receiver.

"This is Lucy Taylor, Secretary of State."

"Miss Taylor, this is Yong-Ho, Minister of Foreign Affairs," the voice on the phone replied.

"Good afternoon, Mr. Yong-Ho. Thank you for taking this call."

"Do not thank me. Our President knows what you are trying to achieve, Madam Secretary. Blaming our country for a pathetic attack on your soil. A failed attack at best. It makes us look weak, and gives you reason to impose greater sanctions—"

"I assure you, that's not the case," Lucy interjected.

"No? Then why do I have a report on my desk suggesting your intelligence agencies blame us? If we wanted to strike the USA, it wouldn't be with gas, Miss Taylor."

Lucy straightened her back. "I am well aware of your capabilities, and while frankly I would very much like to ensure your nuclear program is culled, this is not what our call is about."

"Cull our program?" Yong-Ho chuckled. *"You stand alone. Moscow and Beijing are our allies. You can't even get the Terminal High Altitude Area Defense System off the ground because they tell you it's a regional security risk. They just want to ensure we remain a significant power. They understand the greatness of our country."*

Lucy sucked in a breath and held it, fighting the urge to shout at the man and slam the receiver as hard as possible. Getting

THAAD operational by convincing Moscow and Beijing it was necessary had been one of her main priorities in recent years. It could scupper North Korea's missile program. She hadn't been successful. It was a thorn in her side, and he knew it.

"We're off topic, Mr. Yong-Ho. I wished to speak with you today to tell you that we know it wasn't you. Someone is disguising themselves as your military, and looking to use your country as a scapegoat. We do not wish for war, and we will not blame North Korea for this—openly or otherwise."

There was a long silence before the Minister responded.

"Then we have little else to discuss," he said. *"Make sure your propaganda machines do not apportion this to us or our illustrious leader and there will be no retaliation."*

"We could focus on apprehending whomever is trying to frame you?"

"We will find who is doing this, and deal our punishment under Korean law."

The phone went dead.

Korean law. Whatever that meant. They were notorious for not following UN regulations. Lucy could only hope that they didn't get in the way. She put down the phone.

"We're ready for take-off, Madam Secretary," the purser said before disappearing up into the service area.

Lucy slid back into her seat. She may be going to prison after this, but until then the President had given her full lateral movement and authority. The attack on American soil, the intelligence from Sasha Vetrov and Jonathan Teller—all pointing to an elite terrorist group, the Nine Veils—had tipped the scale in her favor. She needed to be where Jonathan was, there was a plan to catch these bastards, and protect the Huahuqui. But she needed to be on the ground and receive intelligence in real time. Most importantly, she needed to know where the Huahuqui were and where they were headed. Teller would only divulge in person.

The jet's engines roared, thrusting it forward, and Lucy into her seat. It reached take off speed and lifted into the air, off into the night and onward toward Menwith, England.

Location: somewhere on the coast of Mozambique

They were gaining on the Americans.

It was only a matter of time before Takashi and his men would catch up and then be able to capture the creatures themselves. Then Aum could wield the power and kill the benefactors who had so carelessly tried to throw them away like garbage. Takashi would prove that he could lead Aum without Ishii, and that they could bring about the End Times, just as planned.

The stolen Matchedje pickups tore along the dusty road. Takashi stared out the passenger window, his eyes squinted, studying the crystal blue water just a few kilometers away. Mozambique had been like a second home. Strong ties with Japan, and in particular the automotive industry, had meant it was a perfect place from which to operate for Aum. A sham automotive shop was an easy front for their business. Secluded. Mostly unmonitored by western powers.

But now, Chinese investment through the Shanghai-based China Tongjian Investment Co. was displacing the Japanese hold. China had transformed Mozambique into a car manufacturing and exporting country, utilizing Matchedje Motors Ltd—Mozambique's domestic carmaker. The country was filled with Chinese. Takashi hated it. He wound down the window and spat—the wind grabbed his phlegm and flicked it behind the pickup. Stealing these vehicles felt like retribution.

"Master Takashi-san, do we know where we are headed?" a tall, thin man in the seat next to Takashi asked.

"Quelamine," Takashi replied. "There's nowhere else to go from here of any importance. It's a port. They must be heading for a ship. We will find and kill the Beast and take the creatures."

The thin man nodded and clutched his rifle a little tighter.

Takashi scratched at his newly growing, but wispy, beard. Tracking the American's had so far been easy. He didn't need *the system* to give him information. Good old-fashioned connections and interrogation meant that a Pegasus plane wasn't that hard to find. But the trail had cooled after Somalia. And the farther they drove into Mozambique, the colder the trail became. Powering forward was the key. No rest. The Beast was undisciplined and lazy. They would rest. They would stop. Aum Shinrikyo never would.

The pickup crashed over a bump, and Takashi slammed his head into the roof. *"Baka! Hetakuso!"* Takashi yelled at the driver, then smacked him across the back of the head. "You want to get us all killed?"

"Sumimasen deshita Takashi-san!" the driver apologized, wincing from the head strike.

Takashi peered out from the rear window to check on their payload. Four of his men sat in the flatbed, a tarpaulin-covered mass between them. Everything seemed fine. He turned back in his seat.

Taking the Beast head on had not worked. They needed to be discreet. They needed to employ his heritage as *Shinobi*. The benefactors had seen Aum as easy to control. And until now, Ishii had followed their orders to the letter. He saw himself as an elite, a Samurai. Doling out punishments as such. Takashi studied the stump where his finger used to be. No more. Takashi knew his legacy. He was low born, as his ancestors were—originating from the Iga province, dedicated to the training of *Shinobi*—a skill passed down from generation to generation. Now, with Ishii and the benefactor gone, he was free to rule Aum as he saw fit. And it would start with the death of the Americans.

CHAPTER EIGHTEEN

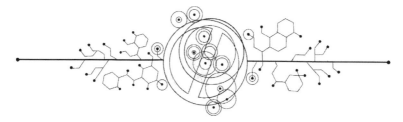

Location: Royal Air Force Base Menwith, Yorkshire, UK

"Stuart Jones," Teller said offering his hand. "It's been a while."

The tall man in a three-piece suit with oiled hair shook Teller's hand with an overly firm grip. "That it has, old boy. What brings you to Menwith? In fact, what brings *me* to Menwith. You weren't exactly forthcoming."

Teller smirked. "Still dressing like a double 0 from the movies I see."

Jones just dipped his brow.

"Is there somewhere we can talk?" Teller asked.

Jones led the way down some narrow corridors and into a small, simple room with only a table and four chairs. The white walls and overhead fluorescent light made the space unbearably bright. It was clear this was an interrogation room.

"You gonna strap me to a chair and break my knees, Jones?"

"Just a friendly conversation, old boy. Take a seat. You want some tea?" Stuart smiled, though it didn't look genuine.

"I'm good."

"So, what's the emergency?"

Teller cleared his throat. "You and I both know you have at least some idea why I'm here. MI5 isn't exactly slack. But neither

211

are you in the habit of sharing information unless asked. I think you might know things that can help me."

Jones offered no outward sign that Teller had hit a nerve.

"You remember a few years back, there was a big hoo-ha about another species more intelligent than us, right here on Earth. At the same time, there was a nasty virus released in the US, and China was on red alert?"

"I recall," Jones said. "You boys covered up what was happening pretty quickly. It wasn't in our interest to get involved."

"Well, you're involved now."

Jones raised one eyebrow. "How so?"

"The other species I mentioned, it's real. Our government stole a corpse of one from the Chinese back in the 40s, and then cloned two live ones, K'in and Wak. Five years ago, the Chinese found out and holy hell broke loose. Turns out the Chinese were infiltrated by a cult called the Green and Red Societies who wanted to use the clones to ... for want of a better phrase ... take over the planet."

Jones sat calmly, his hands in his lap, seemingly unfazed by the information.

"Anyway," Teller continued, eyeing the MI5 agent. "The clones were killed. Collateral damage. The leader of the Green and Red societies was killed. War was averted. We thought that was the end of it. But a few weeks ago, a sinkhole opened up in Siberia and fuck me, would you believe a whole goddamn nest of them were alive down there. They telepathically bonded to some local kids and the kid of a friend of mine. I went in to get them out."

"That would explain the Pegasus explosion on Yamal," Jones said, almost smiling.

"Right. Problem is, we weren't the only ones who knew about the creatures. We've been hit several times by outdated or retired terrorist cells—Aum Shinrikyo, the MYM in Somalia, the RAF in Germany. I think there's a puppet master, someone at the top. They might have even funded the Green and Red Societies back then. Now, I think they're using ECHELON to track us and hit us wherever we go."

The MI5 agent rubbed his hands together. "You have any particular puppet master in mind?"

Teller shifted in his seat. "It's a long shot. But all the attackers had a tattoo—the number nine. My contact in the FSB thinks it's a group called the Nine Veils. Heard of them?"

That made the agent perk up. "Well now. That is interesting."

"You heard of them?"

Jones nodded. "Primarily they've been noted for possible stock market manipulation. Making a killing on some pretty high profile natural disasters and terrorist activities—but usually through stocks that might slip under the radar. Bottled water sales go through the roof after a natural disaster. Anti-radiation tablet stocks soared after the Japanese nuclear power station meltdown. There's a parent company buying these stocks before the event, and we'd linked them to a group called the Nine Veils. But it was only ever a link."

"Well, can we see if they're using ECHELON? It might even be how they're aware of events before anyone else. Tracking terrorist activity through the system."

"Or instigating it themselves," Jones said.

"Can we shut it down?"

"No, don't do that." A woman stepped into the room.

"Madam Secretary," Teller said standing up.

"Secretary Taylor," Jones said, and also stood to offer his hand. "A pleasure."

"You made it," Teller said. "The boys at BAS figured they would set up an official investigation out here in Europe, if I could prove these bastards are using ECHELON."

Lucy nodded. "We're officially on mission now, Mr. Teller. That terrorist group, whoever they are, destroying a government plane and attacking civilians in Washington was enough for the President. You have full leverage and support."

Teller sighed. "Great. That's great." Maybe now he could actually do something for Freya. "But if we're not shutting down ECHELON, what are we doing?"

Lucy nodded. "We need to trace the breech to the source. Find out where they are coming from."

"But the longer the system is up, Freya and the children can be tracked. We're putting them in danger."

"Using them as bait, more like," Jones interjected.

Lucy shook her head. "No, we can send a rescue team to help them. Where are they headed, Mr. Teller? We need to get to them before someone else does. But if we leave ECHELON running, we can catch these monsters, too."

Jonathan stared at the secretary and then at Jones. Leaving ECHELON running could mean they can catch the Nine Veils and perhaps save millions of lives down the road. At the same time, he was risking Freya and the children. Even if they didn't use the sat phone, every communication by everyone else around them could leave clues, ripples in data that signified where Freya was on her journey. *The needs of the few.* Freya hated it when he said that. *Think with your heart,* she'd say.

"I'll lead the rescue mission," Teller said. "You don't need me here, right? Give me a team and the resources."

The Secretary nodded. "Done. Now tell me where they're

going."

"Antarctica. They're going to Antarctica."

Location: en route to La Reunion

The commander—Lauder—had been right. The Batonga had not only been friendly, they'd also been a help.

Catherine had observed them preparing something for Freya, made from some sort of bark. Freya had swallowed the strange concoction with some effort. Whatever it was, it had calmed her somewhat, which was no bad thing. The woman would snap if she was any more highly strung.

But more importantly, with a little chivvying, the tribes' people had given them a contact who had several fishing boats. Under the cover of night, Lauder had led the zoo of Nenets, soldiers, and Huahuqui on the short journey to the Quelamine port. With no more than a few hundred American dollars, he'd then bartered them passage on ramshackle vessels, with captains who asked few questions and were willing enough to head out past Madagascar to the island of La Reunion. Of course, the port was as far as Lauder could come, and so once again the ragtag band was on its own. And once again, Catherine felt like an outsider.

She had not been allowed to travel with the others. Instead she'd been stuck on a boat for two days straight with a bunch of the Nenets elders, one of Tony's men, who she learned was named Tribble, and a few of the Huahuqui—including the one everyone referred to as Freckles.

While Freya had seemed to accept the bond between KJ and K'awin, she had refused to allow Freckles to be too close. Catherine studied the creature through the lens of the camera and took a few snaps. It looked positively deflated, like a lover who had been rejected and had no means of moving on. Catherine had tried cheering up the animal, stroking it and feeding it pieces of fruit from her pack. But each stroke of the animal only told Catherine the same sad story: Freckles only had eyes for Freya.

Catherine sighed and laid back on the sack of god-knows-what that she was using as a pillow. Above, the stars were clear and bright. Without the light pollution from a major city, Catherine could trace the purple and blue streaks that made up the Milky Way. It was truly beautiful. Out here, it was so clear to understand her place in the world. To see what their planet could be like without humankind doing what it does best—pillaging it for all it can give. Being here with the Huahuqui, who were so in tune with the environment, and even the children, was an honor. One that she wasn't going to waste.

The Mozambique fisherman who captained their boat waved his large hand in her face, ruining her moment of reflection. Irritated, Catherine sat up. He pointed ahead to a dark coastline. It was La Reunion. The plan was to approach at night and steal a vessel called the Marion Dufresne. And Catherine was a lynchpin in the scheme.

The small fishing boats were guided to an empty part of the fisherman's wharf just south of the entrance. Catherine jumped out onto the pontoon and made her way to the lead vessel. There, Freya and Sasha met her. Tony and Minya were to stay with the children and the Huahuqui until signaled.

Catherine, Sasha and Freya marched up to the locked gate to the marina. The fisherman had told them that *Pointe Les Galets* had a single night guard who patrolled, and although there was supposed to be twenty-four-hour surveillance, it wasn't vigilantly monitored. In fact, there had been a series of night break-ins on private yachts. And Catherine was the reporter there to cover the story.

On cue, the night guard arrived and noticed the trio of foreigners by the gate. He walked calmly up to them with a gentle smile on his weathered face. Easily fifty years old, he had the composure of man who had seen most things and was used to meeting strangers in the night.

"Forgot to register with the Port Office?" he said, a French lilt accenting his words.

"Yeah," said Catherine. "We just came from the mainland. Got a tip off that you have a robbery happening tonight. On an important ship. We didn't have time to register and it took a while to get here. I'm with the press." She flashed her badge at him.

"A robbery? Really?" The night guard frowned.

"Uh-huh." Catherine nodded. "It's all on a bigger story on the increase in piracy in the area. Can we speak with the Marina Manager?"

The guard shook his head. "He's gone home for the night."

Catherine shot Freya a worried glance. Freya just stared at her, willing Catherine to keep pressing.

"Look," Catherine said. "I know it would be standard that we go wait on the boat and then register in the morning. But, this robbery will happen tonight. And I'm sure you don't want to be the guard who let that happen on your shift. You let us in and you can take the credit. I just want the story."

The guard shuffled on the spot, then pulled out a set of keys that jangled on a ring. He slid a key into the lock and opened the gate. "Okay, show me."

Catherine exhaled hard. "Great, you're gonna be a hero. It's the Marion Dufresne. Can you take us to it? We'll hide on board with my film crew and catch them in the act."

The guard nodded and led them past the Port Captain's office, which resembled the Sydney Opera House, to the other side of the marina. He unlocked a second gate and led them down the pontoon to the large research vessel. Catherine stared up at it.

"It's almost brand new, you know," the guard said. "Maybe that's why these pirates want to steal something from it. The company who owns it; they scrapped the existing equipment, rebuilt the hull, and installed a new gondola and control room. The hull was blasted and repainted as well as some of the ballast tanks. It can accommodate more than one-hundred passengers and forty-six crew."

"Fascinating," Catherine said, rolling her eyes.

"Maybe, you should take a picture of me in front of it," the guard said. "Actually, where's your camera?" He searched the trio, a frown forming across his brow.

Catherine didn't even have time to respond before Freya had launched on the man and pistol whipped him. He slumped to the ground, unconscious.

"Damn, that looked painful," Catherine said.

"He'll be fine," Freya replied rummaging in the man's pockets for the keys. "Here, take these."

Catherine caught the jangling ring mid-air.

"Go get the others and the Huahuqui. Sasha and I will start the engines and get us the hell out of here."

"And him?" Catherine said, nodding at the unconscious guard.

"Well put him near the Port Captain's Office. He'll be fine."

Catherine nodded, then ran off back to the wharf. As she crossed the marina, she thought she saw lights flashing out to sea.

Perhaps more boats? She stopped to stare into the dark, but the flashing was gone. She squinted and gazed for a few more seconds, then, satisfied it was nothing, restarted her jog back to the fishing boats.

Location: unknown

The Doyen stared at the display, lines of code and information streaming across the screen. ECHELON had been invaluable. Monitoring the petty conversations of the average human was time consuming, and infinitely boring. Hearing the mundane lives of ninety-nine percent of the Earth's inhabitants only fed his growing hatred and belief that only the one percent—those who had pierced the Ninth Veil—really deserved to live. But, the time spent was worth it. It meant he could know things about the world far sooner than even most governments, because while they were focused on key words that might shed light on a new threat to their security, he wasn't. He was listening for the tiniest ripples in data. The kind that gave him the edge.

The Fukushima nuclear meltdown was a perfect example. Following the Tōhoku earthquake, ECHELON began picking up communications from panicked workers that the active reactors had automatically shut down their sustained fission reactions. The staff were having problems with the emergency generators that would provide power to control and operate the pumps necessary to cool the reactors. The Western world had not concerned itself with a potential disaster in Japan.

So, his companies bought massive amounts of stock in anti-radiation tablets and apparel—stocks that were low in value since no major meltdowns had occurred since Chernobyl. Then, he just needed to give Fukushima a nudge. Aum Shinrikyo had been the perfect terrorist cell for the job. Defunct, low on watch lists and local. Ishii had been easy to buy with money and the promise of breathing new life into his pathetic belief system. And so, they had entered the facility and shut down the cooling pumps. It led to three nuclear meltdowns, hydrogen-air explosions, and the release of radioactive material across Asia and the Pacific—and his stock value skyrocketed. A massive profit, for little effort.

Of course, the making money was not his endgame. Money merely allowed him to build toward his greater dream. The one set back by the failure of the Shan Chu and death of the clone, K'in, five years earlier.

Now he was closer than ever. A whole nest of Huahuqui could accelerate the plans—if Takashi didn't fuck it up, like the Shan Chu and the Green and Red Societies had. Aum had outlived its usefulness. They had enough orphans now, and soon they would have the Huahuqui.

It was time to put down his dog. The sneaky Jap had tried to stay off the grid. Knowing that the Doyen had ECHELON, Takashi had done his best to hide. But the fool didn't understand how it worked. How the Doyen worked. Everyone left ripples in data, if you looked hard enough. Even if they were off the grid, their environment wasn't. Security cameras in a city. Someone taking a photograph with their cell phone and capturing the scene around them. A single word spoken in the background of a phone conversation. All of these fragments of information could be used to track a person.

"He left Africa, heading for Madagascar," said the woman at the Doyen's side in a soft, but firm, English accent.

"I know," he replied. "How long until the satellite is in range?"

"Not long. A few hours."

The Doyen clasped his hands together and created a steeple with his index fingers. "Good. As soon as you're able, activate it. We can't let him ruin our prize."

"Of course."

"Speaking of which, do we know where they are headed?"

"Given Takashi is likely chasing them, and the last co-ordinates we have for their location, our algorithms suggest they are headed for Antarctica."

"Clever girl, this Freya Nilsson. But this actually works in our favor. Send the GMTU to the most likely place in Antarctica they could go. A team of twenty out of South Africa should do it. Bring me back the Huahuqui."

"Yes, Doyen," the woman said. "My pleasure."

CHAPTER NINETEEN

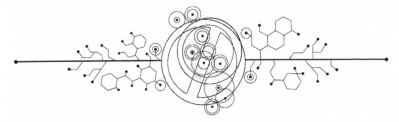

Location: RAF Base Menwith, Yorkshire, UK

The video feed from the commando's headset cam jerked and stuttered. Lucy tried to focus on the images that flashed and streaked across the large plasma screen as the soldier ran from one concealed position to another. Occasionally, he'd swing around to check his men were in line, giving instructions through hand signals only.

"What the hell? Cover your own sector, dammit," the commander hissed into his headset. *"Briggs, get that Jap in line. Fuck."*

"What's going on?" asked the secretary.

"The Japanese aren't following our lead," the soldier at the ops station replied. "They keep breaking formation."

"For God's sake. We don't have time to play who has the bigger dick," Lucy grumbled under her breath.

The special forces team had been pulled together from both U.S. and U.K. marines training in jungle and range techniques at Camp Schwab, in the northern city of Nago, and Camp Hansen, in the central Okinawan town of Kin. The fact that there was even British military training in the U.S. Marine camps had caused some controversy. The fifty-six-year old Japan-U.S. Security Treaty, under which Pentagon troops were stationed in Japan, did not technically provide for the training of foreign forces at U.S. bases there. Deploying US and British Marines on active duty while in Japan, was equally awkward. But they had tracked the source of the ECHELON tap to an office building in Misawa, Tohoku. The boys at Schwab and Hansen were the closest to the target. There was no time to pussyfoot around.

Lucy had made the appropriate calls and been allowed by the Japanese government to instigate a strike. A slight insinuation that Aum Shinrikyo was their responsibility had chivvied the result along. Losing face wasn't an option for the Japanese. However, to ensure all parties were happy, the strike team now also had Japanese military attached. It was not making for a coordinated attack, with the US—UK team and the Japanese team vying for leadership.

"Are they there yet?" Jones asked.

"Just approaching now, sir," replied the ops soldier.

"Good."

Lucy clasped her fingers together and rested them on her mouth, watching the scene unfold on the monitor. It was beyond frustrating. The commander's camera bobbed with his gait, until he was at the door to the office some twenty stories up. The view then spun one-hundred-eighty degrees as he put his back to the wall. Now the feed showed little but the dark of the narrow corridor and the blurry outline of his men lining the walls.

"Breacher up," the commander whispered.

A few moments later, another soldier emerged from the dark carrying a shotgun.

"On my count."

Lucy didn't hear the commander give a verbal count, but after three seconds the camera turned away and two ear-splitting shots were fired. The floor lit up with the blasts and then there was the sound of the door being kicked.

The video transmission once again became a chaotic blur. The breacher appeared to roll to the outside allowing the commander and another soldier on the opposite side of the corridor room to maneuver.

"Fire in the hole!"

"Move, move, move!"

A second later, two blinding flashes turned the monitor white and simultaneous bangs nearly destroyed the speakers in the observation room.

Lucy instinctively flinched and covered her ears.

"US Marines! Stand down!"

More chaos erupted on screen as the commander ploughed into the dark room, his headlamp swinging left and right. Boots stomped on the tiled floors and orders were shouted in English, followed by what Lucy could only assume was the translation by the Japanese soldiers.

And then, nothing but darkness and silence.

Location: aboard the Marion Dufresne II, *en route* to Antarctica

Sasha lay in his cot. It was the first time he had been alone since Yamal. The feeling was strange. While he would normally relish the time to think and to be away from brash Americans, he found himself feeling empty. He couldn't put a finger on why, or even what was supposed to fill the growing void in his chest.

Was it the Huahuqui? Was their mere presence enough to make him bond with a group of strangers?

Not that it mattered. He'd gone soft. Years of being a sleeper agent and a Captain in the FSB seemed to count for nothing when confronted with his past. His own pain as an orphan driving some deep-seated need to protect children. He had no brood of his own, fearing that he would be unable to be a good father. In his mind, never having a father had ensured he would not know how to fulfill the position. But, here and now, he had a chance to save the Nenets children and perhaps recover those stolen from the orphanages.

Sasha shook his head and swung his legs over the side of the cot. He hopped down and made his way to the upper deck. Outside, the air was crisp and cool. A brisk breeze blew from the East, dragging with it a storm that sat menacingly on the horizon. The occasional distant flash of lightning lit up a mass of clouds that obscured the night sky.

The Polkovnik ambled along the edge of the deck. As he approached the midway point, between the bridge and the forecastle, a light banging sound caught his attention. Sasha glanced around, but saw nothing. The banging noise came again. The Polkovnik leaned over the railing. Clanging against the hull was a small boat, tied off and without a passenger. Though difficult to see in the dark, there also seemed to be something else attached to the hull. *A box?* He fished around in his pocket for a flashlight. *What is that?* Sasha's eyes widened. *Plastic explosive?* He scanned the deck for a ladder down but found none. He spun on his heel, only to be met by a painful blow to the temple. The Polkovnik hit the deck hard, but instinctively rolled and avoided the boot than came smashing down where his head had just lain.

With a hard kick, Sasha took out his attacker's legs. The masked man fell backward into the railing but managed to stay upright. Sasha jumped to his feet and launched into an attack. The assailant parried away blow after blow then struck out, jabbing Sasha in the throat. The Polkovnik stumbled backward, clasping his neck. The attacker kicked Sasha in the chest, which sent him sprawling. Sasha, gasping for air, scrambled to his feet but another kick and he hit the deck again, his head ringing.

A blue flash streaked out of the dark, taking out the masked assailant. Sasha blinked away his concussion to see Chernoukh, the black-gilled Huahuqui, pinning the invader to the floor.

Sasha stepped forward, rubbing his neck, then dropped to his haunches and ripped off the man's mask. Angry Japanese eyes stared back at him.

"Who the fuck are you? Aum Shinrikyo?" Sasha shouted at him.

The Japanese man laughed. "Fuck you, Ruskie."

Sasha smacked him in the nose, which exploded with blood. "I'm not going to ask you again."

"You can't stop us," the Japanese man said. "Sōhō is coming. The end for you all."

"Who are you working for?" Sasha pulled the man's hair, jerking his head to the side. A black nine was tattooed behind his ear. Sasha let go of the man's scalp. "The Nine Veils. Is that who?"

The man choked a laugh. "We don't work for anyone, anymore. I, Takashi, lead Aum. We shall bring about the end times. Starting with you."

The man made a show of pulling a small cylindrical object from his pocket and held it up. He then pressed his thumb on a red button.

Nothing happened. A light rain began to splatter the deck as the storm drew closer.

"What is that?" Sasha screamed in his face. "What did you do?"

The man laughed again, and rolled his eyes to the railings.

Sasha stood and peered over the side. The gray lump of C4

now had a flashing red light. "Bastard. How do I turn it off?" Sasha pounced on the man and punched him in the mouth.

"Hey, what is problem?"

It was Nikolaj. He must have followed Chernoukh out from their quarters.

"Get inside, now! *Divay!*" Sasha yelled.

"What?" Nikolaj asked.

The Japanese man began to scream as if his very limbs were being ripped from his body. Chernoukh leapt off, panicked, and scurried back to Nikolaj. Sasha grabbed Takashi by the head, and tried to force him to focus. The attacker's skull was boiling hot. Sasha quickly dropped him. The man began clawing at his neck, tearing at the flesh behind his ear. The tattoo was glowing, the skin blistering and peeling away as Takashi screamed out in anguish.

"Nikolaj, get down!" Sasha dropped his body over the Japanese attacker.

The explosion ripped through the enemy's face and into Sasha's chest. His insides felt as though they had been melted and were pouring through the gaping hole in his rib cage. Sasha screamed and then, the pain was gone and only blackness remained.

"What the fuck was that?" Freya asked the dark of her room.

KJ stirred in his own bed on the opposite side of the space, but didn't wake. K'awin wrapped herself around him a little tighter.

Freya climbed out of her warm bed and pulled on a pair of boots and a jacket, then grabbed the Beretta from under her pillow and crept out. She cautiously tiptoed down the corridor.

A shadow snaked around the corner. Freya raised her Beretta.

"Who's there?" she called.

A man dressed entirely in black came stumbling toward her clutching at his chest. "*Tasukete! Tasukete!*" he cried.

Freya jerked her sidearm. "Hey, back up, man!"

The screaming man kept coming. He tore at the material of his clothing, revealing his naked chest. The number nine was branded into his bubbling skin, the wound glowing white. "*Tasukete!*" he screamed again.

Freya pumped two rounds into his head. He slumped to the floor, but his chest burst into flames. She instinctively turned to run back to the bunk. The force of the explosion behind shoved Freya into the bulkhead. She saved her skull with her forearms, then, head ringing, she stumbled back to KJ.

"KJ, get up, we have to go."

"What's going on, Mommy?"

"There's bad men on the boat, we have to go now." She scooped him up and held him to her chest. "You too, get up!" she screamed at K'awin.

The little Huahuqui scrambled to her feet, her panicked gaze flitting around the room.

"Follow me!" Freya yelled, then powered out of the bunk.

A deafening boom shook the ship, and the alarm began to sound. Freya was thrown to the floor but she managed to shield KJ with her arms. The sound of screeching metal tore into her eardrums as everything began to move.

Freya clambered back to her feet and sprinted down the corridor away from the wreckage left by the dead attacker.

The life boats were the only option. She had to make it. She slid and fell into the bulkhead every few steps as the ship came apart. Seawater began to fill the corridor that seemed to drop away from her—as if the nose of the ship were pointing down.

Freya climbed the stairs and burst out into the night air. A storm had enveloped the ship, thrashing it with wave after wave of pouring rain. Freya squeezed KJ as close as possible and slid toward the railings. She peered over the side.

Several bright orange lifeboats were in the water. They were partially enclosed, having a roof but open sides. From the nearest boat, Catherine, Nikolaj, and Tony were leaning out.

"Jump. We'll pick you up!" Catherine called up, though her voice was almost inaudible.

"Where's Minya? Nikolaj, where's your mother?" Freya shouted down.

"I don't know!" he cried back.

"Shit." Freya adjusted KJ, holding him with one hand and the railing with another. "Baby, we're gonna have to jump, okay? I'll hold on to you. We'll do it together."

"I don't wanna!" KJ cried.

She kissed him on the forehead. She may not survive the fall, but he would be wrapped up in her. "Please baby, you have to trust me."

K'awin nudged Freya's leg, then hopped up onto the railing. The animal stared into Freya's eyes willing her to understand. The creature would take him. Freya's heart beat fiercely. K'awin would be better at getting him there. The little Huahuqui would likely survive the fall better than Freya would. It was perhaps the only way.

"Freya!" came a voice over the storm.

Freya turned and wiped the sodden hair from her face. Minya was on her hands and knees climbing up the slippery deck toward her.

"Freya!" Minya cried again.

"Minya! I'm here!"

The Siberian clawed her way to Freya and then, clasping the railings, climbed to her feet. "I can't find Nikolaj!" she cried over the storm.

"He's down there! In the life boat!" Freya shouted back, her mouth filling with rainwater.

Minya peered over and sighed in relief.

"I need to get KJ down there," Freya yelled. "Can you help me? K'awin will take him."

Minya nodded, and climbed over the railings so that she was hanging on the other side. K'awin followed suit.

"You have to go baby, please!" Freya begged.

KJ clung to her neck even tighter, crying his heart out.

Freya stared into Minya's eyes, the stare of a mother: *please.*

Minya nodded, then began to pry KJ from Freya. KJ fought and cried, but eventually Minya managed to separate them.

The ship creaked and jerked forward, the nose diving into the ocean and the rear end pointing skyward—its exposed engines deafening as they churned nothing but air. K'awin slipped and fell into the cold sea below with a splash. Minya lost her footing and nearly dropped KJ, but managed to hold him with one arm, the railing with the other.

Freya leaned farther over the barrier. The lifeboat had now drifted too far away, the storm dragging it out to sea. She grabbed hold of Minya's wrist with one hand and reached over with her other for KJ. Minya lifted KJ just a little so that Freya could reach him. Freya clutched at his soaking wet shirt and held on.

"You have to climb back up, baby!" Freya said, but a rumble of thunder stole the words.

Minya's fingers slipped away from the railing. Freya tightened her grip on her friend now dangling above the angry ocean, and yelled in frustration. The metal railing dug into her ribs as she bore the full weight of Minya in one hand and KJ in the other.

"Baby, you gotta climb!" Freya called to KJ, but he continued to cry and hold onto her arm.

The ship shifted again, metal squealing on metal above the storm.

Freya's grip weakened, spasms in her arms and fingers beginning to form. She could only hold one of them.

Minya looked up at Freya, her eyes glassy and full of fear. Freya stared back, her heart pounding. And then, she made the only decision she could. "I'm sorry," she mouthed, and let go of Minya.

In what felt like slow motion, Minya fell in fear-stricken silence. Tumbling down, she smacked her head on the side of the ship several times before her limp body slapped the water's surface. Then she was sucked beneath the black waves.

Sobbing, Freya grabbed KJ's sleeve with her now free hand. "Baby, please you have to climb up."

A deafening boom of thunder and flash of lightning filled the air. KJ shrieked and thrashed. His shirt ripped and tore off in Freya's hands. Her heart hammered in her chest as she watched in horror as her son plummeted, screaming into the sea.

Freya had dropped them both.

The lifeboat rocked like a toy on the waves, deluged by heavy rain and battered by the squall. The roof offered some protection, but they couldn't close the sides yet. Not without looking for the others. Catherine scrambled from one side of the boat to the other, searching for Minya or KJ. There was nothing. "Fuck, fuck, fuck!" she screamed.

"Look!" Tony said.

As the Marion Dufresne sank, Catherine watched Freya try to stay above water by climbing to the aft portion of the vessel and scaling the oceanographic crane. "What is she doing?"

"We have to find my mother!" Nikolaj shouted. "Where is she?"

"I don't know!" Catherine screamed back. What the hell were they supposed to do? They couldn't find anything in this storm. Catherine clung to the side of the lifeboat, leaning out as far as she could as if it would help her see one more inch—an inch that would matter.

"She jumped!" Tony yelled.

Catherine shot her head up to see Freya, her arms across her chest, plummeting toward the ocean. A soundless splash and Freya disappeared from sight. Catherine stared wide-eyed, her breath held. Then, after a few moments, Freya resurfaced and Catherine exhaled.

"We need to get to her!"

"How?" Tony called back.

The lifeboat jerked forward. Once. Twice. Catherine searched the perimeter until she saw Freckles and several other Huahuqui pushing at the hull, aiding the weak outboard engine. They were driving them in the right direction.

"Yes! Thank you!" Catherine yelped.

Slowly the lifeboat stuttered against the waves toward where Freya had splash landed. A blue flash of skin at the surface caught Catherine's eye. Then again. K'awin burst from the sea and landed out of breath in the lifeboat. Catherine immediately pawed at the animal. It didn't seem to be hurt, but its arms were wrapped around something. The reporter peeled back K'awin's limbs. Clasped to her body was KJ.

Catherine pulled him away and listened for breathing.

He was unconscious, but alive.

Catherine yelped with joy. She tore off her jacket and wrapped it around the boy, before shoving him into the arms of one of the Nenets women. "Okay, now the others!"

As the lifeboat drew close enough, Freya dipped below the surface again. This time, she didn't come up. The blue, speckled, body of Freckles shot past and then disappeared beneath the waves. Catherine gripped the side of the lifeboat until her knuckles were white. She scanned the water, wiping away her sodden orange locks while the storm raged on.

"There!" Catherine said.

Closer to the Marion Dufresne, Freya reappeared, pushed up by Freckles. The woman seemed disorientated and totally unaware of who had just saved her. The reprieve was short-lived. With a screech so loud it could be heard above the storm, the oceanographic crane split under its own weight and crashed into the ocean beside Freya—and on top of Freckles. The creature's head caved in. The debris slipped into the ocean dragging Freya and Freckles's lifeless body with it into the deep.

"No!" Catherine cried out.

She clawed at the water, trying to paddle to where Freya had disappeared, but the storm was growing stronger. The wind dragged the lifeboat farther and farther away. Even the Huahuqui who had been pushing became tired and had to climb aboard to rest.

The lifeboat rocked back and forth, and the rain fell hard.

Tony held a searchlight over the water, but its pathetic beam of light lit up only the smallest of patches. Inch by inch, they drifted away until Catherine could only make out the silhouette of the Marion Dufresne, its nose in the ocean and its ass in the air. Breathless and defeated, she slumped back into the bow and closed her eyes.

"There!" Tony shouted. "She's there!"

Catherine jerked into action, her eyes wild, and scanned the area of ocean at which Tony had the searchlight pointed. Sure enough, there was Freya, floating face up.

K'awin came alive and dived back into the water to fetch Freya. The Huahuqui pushed Freya along until she reached the side of the lifeboat. Tony slipped his strong hand under Freya's armpit and pulled upward. She was lifted from the water and into the bow, panting, coughing, and twitching.

"KJ ... have to find KJ," Freya said.

"Cover her, someone cover her," Tony commanded.

"I got it," Catherine said, sliding the blanket over Freya. "Are there any more?"

"I don't think so. I only saw her," Tony shouted back.

Freya lay in the boat, covered in a thermal blanket, her eyes screwed shut. "I'm sorry, Kelly," she whispered. "Our son. I'm sorry ..."

"He's here, Freya. KJ is here," Catherine said.

But Freya didn't respond as she fell unconscious.

Location: RAF Base Menwith, Yorkshire, UK

"Sweet Jesus," the commander said. *"Base, are you seeing this?"*

Lucy did see it. She stared at the screen, her stomach in knots.

She opened her mouth to speak but bile rose in her throat, stealing her will to talk. "Steve …" was all she could manage.

"You know him?" Jones asked, his brow tight.

Lucy caught her breath and nodded. "His name is—was—Steven Chang. He was a friend."

In the center of the open plan office space, now lit by the overhead fluorescent strip lights, was a gnarled tree with a thick gray trunk and bushy green canopy that touched the ceiling some ten feet above. Coiled around the heavy stem was Steven—his spine, arms and legs broken to contort his body into the desired shape.

The commander stepped forward to examine the grotesque display. Now that he moved slowly, the feed from his camera was clear—too clear. Lucy could make out carefully carved scales in Steven's skin, his face wide-eyed and pallid, his jaw broken, as if to mimic the floating lower jaw of a snake.

Lucy coughed and vomited into her hands.

"Madam Secretary," Jones said, handing her a handkerchief. "You can leave, you don't need to see this."

Lucy wiped her mouth and hands. "No. No, I need to stay."

She forced herself to look back at the screen. *Steve, what did they do to you?*

"There's something in the branches of this tree," the commander said. *"A box."* He pointed to it, and his camera followed his gaze.

There in the lower branches of the tree was a wooden cube, each side around a foot long with a geometric pattern carved into it.

"What's that?" Lucy asked.

An barely audible conversation could be heard on the other end, the commander conversing in pidgin Japanese. Finally, he spoke into the microphone again. "Our friends here say it's a puzzle box. The last one they saw that looked like this took nearly four-hundred moves to open, and took months for a grandmaster to crack. I don't know if there's even something in here—an answer or a bomb. In fact, we're going to have to get the local bomb squad in here."

"Dammit," Lucy said, regaining her composure. "And there's nothing else? No server, nothing to indicate this is the source of the ECHELON breach?"

"Not a damn thing. There's probably a decoy hidden in here somewhere, but given our little gift here, this is just a way to waste our time. They were never here."

Lucy exhaled loudly and clenched her jaw. "Teller better be able to get to Freya before these sick bastards do—the Nine Veils. I'm going to personally make sure they pay for this."

Location: unknown

"The message has been delivered," the woman said. "To both parties—the Americans and our little Japanese friends. Takashi's team is dead."

"Good," replied the Doyen, a cruel smile spreading across his face. "The Americans will be deciphering our little gift for a while. And as for Takashi, I'm happy to hear the embedded chemical explosives worked well."

"They still managed to destroy a ship in the Southern Indian Ocean. Satellite imagery suggests it had the Huahuqui on board."

The Doyen paused, clasping his hands together in thought. "Are any survivors confirmed?"

"The satellite needs to pass over again to see. But, they are annoyingly resilient. I believe them to still be alive," the woman replied, her tone firm.

"Do not be angered at their ability to survive," the Doyen soothed. "This very fact is key to why we need them. You let your hate cloud the greater purpose."

The woman didn't respond.

"The Huahuqui are still alive, and their fearless leader will do the only thing she knows how: finish her mission. Keep the GMTU on target for Antarctica."

"Yes, Doyen."

The woman turned and left the leader of the Nine Veils in his dark room, save the faint blue glow emanating from his desk.

CHAPTER TWENTY

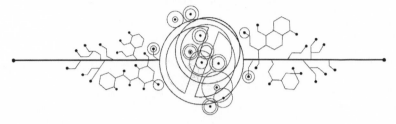

Location: Somewhere on the Southern Indian Ocean

Freya slowly opened her eyes to see a white, plastic ceiling. Her stomach churned as she rocked back and forth. It all came rushing back. She was pulled from the ocean into a lifeboat. Minya and KJ falling to their deaths flashed in her mind. Her heart cramped and she screwed her eyes closed. "KJ ..." she whispered.

"Mommy?"

Freya frowned and moaned. She could still hear his voice.

"Mommy?" came the voice again.

Freya's frown deepened and then she opened her eyes. There, hovering above her, was the small, pink, round face of her son— and then pushing her way in to see, the even fatter round face of K'awin. The creature panted like a dog and stared down at Freya.

"KJ?"

"Mommy!"

Her son threw his arms around her and squeezed harder than Freya could remember he had done in a long time. She hugged him back, clasping his tiny body to hers, and choked on her own sobbing. Her arms twitched and jerked, overpowered by her emotions.

"Are you okay, Mommy? You're shaking."

Freya sniffed back her tears. "I am now, Mr. Man."

"K'awin saved him," came a soft voice.

Still holding KJ, Freya pulled herself up to a sitting position and turned to see Catherine strapped into one of the sixteen seats next to Tony Franco.

"Practically drowned herself doing it from what I saw," the reporter said.

Freya cast her gaze at K'awin who sat close without interfering—as if the animal knew this was a mother-and-son moment. Freya gazed into the Huahuqui's gentle eyes, then opened her arms wide.

Unsure, K'awin blinked and smacked her tiny lips together a few times then edged forward. Freya put her arms around the animal and pulled her close, squishing KJ between them. A warmth and feeling of love spread through Freya. She hadn't lost him. He was alive. It was unbelievable.

But as the beautiful moment washed over her, Freya caught a glimpse of Nikolaj. He sat next to Chernoukh with his knees tucked up under his chin. He watched them with sad eyes. Freya broke her embrace, but held onto KJ and shuffled toward Nikolaj. She reached out to touch him, but he pulled back.

"I'm … I'm …" she began.

Nikolaj sniffled and studied her before speaking. "It is not your fault. You tried. It was accident." He seemed to want to stay put, but leaped forward into her arms and cried.

Freya hung onto his shaking form, guilt coursing its way through every fiber of her being. She opened her mouth, but no words came. What was she supposed to say? With both boys in her arms, Freya turned to see Catherine and Tony. "Thank you, for finding me. And my son."

Tony nodded. "We can't take all the credit. Freckles kept you from drowning, at least for a while. Then K'awin saved you."

Freya sighed and allowed a small smile, scanning the lifeboat for the little Huahuqui. In each seat was a Nenets, with a Huahuqui at their feet. But when she couldn't see Freckles, her gaze returned to a solemn-looking Tony. Freya's smile faded. She glanced at Catherine for an answer. The reporter just shook her head.

"Damn," Freya said under her breath.

"Where's Svetlana? And Ribka?" KJ asked.

"They're okay, KJ." Tony said. "They're on another lifeboat. I put them there myself."

Freya peered from the open side of the lifeboat. She hadn't noticed, but there were two others floating nearby. Both were carrying Huahuqui and Nenets. "What happened back there? How many did we lose?"

"I think it was Aum," Tony said. "They were planting C4 all over the ship. When the first explosion hit I had to get the lifeboats down. They're on manual release. I only managed three. Then I got as many of the kids and the Huahuqui off the ship as I could. The motors have kept us grouped, but they only run for twenty-four hours. We're about out of juice."

"We actually only lost a few people," Tony continued. "Important ones. Not that everyone's not important, but, well …"

"We lost Sasha and a couple of Tony's men, too," Catherine added.

Damn. Sasha. And Minya, because of me, Freya thought.

"Sasha saved me from man who exploded," Nikolaj piped up.

"Yeah, what was with that?" Freya asked, trying to focus.

"That's the weird part," Tony said. "They seemed to self-combust. Explode right in front of us. Their tattoos glowed, then *boom!* Minced Jap terrorist all over the walls."

"Sounds to me like their puppet masters didn't want them to blow us up," Catherine said.

"If that's right, the Nine Veils, or whoever these bastards are, are still after us. And we're sitting ducks," Freya said. "We'll never make it to Antarctica."

"But maybe we can make it there," Tony said, motioning to behind Freya.

A few miles off the port bow was a series of small islands, the ocean chop around them stronger than where they currently sat.

"Any idea where *that* is, Tony?" Freya asked, shivering a little.

"From our last coordinates coming from La Reunion, I'm guessing those are the Kerguelen Islands."

"Any chance there'll be help there? Or a place to at least get supplies?" Catherine asked.

Tony shook his head. "They're among the most isolated places on Earth. The main island, Grande Terre, is surrounded by another three hundred smaller islands. There are no indigenous people, but I did hear there is a group of fifty or so scientists based in *Port-aux-Français*. Which is probably on that big island right there." He pointed to the closest and largest land mass.

"Then we head there," Freya said. "Use the last of the fuel."

As they approached the inlet, the sheer size and frozen bleakness of the island came into sharp focus. From the lifeboat Freya could see a gargantuan snow-covered peak, steep fjords and peninsulas. The main island appeared to be ringed by hundreds of smaller ones. Penguins stood on the shore like rows of soldiers and seals popped up from the ocean to investigate the bright orange boats. But there was no sign of people. Tony had mentioned these islands were also called the Desolation Islands. It was easy to see why.

Next to the gravelly shore, on a patch of short grass a few square miles across, sat a scattered collection of metal boxes and billets that barely passed as buildings. Freya surmised they must comprise the research station, though it appeared abandoned. Just like the large vessel tied up to the only pontoon.

The gravel crunched under the weight of the lifeboats as they came ashore. Satisfied they were stable, Freya wrapped up in the thermal blanket, locked KJ to her chest, and jumped down to the ground. She stretched her legs and groaned.

Catherine and Tony dropped down beside her.

Freya was about to suggest that the Huahuqui stay put, but they were already climbing out. They, too, probably need to stretch their limbs. Freya patted herself down for a Beretta but it was gone. "Hey Tony, you got a spare sidearm?" she called over her shoulder.

Tony shook his head. "Sorry, just this one." He lifted up his Glock.

"Damn, then I guess you take the vanguard."

Acknowledging the request, he signaled to the last of his men who had exited the other lifeboats. They took up the lead, weapons drawn, ensuring the children and Huahuqui were behind them. Carefully, the menagerie crept toward the dock.

From one of the small billets, an angry looking man in a thick wool hat and large jacket emerged waving his arms and shouting something in French. *"Qui êtes-vous? Que voulez-vous?"* But as he came closer, his pace slowed and his shouting stopped. Instead, his jaw slackened and he stared at the thirty or so giant blue axolotls padding across the gravel toward him. *"Que ... "* was all he could say.

"My name is Freya Nilsson," Freya called out without stopping. "We need your help."

"Who ... who are you? What, what are zose t'ings?" he stuttered in a thick Parisian accent.

Freya thought on her feet. These islands were isolated, and it was likely the scientists were also isolated. She could say anything she wanted. The remoteness of this place might also mean it would be difficult for the Nine Veils to track the Huahuqui.

"We were on the Marion Dufresne. We are on a mission from the US government, in collaboration with Russia, to relocate a recently discovered species to Antarctica. There was ... an accident. Our ship went down." It wasn't a total lie. The best lies had some truth.

"New species?" the Frenchman said, frowning with big black bushy eyebrows.

"Yes. They're called the Huahuqui, and they're quite sentient. They live in arctic conditions, and were found in a sinkhole in Siberia. But the political situation meant they couldn't stay. We are moving them."

Freya signaled for Tony and his men to lower their weapons.

"Zis is, remarkable," the scientist said, his curiosity driving him closer still. "Can zey speak? Do zey communicate?"

"They do," Freya said. "With each other, but also the children." She motioned to the Nenets. "Please, can you help us get to Antarctica?"

The man didn't speak, his gaze fixed on the Huahuqui.

A short Chinese man burst from the same billet that the Frenchman had come. "Pierre, what's happening here—"

Pierre turned, mouth still agape, to face the Chinese man. "Um, zese people are from America. Zey say zey are 'elping ... zese

… t'ings relocate to Antarctica."

"I'm Freya—"

"I know who you are," the Chinese man said, his face etched with disbelief and the faintest of smiles. "And I know what they are. But how? The only one was killed …"

"Wait, who are you?" Freya asked.

Tony raised his Glock, but Freya shook her head so he lowered it.

"My name is Yen," the man said. "For a long time, we fought to keep the knowledge bringer from the man you knew as the Shan Chu, or maybe Jia-nghù Tsai—though his real name was Masamune Sagane."

Freya's eyes widened. "You're with the Green and Red Societies? The good side, at least. With the scientists?"

Yen nodded. "Yes. I am."

Freya sighed, then laughed out loud. What were the chances of meeting an ally on Desolation Islands of all places? In the middle of nowhere, half frozen to death, they had found a friend. But not just any friend, someone who actually understood the Huahuqui.

"Who is this guy, Freya?" Tony asked.

"That's a long story."

"Yes, it is. Come," Yen said, beckoning them. "Come inside. We need to get you warm, and you need to tell me everything that's happened."

Freya nodded, shifted KJ on her chest, then marched after the little Chinese man. She allowed herself a small grin when she caught a glimpse of Pierre watching in silent awe as a train of strange blue creatures padded by, each one seeming to acknowledge him on their way.

It was surprisingly warm inside the metal shack that Pierre and Yen called home. The other scientists had left for the summer. The two remaining men were to hold the fort until the group returned in a month. Everyone was offered beans and bread, which they happily scoffed down. KJ sat with Svetlana and Nikolaj, and talked among themselves, but in Aymara, so only they could understand. Of course, their Huahuqui were right beside them.

Freya spent nearly two hours explaining what had happened over the past few weeks. Yen sat calmly, absorbing all of the information and occasionally asked a question or two to clarify his understanding. Pierre, on the other hand, said nothing. He simply stared at the Huahuqui with wide and fearful eyes. Once Freya had finished, she took the opportunity to finish her own meal, scooping up the beans with the bread and shoving them into her mouth. *Kelly would be proud*, she thought.

"We had long wondered how Sagane had suddenly come into such money," Yen said. "Controlling a triad faction was one thing, but he had resources and the ability to infiltrate the highest places in our government. The plan to destroy the ozone above America with a nuclear weapon was too sophisticated for him. That must have been what his benefactor wanted. But it seemed he went rogue—chasing after the knowledge bringer clone on his own. When he was killed, we lost the ability to find out more."

Freya nodded. "We thought there may be some connection. The Nine Veils having a hand in what the Shan Chu was up to makes sense. They missed the opportunity last time. They're hell bent on finding us this time."

"Well, we can't let that happen, can we?" Yen said, smiling.

"So, you'll help us?" Freya asked.

"I will indeed. Can I ask where in Antarctica you were headed? Do you have a base?"

The question stabbed at Freya's mind. She hadn't considered that at all. Her only thought had been to get to the frozen continent—not what she would do once there. The thought caused her to laugh out loud.

"Something funny?" Tony asked.

It wasn't funny. But she felt like a joke. Her fear of losing KJ; her desire to keep him safe at all costs had made her impulsive and rash. She'd dragged KJ halfway around the world, sacrificed her best friend, and gotten countless people killed in the name of protecting her son. And with no plan of what to do when she arrived at Antarctica. Freya had become just like Kelly—all heart and no brains. Both Minya and Jonathan had tried to tell her and she didn't listen. Now Minya was dead, Jonathan had left, and KJ was in mortal danger. She needed to get a grip.

Freya's smile faded. "I don't have a specific place in mind. I guess I just needed to get there. I'm open to suggestions."

"Good, because I have an idea," Yen said. "Have you heard of Lake Vostok?"

Freya shook her head and glanced at Catherine and Tony. From the look on their faces, they hadn't heard of it either.

"Lake Vostok is actually subglacial. It sits four-thousand meters *under* the ice and can only be accessed because our team has been drilling there for years. Up until a few months ago, we were banned from drilling within four-hundred feet of the lake for fear of piercing it," Yen said, his voice rising with excitement. "You see, Vostok Lake was believed to be locked away for tens, maybe hundreds, of millions of years. It represented a climatologists and evolutionary biologists dream come true. Even NASA got involved."

"NASA?" Freya asked, her nose scrunched up. "And you said, up *until a few months ago*. What happened a few months ago?"

"Right, well, while Vostok is a goldmine to understand our history, it may also help us understand the future. Vostok Lake is believed to be representative of the conditions found in the oceans under Europa's frozen surface—you know, Jupiter's moon."

"What has this got to do with us, Yen?" Freya asked growing impatient.

"Yes, I'm getting there. At Caltech and the Jet Propulsion Labs, which design and operate most of NASA's planetary spacecraft, a team of six engineers developed a small metal probe called a cryobot that emits chemicals to create a sterile zone around itself, allowing it to burrow through the ice using a high-pressure jet of hot water to clear its path, take samples, and transmit collected data back to the surface. Against the advice of the head of SCAR, who said they were short sighted and would risk exposing the lake to surface contamination, they tested the cryobot. What they didn't expect to find was an environment. It's near perfect—arctic, wet, and well protected."

The Frenchman snorted. "Perfect? Vostok is an oligotrophic extreme environment."

"What the hell does that mean?" Tony asked.

"It's like ze ice-covered ocean of Jupiter's moon, Europa," Pierre replied.

"So, it's inhabitable?" Freya asked, her eyebrows raised.

"Not necessarily," Yen interjected. "We can probably hide you at the Russian Vostok base for a while. But to take advantage of Lake Vostok itself, we will need to create some kind of biome and acclimate it to the surface."

"What do you mean, acclimate?" Tony asked.

Yen shifted in his seat. "Normally, the water itself is supersaturated with nitrogen and oxygen—fifty times higher than found in ordinary freshwater lakes. And it's the coldest naturally occurring liquid water on Earth at -3 °C, below freezing temperature. A combination of the pressure from the continental ice above and geothermal heat from the Earth's interior keep it liquid. But now that we've broken through and created tunnels, the pressure will equalize somewhat. If we build a biome over it, we can control the acclimation."

"That's a long shot. It will take time and money and support from someone," Freya said, shaking her head.

"The whole thing is a long shot," Catherine piped up. "But what choice do we have?"

"And you forget that the Green and Red Societies are invested in this. We have money. No one can tell us not to build a biome over it. Antarctica isn't owned by anyone. The research can even still continue, if done right."

Freya searched the faces of the scientists, then Catherine and Tony. They stared back, waiting on her leadership. *Minya died for this. Sasha died for this.* She cast her gaze to KJ. He sat with one arm around Nikolaj. KJ would never be safe if she didn't take control of the situation. They had a potential base, fortressed like no other. Politically, no one could touch them on Antarctica. And now, she even had financial backing from the Green and Red Societies.

"Do you have enough thermal gear for all of us?" Freya asked.

Yen nodded.

"So how do we get there?" Tony asked.

Pierre pulled out a crinkled map and laid it on the floor. Using a thick red marker, he circled their location on the Kerguelen Islands, then drew a line across a short stretch of the Southern Ocean to a small settlement on the closest coast of Antarctica, before squeaking the pen to Vostok station inland. From the simple sketch, it seemed like a short, straight route.

"That's not so bad," Tony said.

The Frenchman snorted.

Pierre began tracing his finger along the line. "We take our research vessel, and head for Mirny, here, on the coast. That's two-thousand kilometers in arctic conditions. With our boat's speed, that's a three-day journey at best. Then a land transport route to Vostok. That's another two days of travel."

Freya sighed. "Jesus, can't we just fly?"

Yen shook his head with a smile. "Not if you want to stay off the radar, but don't worry, you're in good hands. I'll get a message ahead to the station to expect us. I'll keep it ... discreet. You take your time to recoup on the trip, and to acclimate. You'll need to. Vostok is the coldest place on Earth."

CHAPTER TWENTY-ONE

Location: Hercules Plane over South Africa

It was taking too damn long to get there.

Jonathan tapped his feet in the hold of the Hercules. He was surrounded by his crack team of twenty men, decked out in arctic combat gear—everything from their ballistic helmets to their assault rifles painted in avalanche white and blue to disappear into the snow if needed.

He didn't doubt the skill of his men. They could do their job. But was twenty enough? What kind of force would be hounding Freya? Until recently, the Nine Veils had been puppeteers. But now—now they'd made a bold move. They'd made a statement. Lucy had been frantic in her last transmission. An orchestrated display provided by those sickos for the strike team to find—the body of her murdered friend. The Nine Veils were no longer willing to wait in the dark.

The question was: why make that move now? They didn't have the Huahuqui, did they? Was he already too late? Or were they so confident that they would obtain their prize. There was no word from Freya or Tony. For all Jonathan knew, he was hurtling toward Antarctica to find the dead body of the woman he loved.

Teller checked his watch. By his calculations, they were just over South Africa. Pulling the team together and insisting on leading it had cost him time—cost Freya time.

"Sir, satellite imagery has picked up a ship on the northern coast of Antarctica," came the pilot's voice over the headset. *"Seems to be a research vessel docked at Mirny. HQ says no research vessels due at Mirny for another month. Could be our guys."*

"Roger that," Jonathan said.

That was positive. They'd picked up a ship. Freya might be safe after all.

"There's something else though, sir."

The contents of Teller's stomach seemed to rise. "What do you have?"

"Another ship, heading for Mirny—fast. Definitely not a research vessel, sir. It's strange, almost didn't pick it up."

There is was. Confirmation Freya was being chased.   By someone in a stealth vessel no less. And they were a damn sight closer to her than he was. Leaving her had been a mistake. He should be there now, with her. Instead, he'd run off to solve the puzzle. *Head over heart*, that's what she'd said. Freya was right. He couldn't let the job go, and now she might pay the ultimate price.

Jonathan clenched his jaw and yanked in frustration on the safety harness.

"Sir?"

"Just make this damn thing go faster."

Location: Mirny-Vostok Route, Antarctica

The three-day trip from the Kerugelen Islands to Mirny had been uneventful—in that they had not been attacked. The ocean chop and unforgiving ice were near unbearable, rivaled only by her constantly convulsing, seasick stomach. The ship crested and fell from waves as tall as buildings.

Yet, against the elements everyone else seemed to forge ahead and focus on the last leg of their journey. The scientists learned all they could about the Huahuqui, taking pictures and studying their morphology, while Freya and Tony crouched over a map of Antarctica, talking with intensity about their plan of action upon arrival at Vostok. Catherine had wanted to join in and ask questions, even offer help, but she still felt unwelcome, and as they approached the coast of Antarctica, a paralyzing bitter cold had crept over everything and everyone. In the end, it drained all desire to converse.

Although clad head to toe in black arctic gear, supposedly wind and snow proof, Catherine shuddered for the hundredth time. The cold seeped deep into her bones and made its home there such that no amount of rubbing her arms and legs made the slightest difference. She sat with the rest of the ragtag band in the hermetically sealed Kharkovtchanka, a giant, ex-soviet monstrosity of a truck riding on two enormous treads, as they powered through another snowstorm along the well-worn route from Mirny to Vostok.

The Huahuqui huddled together with their children in one giant heap, keeping each other as warm as possible. Even for these Yamal-adapted creatures, Antarctica appeared to be a little too much. Pierre and Yen had covered them in thermal blankets just to be sure. Freya even accepted the invitation to snuggle in, and was asleep tangled up with K'awin and KJ. Catherine studied Freya's twitching arms and legs. The jerking may have been mistaken for Freya dreaming, perhaps reliving the death of her friend, but Catherine had seen her ability to control her limbs gradually fail over the past few weeks. Something else was at play.

Only Tony Franco remained awake. He was always awake. Possibly the most dedicated man she'd ever seen. Like a loyal dog, he did his duty and never seemed to want recognition for it. He'd gotten them from Yamal to here, and taken a bullet in the process. And not once had he complained. He followed instruction from Freya, Teller, and even Sasha—when he was alive. He was a man without an ego. Was that even possible?

"Something on your mind there, O'Conner?" he asked, with a slight smirk.

Crap, was I staring? Catherine thought. "I was just considering how lucky we are to have you along with us. I don't think I've ever said thank you."

Tony shrugged. "Just doing my duty, Ma'am."

"But it's not just your duty, though, is it? This is far beyond your duty."

"I disagree," he said, though his tone carried no threat of an impending argument. "Teller gave me instructions to protect Freya and the kid. And that's what I'm doing, 'cause he'd do it for me. It's a code. You protect your team no matter what, including orders from above—though I screwed that up on the boat from La Reunion. Our giant salamander friends over there saved the day."

"You're doing a good job, Tony." Catherine smiled, although it broke into a fresh bout of teeth chattering. "You never told me what you think about the whole Huahuqui thing. Our *salamander friends*, as you call them."

Tony seemed to muse on this for a moment. "I'm not sure what I think, to be honest. They seem to be harmless. And the kids are attached to them, ya know? They seem happy. My life was a bit fucked up when I was a kid. Grew up in West Philly. Could have used a friend—even a big wet one—once in a while."

Catherine laughed.

"Besides. Isn't it our job to protect kids? Isn't it why we go to war? To make sure our kids have a safe future?"

"Never thought of war that way," Catherine said. "You have kids?"

Tony shook his head. "Nah, married to the business. Though right now, I feel like I adopted a few."

"Can I ask you a question? I didn't want to interrupt you and Freya before."

He clapped and rubbed his gloved hands together. "Shoot."

"What were you and Freya talking about on the boat. You were sketching something out on the map."

"Phase lines," he said without skipping a beat.

"Phase lines?"

He nodded. "Yeah. Look, so far, these Nine Veil bastards have been able to nail us at almost every turn. You think they won't be able to get to us at Vostok?"

That's exactly what Catherine had thought. It's why she'd suggested Antarctica in the first place. Politically neutral. No military presence. Remote. "They'd come after us there?"

"You gotta assume that. And we have no idea when, or if, help is coming. According to the scientists, Vostok is a small collection of box-like structures and some machinery—drills and trucks. There's two ways in and out. Along this route, and by plane or helicopter from the West. If we just sit there and wait, we're boxed in with nowhere to go. So, we have to build in phase lines—points at set distances from the main camp that can be used to slow down the enemy and hopefully take out some of their people before they get to the kids and Huahuqui holing up at the station."

"You're talking about booby traps?"

"Kinda, yeah. We have a few of my guys here, but that's it. So, we need to improvise. We talked to the scientists. There's some machinery we can use, and this big-assed box on wheels, too." He motioned to the inside of the Kharkovtchanka.

A knot formed in Catherine's stomach. "Can I help?"

"I don't know, can you?" Freya pried herself carefully from the huddle, ensuring her son stayed asleep.

"Hey, look I just wanna help—"

"I know you do," Freya said. "I'm genuinely asking you."

Catherine stared at the woman, studying those big green eyes that studied her right back.

"Look, I was a bitch," Freya said. "I'm sorry. You've helped a few times now and I haven't acknowledged it. I can't afford to ignore any suggestions right now. If you think you have an idea, I want to hear it."

Catherine swallowed the dry lump in her throat. She did have half an idea. "You heard of RTGs?"

Freya and Tony shook their heads, breath misting the air.

"Right, well you know I was involved in environmental journalism. A while back there was a big *hoo ha* about radioisotope thermoelectric generators, RTGs, which were delivered to Antarctica at the end of the 1970s as a component of unattended automatic geophysical stations. The environmental agencies got involved and wanted a complete inventory of where they were, and to even remove them."

"What are they based on, these RTGs?" Freya asked.

"Strontium-90 is the isotope of choice. Produced from nuclear fission. It's a beta emitter. There have been dozens of cases of radiation poisoning in Russia from civilians coming across abandoned RTGs. It's a big deal."

"Can we do anything with that, Tony?" Freya asked.

He rubbed his chin in thought. "Well, we can rig up a dirty bomb maybe? The explosion would be bigger than normal. Give us a wider kill zone. But the radiation wouldn't kill anyone immediately—if at all. We ain't got time to wait a few days for them to start throwing up from sickness. Maybe if we make it easy to see, it'll help slow them down. Psychological warfare. We put it out on the only road in and out for them to see and feel they have to dismantle."

"It's better than nothing," Freya said.

"You know …" Yen said, from the corner. Catherine hadn't noticed he was awake. "We would have passed an RTG a kilometer or two back. There's an old one just off the main route."

Tony stood, pulled his hood over his head and zipped up his thick coat. "Then let's stop this thing and let me out. I'll rig the RTG and then make it back to you. I'll even see if I can set a few traps on the trek back to Vostok."

"Take ze snowmobile from ze trailer," Pierre said. "It'll be faster."

"Sure. Private, you're with me." Tony pointed to one of the remaining six members of his crew, who immediately stood and waited.

The Kharkovtchanka ground to a halt, and the rear door squealed open. The bitter wind blew into the hold, stabbing at the exposed faces of the occupants.

Catherine took a sharp breath. "Jesus fuck, that's cold."

"Okay, I'm out. I'll meet you at the station." With that, he and the private jumped down into the snow and slammed the door shut with a *clang*.

The ruckus outside indicated the snowmobile was being pulled off the trailer, then the engines of the Kharkovtchanka roared to life and they once again began to trundle at thirty kilometers an hour toward Lake Vostok.

Catherine rubbed her arms and searched for eye contact with Freya.

"Something else?" Freya asked.

"Look, you and I aren't the best of friends, and you don't have to answer me, but are you sick? The shaking is becoming worse."

Freya examined her hands, opening and closing her fists. "Yeah, I am," she said without looking up.

"How sick?"

Freya checked to see that KJ was asleep before speaking. "Sick. Ten months, ten years. No one knows."

"There's nothing to be done?"

Freya shook her head.

"I'm sorry."

"So am I. Right now, I can't think about it. We need to fortify the station. Those bastards are coming for these kids, my kid. And I wanna be ready."

CHAPTER TWENTY-TWO

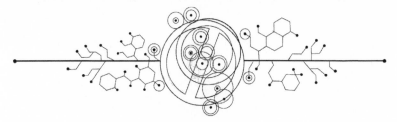

Location: Vostok Lake, Antarctica

It was worse than Freya had imagined. The idea of bringing the Huahuqui and the Nenets children, and KJ, to this frozen desert had seemed logical. But now that they were here, it seemed like the biggest mistake of her life. KJ clung to her chest for warmth. Every time another gust blew by, KJ gripped her like a vice and squealed through the thick scarf wrapped around his face. Freya rubbed and patted and did everything she could to warm him, though her arms were tired and the twitching was only becoming stronger.

She surveyed their supposed haven. A barren frozen wasteland, a flat, white desert capped by a bright blue sky. The only visible rocks within hundreds of miles were small black pebbles—the remnants of shooting stars, according to Pierre. Freya scooped one up.

"Here, Mr. Man. This is a shooting star that fell to Earth."

He pried himself away from her chest long enough to take and inspect it through the ill-fitting goggles on his face. "Like the ones we wish on?" he asked, teeth chattering.

"Yes, baby. Make a wish."

KJ rested his hood-covered head against her chest again. "I wish you to get better, Mommy," he whispered.

Freya's chest tightened and tears welled up. He knew? Of course he knew. He was smart. Trying to hide it from him was another mistake. Freya seemed to be making a lot of them. She opened her mouth to tell him she'd be okay, but it was a lie. And he deserved more. So, instead, she said nothing and hugged him tighter.

"We need to go in," said Yen. "We'll leave the kids in the Kharkovtchanka." He then marched past a graveyard of abandoned machinery toward the drill housing.

Freya nodded, cleared her throat, and followed him.

Inside it was a little warmer. KJ slid off her chest and meandered around, inspecting the tiny dark room. He stopped and examined a wall with champagne corks stuck it. Next to each one was a depth recorded in permanent marker. The last one said, "breakthrough 2017".

Yen shook the hand of the only man in the room. "This is Francois. Francois, this is Freya Nilsson."

"Bonjour," the thin man said. His eyes were ice blue and as cold as the world around them.

"Bonjour," Freya replied. "Thank you for taking us in."

"I'm not sure what else we could do," he replied, his tone flat.

"I'm sorry for bringing this to you. We really had no choice."

"So now what?" Francois asked, rubbing his short gray hair.

"How many of you are here right now?" Freya asked.

"Five. Me, a couple of Russians, and two Chinese scientists."

Freya frowned. "I thought there were thirty or so?"

Francois shrugged. "Depends. Sometimes yes, sometimes not. Now, we're five."

"Okay, we don't have time to waste," Freya said. "Is there any way to fortify this place, in case we're attacked?"

"Attacked?" The color drained from Francois's face.

Yen placed a hand on the man's shoulder. "I told you what, who, we have with us. And some people want to take them. We need to find a way to protect them."

Freya nodded. "Right? Yen said something about the lake being protected? Below the ice?"

Francois shook his head. "There's no way to get down there. We broke through, but the passage is only big enough for our probes. No way to get people down there. That'll take months of digging."

"Goddammit," Freya said, clenching her jaw.

A distant boom sounded outside.

"What the hell was that?" Francois asked.

Freya shot Yen a worried glance. "Tony?"

Yen nodded. "The RTG."

Freya scooped up KJ and pushed through the old brown door. Against the brilliant blue sky, a pillar of black smoke rose into the air. She stared, unable to think or move. They were coming.

The drone of a snowmobile engine grew louder. Tony burst over a small snow drift, his vehicle lifted into the air and then crashed hard into the ground. He waved his arms, shouting at them. "They're coming!"

Freya jerked to life. Instinctively, she ran straight for the Kharkovtchanka and yanked on the door and climbed inside. She placed KJ on the floor next to K'awin, and dropped to her haunches to stare the little creature in its big blue eyes. She placed her hand on its head, and felt a wash of emotion—fear and confusion—pulsate up her arm and into her body.

"You take care of him, you understand me? Keep him in here. It's the safest place to be. Do you understand me? I need you ...

K'awin … please."

The little Huahuqui ruffled her gills and padded closer to KJ taking him in her stubby arms. She smacked her lips together. The emotion changed from fear to determination and Freya could feel she was understood.

"Thank you," she whispered, before taking her hand from the creature and placing it on the cheek of her son. "I love you, Kelly Junior. Never forget it. Stay in here. Look after the other kids for me, okay?"

KJs eyes were aglow again, his proximity to K'awin and the other Huahuqui already manifesting its effect. "Okay, Mommy. Protect the other kids."

Freya kissed him on the forehead, then stood and beckoned the last four of Tony's men to follow her.

"What about me?" Catherine asked.

"Stay here with them. Make sure they stay put," Freya said. Then added, "Please, keep them in here."

Catherine nodded.

Freya and the soldiers dashed out the door, slamming it behind them, and joined the gathering group outside where Tony had just pulled up.

"We build a perimeter," Tony said, out of breath to the group huddled by the drill. "There's three WWII trucks at the back of the station. We pull them around to cover us between the East Camp and the old aircraft radar building."

Freya nodded. "They're coming down the Mirny-Vostok route. It's a funnel. We can try and pick off as many as we can from the safety of the trucks. Yen, you take Pierre, Francois, and the rest of the scientists to the generator building. Lock yourself inside and stay there."

"Pierre will do that. I want to help," Yen said.

"Help how? We don't have time for this."

"The cryobot. It uses a laser. It'll be a bit like a short-range sniper rifle from here. I can operate it. Just put me on the back of a truck."

"Fine. Okay," Freya said. "Pierre, you take them."

The Frenchman nodded and scurried off with the remainder of the station scientists.

"Should we have given them a gun?" Yen asked.

"Can't spare one," Tony said cocking his rifle. "We need everything we have. By the way, I laid a few mines in the deep trenches left by these trucks a couple clicks out. The snowmobiles get stuck in them, too. Should help slow things down a little."

"And then we just pick them off," Freya said. "Did you see how many there were?"

Tony shook his head. "No idea. They were in Trekol-like vehicles. Must have been dropped from a ship or plane near the coast."

"Okay move, let's go," Freya ordered.

The team scattered. Tony's men ran off to the last phase line. Freya took one truck, while Tony and Yen stole the remaining two. They started the gigantic engines, black smoke puffing from the exhausts, and steered the heavy vehicles into a semi-circle around the station, facing the only route in.

They killed the engines and clambered into the flatbed-backs.

Freya lay on her stomach, the sight of her rifle pressed against her right eye.

On the horizon, like an army of black ants, they came. Five or six Trekol-like vehicles speeding toward them. Unlike the monstrosity she had come in, the enemy vehicles pounced and sprang over the terrain like gazelles on the Serengeti. Freya slowed her breathing, and tried to stop her hands from twitching, but the view in her sight kept skipping with each micro movement of her fingers. They'd need to be a lot closer for her to hit them.

One of the trucks struck a landmine. The explosion was deafening. The vehicle upended and flew into the air before crashing into a useless heap in the snow. A whoop from Tony's truck hailed his delight. Through her sight, Freya spied several soldiers climbing out of the wreckage and then stomping toward her as if they had sustained no injury at all.

"Come on you bastards," she whispered.

"You see them?" came Tony's voice over the walkie-talkie.

"I see them," Freya replied.

"They're half a mile ahead," came another voice. Freya didn't know his name. One of Tony's crew at the last phase line.

The black vehicles drew closer, then ground to a halt. Each vehicle released four or five soldiers dressed in arctic combat gear. They fanned out and came straight for them. The vehicles began rolling forward again.

"Take those bastards out, Xavier," Tony ordered.

"Affirmative. Rock and roll, boy—" The line squealed and the transmission ended in a mix of cries and gunfire.

"Xavier? Xavier!" Tony called through the walkie-talkie.

Nothing.

"Fuck, they were made."

Freya pulled the sight tighter to her eye and quickly scanned the horizon. The soldiers were still coming. Their faces were covered in a full-face helmet the likes Freya had never seen. She grabbed for her radio with one hand. "They're some kind of special ops. I'm not even sure if a head shot will do it. They'll have to be

263

at least half a mile closer."

"*Affirmative.*"

Freya watched intently as the figures became larger in her sight. They walked in straight lines with the vehicles bringing up the rear. Slowly and purposefully, they marched forward.

Freya clenched her jaw. "Can't wait any longer." She levelled the cross hairs on the head of the closest soldier and squeezed the trigger.

Crack!

Not even close. The snow at the soldier's feet puffed up as the bullet struck.

As if able to determine exactly where the shot had come from, the enemy soldier and three others around him, raised their weapons and showered Freya's truck in ammunition.

"Jesus, is my position that obvious?"

"*I got your back,*" Tony said, his voice crackling over the walkie-talkie.

"*Here goes nothing!*" Yen said.

A series of well thought out shots fired from Tony's truck, mixed with ear-piercing squeals from Yen's laser. Most missed their target, but three soldiers went down hard.

"*Yahoo!*" Tony yelped over the radio.

A laser blast struck a soldier in the head, taking his helmet clean off and sending him sprawling into the snow.

"Good shot, Yen!" Freya said. She readjusted her sight to track where the enemy had gone down. The view was a little shaky from her trembling hands, but eventually she found him, dead, face up in a snow drift. *Oh God, no.* She grabbed the walkie. "Tony, Tony!"

"*What's up?*"

"Jesus, Tony, we have a problem. They're kids, Tony."

"What are you talking about?"

"They're fucking kids. Fifteen tops. I just saw one without his helmet!"

"Are you sure?"

Freya peered through her sight again, finding the fallen enemy. He was still there, his puppy fat-covered face spattered in blood. She screwed her eyes shut, wishing the image away. She grabbed for the radio. "I'm sure. Jesus, Tony. What do we do?"

A fresh bout of firepower rained down on her truck.

"We have to retaliate, Freya. They will kill us."

"But they're kids! How can we—"

The door to the Kharkovtchanka clanged open. Freya turned to see the Huahuqui, their children on their backs, spill out of the vehicle onto the ground and tear out in front of the station between the trucks and the enemy. At the very front was KJ, riding K'awin like a horse. Catherine came tearing after, screaming for them to come back.

Freya leapt to her feet. "KJ, what the hell do you think you're doing?"

Her son didn't respond.

The mass of creatures and child riders fanned out until they had formed into one long line in the shape of an arrow head—KJ and K'awin at its tip, with Svetlana and Ribka and Nikolaj and Chernoukh at its sides.

"KJ, get back here!" Freya leapt down from her truck and sprinted toward her son.

A strong electric blue haze enveloped the Huahuqui and the children as they began chanting in Aymara.

"Taqpach jaqejh khuskat uñjatatäpjhewa munañapansa, lurañapansa, amuyasiñapansa, ukatwa jilani sullkanípjhaspas ukham

uñjasipjhañapawa, " they chanted over and over.

Freya's movements became sluggish as she drew closer until she was unable to move at all, her limbs frozen. She could only stare, wide-eyed, as the air filled with the electricity pulsating from the children. Her focus was drawn to the oncoming soldiers. Like her, they had ground to a halt and seemed unable to move. They stood in regimented rows. A few removed their helmets in apparent awe, but once close enough were also frozen to the spot. Freya studied their young faces. A child army. Her stomach convulsed. She refocused on her son, but could only see the back of his head.

Then, something switched on inside Freya's head, and while the children's words were still Aymara, she could understand their meaning.

"All human beings are born free and equal in dignity and rights. They are endowed with reason and conscience and should act toward one another in a spirit of brotherhood."

They were reciting Article One of the Declaration of Human Rights. Could they really stop the soldiers? Could they convince them, through a bond, that all of this was wrong? Had Freya again underestimated her son?

Freya's limbs were allowed a little movement. She scanned the Huahuqui. The blue haze had faded, just slightly, but faded. It was too tiring. Keeping the hold on the soldiers. The children couldn't hold it.

"KJ!" Freya called out.

He turned to face her, his eyes glowing brighter than burning magnesium.

"KJ, baby, it's me—it's mommy. You can't hold this, and when you let go, they're gonna hurt you. Come to me, baby. Please." With great effort, Freya was able to lift her arms toward him.

"Mommy?" he said.

"Yes, Mr. Man—"

A thunderous drone filled the air. KJ turned away and looked to the sky, as did all the children and Huahuqui. Freya's ears burned with the sound and she too followed it to its source high above them.

Hurtling toward the ground was an LC130 Hercules plane, a large American flag adorning its fuselage. The plane crashed hard into the ground behind the line of soldiers, and crushed two of the enemy vehicles in its path. The enormous plane bounced like a toy against the hard ground, skidding and screeching, throwing snow, ice and black pebbles across the landscape.

"Jonathan," Freya said under her breath.

The Huahuqui scattered, the blue haze vanished, and the children screamed.

Freya ran for KJ. Dodging scared creatures and children, she ploughed on through the chaos. A helmetless child soldier sprinted for KJ's location. Freya reached her son first, tore him from K'awin's back and spun into a roundhouse kick that hit the boy soldier in the jaw. He tumbled to the ground but, unfazed, quickly climbed to his feet.

He came at Freya again.

"I don't want to hurt you!" she shouted at him.

He didn't answer.

K'awin leaped onto the boy and pinned him to the ground. The soldier fought and struggled but couldn't get up.

Freya turned around and headed for the Kharkovtchanka.

"Svetlana!" Nikolaj cried.

Freya spun around to see Svetlana and Ribka descended upon by five boy-fighters. They injected them both with something, and immediately their victims went limp.

"We have to save her!" KJ cried.

"I'll go back for her, but now I need you safe." She ran for their armored vehicle.

K'awin caught up beside them and effortlessly slipped under Freya, who grabbed one of the animal's gills with a free hand. The Huahuqui powered forward and leaped into the Kharkovtchanka leaving the fray behind them.

No sooner had she set KJ down, but the clanging of military boots sounded behind her. Freya spun and K'awin crouched defensively over KJ.

"Jonathan!" Freya threw her arms around his neck. "You came. How did you know where to come?"

"I'm a good guesser," he said, squeezing her tight.

Freya let go and stared at him. "We have to get the others. They're taking the children. But they're kids themselves, don't hurt them. Just, just stop them."

They peered from the doorway to survey the battlefield. It was already dissipating. The remaining Nine Veils soldiers had retreated and were boarding the last two vehicles. Freya watched, hanging on to KJ at her side, as Teller's force rounded up the Huahuqui and corralled them back toward East Camp.

Freya scanned the area, her heart pounding, mentally counting the Huahuqui. "That's not all of them, they've taken some. We have to go after them."

"In what Freya? I just crashed my bird into the ground. They've got those Trekol-looking things. We've got nothing that fast. We know who they are. We'll find them."

Freya's heart sank. She picked up KJ and held him on one hip, pressing him to her. From the safety of the Kharkovtchanka she watched, guilt ridden, as the enemy vehicles raced off into the distance. Her gaze fell to the remaining Huahuqui and children, milling around like lost sheep, crying and warbling at the loss of their family, Teller's soldiers doing their best to keep them penned in. Nikolaj stood beside Chernoukh, vacant and despondent.

"We have to find Svetlana, Mommy. She needs us," KJ said.

Freya turned to look her son in the eyes and held his chin in her shaking fingers. "We'll find her, baby, I promise. We'll find her."

EPILOGUE

Location: Alpha Base, Antarctica, one year later

Freya stared up at the crystal-clear polygons of glass that formed Biome One of Alpha Base, shielding them from the harsh Antarctic environment. It was now a scientific holy place akin to Mecca. Anonymous funding from the Green and Red Societies to ensure the Huahuqui had an official residence was then matched by the National Science Foundation in the US, the Natural Environment Research Council in the UK, and various other European organizations, working together under the Scientific Committee on Antarctic Research, to ensure that research could still be carried out in the lake below. The Huahuqui would assist in understanding the discoveries they made.

The Antarctic Treaty was dissolved. All member countries had agreed that this was the best place for the Huahuqui and the Nenets children. No more black boxing. No more experiments on them. Without even trying, the ancient knowledge bringers had brought nations together.

A new treaty had been signed: The Rubicon Accords. A fitting name. There was no going back. A line had been crossed. The Huahuqui were now part of the world again—for better or worse. It was a future that scared the living hell out of Freya. Her son, KJ, was at the very front of this new world venture. KJ's bond with

K'awin had grown stronger and stronger. Separating them would have done more damage than good. So, if she couldn't control that, she could at least be part of the team that led the Alpha Base project.

She watched her son from across the foyer, now six years old but somehow much more mature in his ways. He marched across the newly tarmacked path. As ever, K'awin padded along beside him. He was off to school, if one could call it school. Some of the best professors in the world had come to teach there—and learn from the Huahuqui. KJ was already several grades ahead of where he should be. His most recent undertaking had been to learn the basics of nuclear physics. His professor, Mrs. Gray, had suggested it. He was now fascinated with the Chernobyl power plant meltdown in the 80s.

KJ waved as he skipped by and was joined by at least five of the Nenets kids and their companions. They all now spoke several languages, but usually the kids slipped into Aymara when conversing among themselves. Ten paces behind, Nikolaj trudged slowly toward the classroom. Chernoukh was at his heel, the creature's black gills bobbing with its gait. Freya lifted a hand to wave, but it became an awkward half gesture. She pulled her hand close to her chest, lest it decide to start jerking all on its own, again. Nikolaj glanced at her but didn't respond.

"Still not talking to you, huh?" Jonathan said as he approached from the entrance to the habitat dome.

Freya shook her head. "He doesn't talk to anyone anymore."

"It's not your fault, you know."

"Yes, it is," she snapped back. "I gotta watch out for him. At least until ..."

"And you are," Teller said putting a hand on her arm to calm the spasm that was beginning to form. "He lives with you and KJ. You take care of him as best you can. He'll come around. It's a healing process, you know that."

Freya nodded and rolled her eyes. "Yeah."

"C'mon. We have a briefing meeting to make."

Freya started after Teller toward the operation dome. As they approached the gated entrance, a lively woman with bright orange hair came bounding out, her video camera in hand.

"In a rush, Catherine?" Teller asked.

"Sorry," she said, without stopping. "I have to do a live feed and I'm running late. I'll catch you in the mess hall, okay?"

"Sure," Teller said. "See you later."

Catherine gave Freya a curt nod, and jogged off toward the foyer.

"You two okay?" Teller asked as they continued on.

"We have an understanding," Freya replied. "And she's doing a good job reporting on what's going on in here. We have to keep it public. No black boxes."

"Apart from this one," Teller said as they passed through the first security gate.

Freya sighed. "Yeah."

The change from bright blue sky to the fluorescent lighting of the corridor into operations took a few seconds to come to terms with, but eventually Freya's eyes adjusted. "They're still coming, you know," she said, boring a stare into the side of Jonathan's head.

"The boats?" Teller asked.

"Daily. I don't know how they're making it across the rough ocean. Hell, I don't know how many haven't made it. They're calling it a pilgrimage. To see the Huahuqui and be saved."

Teller sighed. "We don't allow a large military contingent here, but they control most of the illegal visitors. We can't get them all."

"They should use the approved routes."

"Yeah, tell that to the millions of refugees who cross borders the wrong way every day," Teller replied, swiping his key card through the scanner.

The door slid open.

"I guess you're right," Freya said, then stepped into the control room.

The CR always felt strange to her. Unlike the other domes, it was not made of glass. Concealed from the outside world, it was like a remnant of the secret facilities she knew so well and had opposed for Alpha Base. For the most part, she'd won. But the operations dome had been the compromise. The single wall of the circular space was covered in flat screens displaying all manner of information about Alpha Base. Everything from the productivity of the solar panels to the performance of the irrigation system and the yield of the crops.

There were cameras in every corner of the base, with all of the feeds monitored there in the CR. The most interesting feed came from the cameras placed four kilometers below the ice: in the fortress that was the home of the Huahuqui. The acclimation project had worked well and so while the juvenile knowledge bringers spent much time with their human companions, the adults often dwelled in the depths, enjoying the quiet.

Freya sat beside Jonathan at the main monitor. Her right leg twitching so she crossed her leg over it to quell the tremor. A few key punches later and Lucy Taylor's face filled the bright screen.

"Madam Secretary," Freya said.

"Freya, Jonathan. Good to see you. I hear all is going well."

Jonathan nodded. "As well as can be expected. Good to see

you're not in an orange jumpsuit."

The secretary gave a tired smile. "The president is a good man. We have bigger problems, and my personal knowledge of the situation has thus far kept me out of jail." Her smile opened up a little. "As it has for you, Mr. Teller."

Jonathan smirked.

"We still need more border controls, to stop the pilgrims," Freya blurted out.

The secretary bobbed her head in agreement. "I know. We're doing our best. Too many ships are going down. We'll find a way."

"Do you have any more news?" Jonathan asked.

"I'm afraid not. The longer time goes on, the colder the trail gets. They've disappeared into thin air."

Freya pulled her ponytail tighter. "They took a bunch of the Huahuqui and children, which makes them a bit conspicuous don't you think? You're telling me the NSA, British Intelligence and all the other agencies can't find these bastards?"

"We're doing our best—"

"Yes, you said that. But if they come for my son—"

"We'll be ready," Teller said, his tone soft.

Lucy nodded. "Indeed. You may not have much military on the island, we but have the coast covered from the sea and air."

"Yet pilgrims still get through," Freya quipped. "What about the orphanages? Didn't that lead anywhere?"

"We've been working with the FSB," Lucy replied. "But it seems that operation dried up. Intelligence tells us the Nine Veils were using orphans to build some kind of retro-engineered, genetically enhanced, army to sell to the highest bidder. By organizing terror attacks across the globe, they could ensure a steady stream of need for their army—resistant to chemical weapons and superficial physical injury. When they found out about the Huahuqui, it was too good an opportunity to miss. A way to boost their militia."

Teller took a deep breath. "So, they used terrorist cells, and blamed North Korea, all just to keep us distracted? Keep us away long enough so they could take the Huahuqui? Dammit. I'll tell you what, though, now that we know about them, I don't think they'll be setting up auctions anymore."

Lucy nodded. "I'd agree. But we may have another problem. You remember what they did to Steve Chang?"

Freya and Jonathan nodded.

"The cryptologists at the NSA opened the puzzle box. After it was deemed not to be a threat, it then took a team to decipher one thousand moves to solve it. Inside was a single note in Aymara: *the future is behind us.*"

"What the hell does that mean?" Jonathan asked.

"Aymara doesn't consider time in the way that we or most languages do," Freya said. Her heart hurt as there was only one reason she knew this. "The children speak it with each other. It's a language that many linguists believe was designed. It can be used to program computers. But unlike us, the Aymara don't really consider time as a thing that we move through or moves with us, but as a state of knowing or not knowing." She sighed. Minya's words, her knowledge, fell from Freya's lips but they didn't seem to carry the weight of her late Siberian friend. "When they speak, it sounds like the future is behind and the past is in front. What they mean is the past is known to them and the future is not."

The secretary nodded. "We believe it's a warning. But that's not all. The symbolism in that set up just keeps coming. Multiples upon multiples. Even down to the tree Steve was … well, it's a banyan tree. It's a tree who's seed only grows when it germinates in the crack or crevice of a host tree or human edifice. The boys here in Washington are afraid the Nine Veils were just trying to place enough soldiers in the defense lines of major powers for something bigger. The question is: what's their endgame?"

"I'll bet my bottom dollar their endgame hasn't changed." Jonathan rubbed his jaw. "Now they have Huahuqui, maybe they've just changed *how* they're going to realize whatever it is they're aiming at."

Freya closed her eyes and tried to lose herself in the darkness, the conversation between Lucy and Jonathan melting into the void behind her eyelids. Despite everything they were trying to achieve at Alpha Base, no one was safe. Whether she wanted it or not, war was coming—and coming for her son and Nikolaj and all the other children. But, each day that passed, she lost more control of her limbs. Each day, she was less able to protect them. Ten years. Ten months. There was no telling.

"Did you hear me?"

"I'm sorry, what?" Freya asked, opening her eyes.

The monitor was off and they were in relative darkness. The conversation with the secretary must have been over.

"I was trying to ask you something," Teller said.

Freya scrunched up her nose. "I've already said no. The doctors offered to look into my Huntington's using Huahuqui DNA. KJ is clear, and that's all I care about. Don't you remember what happened with Wak and Vic—"

"You wanna shut up and let me speak?" Jonathan interrupted. "Like I was saying—" he pulled a small box from his pocket. "I know this isn't romantic, with candles and whatever, but none of that stuff means anything. All that matters, is that I love you.

Always have, always will."

Freya stared blankly at Jonathan. His words swam in her head but made little sense. She took the box and fumbled with it a little before slowly opening the lid. Inside, was a metal ring clip with a quarter inch, hand-polished black stone—a fallen star from the wasteland outside—held in place with a soldered claw.

Teller scratched at his neck. "Yeah, so, I'm sorry about that. But diamonds are kinda scarce around here, and we're not getting back to civilization any time soon."

"But why? Why would you ... you know ... I ..." Freya stammered, without looking up. "A journey like this, where you know the end is coming, it's best to do it alone. I finally understand Kelly, now. He wasn't protecting himself, he was protecting others from hurting when he was gone. Because he knew it would be soon. I don't want to hurt anyone else."

Jonathan took Freya's free hand in his. It trembled, though Freya couldn't discern if it was the Huntington's or her sudden anxiety.

"Well, if that ain't the biggest pile of horseshit I've ever heard," he said, trying to meet her gaze. "How much hurt did his death leave behind? No man, or woman, is an island Freya. I told you, I love you. I may not be Kelly Graham, but he's gone and I'm not. I want to be the one to see it through, for however long to, well, whatever happens next. And in the end, I'll be there for KJ, too."

"KJ ..." Freya raised her eyes to see Jonathan's expectant face. "You'd look after KJ? When, I mean, after—"

"I would," he said softly.

"And Nikolaj?"

Jonathan gave a soft chuckle. "And Nikolaj."

Freya glanced at the makeshift ring one more time, then back to Jonathan where she held his gaze, searching his strong hazel eyes. KJ would grow up to be willful like his father. He needed guidance, a role model, and Jonathan was a good man. He may have been more in his head than his heart—an antithesis of Kelly Graham—but with war coming, and with Minya gone, there was no one better to teach KJ.

"Yes," she whispered. "Okay, let's do it."

Location: unknown

Svetlana shivered uncontrollably, her skin prickled and cold, as she shuffled along the white corridor. Ribka had been allowed to pad alongside her. Svetlana felt the fear pouring from the Huahuqui, its gills flaccid and drained. She placed a shaking hand on her companion's head, but it gave no comfort. Her own fear melded with that of Ribka's, amplifying the heart-crushing emotion.

The two young, but well-built, soldiers at her sides marched with purpose. Their heavy boots were loud on the stone floor and their gear rustled with each wide step. Both wore helmets that obscured their faces and carried large black guns, though Svetlana had no idea what kind.

They reached the end of the corridor and stopped at a set of double doors with no hinges. Svetlana scanned them, noting that there were also no door handles or locks. They had not been to this room before. In fact, they were only ever allowed in the training camp, or into the lab for the weekly check-up. Despite all the needles and tubes that were inserted into her and Ribka in the lab, *this* place scared her more.

With a slow and purposeful *whoosh*, the doors slid open revealing a dark room with a large desk and no windows. The only source of light emanated from the small table; it glowed like a dying star that had been plucked from the sky and brought to Earth. A shove almost toppled Svetlana into the room, but she managed to save herself and instead stumbled a few steps inside. Ribka followed suit, sidling up to Svetlana and rubbing her snout on the Nenets girl's leg.

Svetlana stroked the top of Ribka's head.

As her vision adjusted to the light, Svetlana saw the luminous object on the desk was not a star, but a round, jelly-like ball in a sealed transparent box. It glowed blue, with hints of green inside, and pulsated ever so slightly—as if it were alive. The fluorescent light lit a large leather chair that faced away from her. Behind it was an ornate carving of a gnarled, twisted, leafless tree with a thick scaly snake wrapped around it's trunk.

The chair slowly and silently turned around. A man with narrow waist and broad shoulders sat in the chair. Most of his features were concealed in shadow—the orb only illuminated the lower half of his bearded face.

"Do not be afraid, child," said the man in a voice as deep as the ocean. "I am the Doyen."

Svetlana didn't speak, but her legs trembled. She needed KJ so badly, but he hadn't come. No one had come.

"You are quite safe. In fact, you are better than safe. You are among those of us who see your true potential. To be a god among men. Or goddess among women, if you will. To exist beyond the Ninth Veil. I am led to believe you in particular show much promise. That other boy in training, both of his arms broken. Impressive."

His words were meant to be soothing or perhaps encouraging, but his voice carried such weight that it shook Svetlana's insides.

She didn't want to hurt the boy, they made her—forced her—to stamp on him when he was already defeated. A warm trickle meandered its way down the inside of her leg and created a pool around her feet.

"I understand you lost your mother," the Doyen continued. "This will not do. Every child needs a mother. Who else can guide you through this festering shit hole we call life? So, I have a gift for you."

From within the darkest corner of the room, a woman slipped out of the shadows. Her hair was golden and her eyes azure. The glowing orb on the table threw tortured shadows across her face, sharpening her already angular features. On her chest lay an inverted crucifix that the woman toyed with between her finger and thumb.

"This is Miss McKenzie," the Doyen said.

The woman nodded with a cruel smile. "You can call me Victoria."

The doors behind Svetlana slid closed.

Acknowledgements

Thank you to the following people for beta reading early drafts:

Tess Burnside, Marina Diner, Alexandra Doe, Kelly Hambly,
Julieanne Lynch, Chris Rapier, Jonas Saul, Sam Walford,
Dominica Worthington

A big thank you to Jonas Saul for his developmental edit.

As always, I must thank my agents Italia Gandolfo and Renee C.
Fountain, as well as the Vesuvian Books team – especially Liana
Gardner.

AUTHOR BIO

Gareth Worthington holds a degree in marine biology, a PhD in endocrinology, and currently educates the World's doctors on new cancer therapies. Gareth has hand tagged sharks in California; won in the Science Fiction Category at the 2017 London Book Festival and won honorable mention at the New York Book Festival 2012 and 2013 for his writing; and trained in various martial arts, including Jeet Kune Do, Muay Thai, and MMA at the EVOLVE MMA gym in Singapore and Phoenix KampfSport Switzerland.

Born in Plymouth UK, Worthington currently resides outside of Zurich, Switzerland.

www.GarethWorthington.com

www.ChildrenOfTheFifthSun.com

CHILDREN
OF THE
FIFTH SUN

2012 WASN'T THE END
IT WAS THE BEGINNING

"INSANE! A WILD RIDE RESEARCHED ON PAR WITH A MICHAEL CRICHTON NOVEL."
—Jonas Saul, bestselling author of the Sarah Roberts Series

GARETH WORTHINGTON

CHILDREN
OF THE
FIFTH SUN

IN ALMOST EVERY BELIEF SYSTEM ON EARTH, there exists a single unifying mythos: thousands of years ago a great flood devastated the Earth's inhabitants. From the ruins of this cataclysm, a race of beings emerged from the sea bestowing knowledge and culture upon humanity, saving us from our selfish drive toward extinction. Some say this race were "ancient aliens" who came to assist our evolution.

But what if they weren't alien at all? What if they evolved right here on Earth, alongside humans ...and they are still here? And, what if the World's governments already know?

***

Kelly Graham is a narcissistic self-assured freelance photographer specializing in underwater assignments. While on a project in the Amazon with his best friend, Chris D'Souza, a mysterious and beautiful government official, Freya Nilsson, enters Kelly's life and turns it upside down. Her simple request to retrieve a strange object from deep underwater puts him in the middle of an international conspiracy.

A conspiracy that threatens to change the course of human history.

CHILDREN
OF THE
FIFTH SUN
RUBICON
THE AGE OF MAN IS OVER
AWARD-WINNING AUTHOR
GARETH WORTHINGTON

CHILDREN
OF THE
FIFTH SUN
RUBICON

The age of man is over.

It has been seventeen years since the Nine Veils abducted the
Nenets children and their bonded Huahuqui. Despite years of
searching by Jonathan Teller and the NSA, nothing has been heard
from the clandestine organization or the abductees.

KJ Nilsson, the remaining children and their Huahuqui—collectively
known as the Stratum—have grown up in relative safety at Alpha
Base, Antarctica. Thanks to the work of Lucy Taylor, now President
of the United States, the Stratum are to be recognized as a unique,
symbiotic, race and legal citizens of several great nations.

But things do not go as planned when the Nine Veils come out of
hiding—with their own army of Huahuqui—determined to become
the most elite power on the planet.

Now, KJ and his fellow Stratum must prove they deserve their new
status by defending the citizens of Earth against their own kind.
Whoever wins, the age of man is over.